your
chariot
awaits

Other Novels by Lorena McCourtney

Invisible
In Plain Sight
On the Run
Stranded

your chariot awaits

Book #1
An Andi McConnell Mystery

Lorena McCourtney

THOMAS NELSON
Since 1798

NASHVILLE DALLAS MEXICO CITY RIO DE JANEIRO BEIJING

Published in Nashville, Tennessee. Thomas Nelson is a trademark of Thomas Nelson, Inc.

Thomas Nelson, Inc. titles may be purchased in bulk for educational, business, fund-raising, or sales promotional use. For information, please e-mail SpecialMarkets@ThomasNelson.com.

Library of Congress Cataloging-in-Publication Data

McCourtney, Lorena.

    Your chariot awaits / Lorena McCourtney.

      p. cm. -- (An Andi McConnell mystery ; bk. 1)

    ISBN-13: 978-1-59554-279-3 (softcover)

    ISBN-10: 1-59554-279-5 (softcover)

    1. Older women--Fiction. 2. Washington (State)--Fiction. 3. Christian fiction. I. Title.

PS3563.C3449Y68 2007

813'.54--dc22

                            2007032725

Printed in the United States of America

07 08 09 10 RRD 6 5 4 3 2 1

1

I flopped into a chair at a corner table, glad the little bakery/coffee shop was almost empty. Today not even the aroma of maple bars, apple fritters, and fresh-baked bread could burn through my fog of doom and gloom.

"Hey, it's the middle of the afternoon. What're you doing here?" asked Joella, who was my next-door neighbor as well as a waitress here. She looked at me more closely as she set a cup of my usual French roast blend on the table. "Something wrong?"

"I thought the most traumatic event of the week was going to be my birthday." I fished a paper out of my purse and spun it across the table. "Wrong."

Joella grabbed for it, but it sailed right on by and landed under the only other occupied table. A guy in khaki pants and T-shirt emblazoned with a picture of a sailboat picked it up. He read it as he walked over to my table.

Indignation joined my funk. "Hey, what're you doing? That's private!" I snatched my paper back.

Joella patted my shoulder. "Don't mind Fitz. He used to play a detective on TV. He's nosy about everything."

"I'm not nosy," the guy protested. "I'm just *interested*. And it pays off. I spotted a carjacking suspect in the Burger King parking lot a couple weeks ago, let the cops know, and right away they nailed him."

"That doesn't give you the right to read other people's private papers." I held the letter close to my chest.

He ignored my complaint and stuck out his hand. "I'm Keegan Fitzpatrick, usually known as Fitz. I live with my son on the *Miss Nora* over at the marina." He tapped the sailboat on his chest, which I now noted had "Matt's Sailboat Charters" arched over it, and "Sail into Adventure" below.

When I offered only a grumpy stare in return, Joella identified me.

"This is my landlady, Andi McConnell. She lives in the other half of the duplex. Don't mind her. She's a little irritable because she has a birthday coming up this weekend. She looks pretty good for ninety-seven, don't you think?"

He looked me over, speculating about what birthday it actually was, of course. I saved him the trouble.

"I'm going to be sixty, okay? The big six-o. Six decades. Sixty percent of a century: 21,900 days."

"You figured out the *days*?" Joella's tone was somewhere between appalled and incredulous.

"Does that include leap years?" Fitz inquired.

"I guess I forgot leap years."

"Then you'll have to add—"

"Never mind."

"Doesn't matter anyway," he said. "Because sixty is prime time. Enjoy it."

"Right," Joella agreed.

Like she'd know. Joella is all of twenty, slim-thighed and sparkly eyed, with magazine-ad skin and bouncy blonde hair.

"So how old are *you*?" I challenged Fitz. Not that I cared, but I figured he may as well have a taste of his own nosiness.

"Sixty-three," he said cheerfully. "That's prime time too. Although I've never gotten around to figuring how many days it adds up to."

I had the feeling that when Fitz was ninety, he'd still be proclaiming *prime time*. On some days I might find that endearing. Not today, especially when he was slyly poking fun at me. But he did look reasonably well preserved. Gray hair thinning on top and a fairly weather-beaten face, but a trim physique and sharp blue eyes that looked as if they didn't miss much.

"And I'd say you have more to be irritable about than an upcoming birthday." He nodded toward the paper I was still clutching.

Joella's perky brows lifted, and I handed her the by-now somewhat scuffed and crumpled letter. She studied the words that were about to change my life.

"So the rumors that have been going around for so long were true," she murmured.

"Worse than true." For weeks rumors had rampaged around the corporate headquarters of Friends & Neighbors Insurance about an imminent merger with another company. The rumors had been much too kind. This was no merger; it was a shark attack. Corporate murder. Mass execution.

Okay, maybe that's a little melodramatic, but it was a disaster for most F&N employees. Certainly for me.

"They're closing down and letting everyone go?" Fitz asked.

"They let us leave early today, to absorb the shock, I guess. Friday's our last day. Free Fall Friday, everyone's calling it, because that's where it puts most of us. A few executives are being transferred to the new main office down in San Diego. And they're keeping a handful of people on here to wind things up and turn off the lights."

"I had my house in LA insured with Friends & Neighbors before I sold it," Fitz said. "They were a good outfit. Paid off right away the only time I had a claim with them."

"It's a nice letter," Joella offered. "A very polite letter."

I groaned. Joella is the sunniest, most even-tempered person I know. She always sees that proverbial silver lining. Me, if I can even scratch around and find the silver lining, I invariably spot the tarnish on it.

It's an odd relationship we have, I suppose, considering the difference in our ages. I feel almost fiercely motherly toward my daughter, Sarah, and fiercely grandmotherly toward her daughter, Rachel, who is only a couple years younger than Joella. But with Jo I feel more . . . what? Unlikely as it sounds, more *sisterly*. In fact, she's so mature and sensible and good-hearted that it sometimes feels as if she's taking me under her wing. Like the time I came down with some miserable flu thing, and she was right there with tissues and chicken soup. And she'll make a wonderful mother. Though I'm always careful not to say anything to influence the big decision she'll soon have to make in that area.

Sometimes I think Jo deserves a medal for her sunny attitude. Sometimes I'd like to turn her upside down and shake her and yell, "There's a bad side to everything. How come you can't ever see it?"

But she was right about this. It *was* a polite letter. All done in very proper corporatespeak. It assured me that the termination was in no way a reflection on my capabilities as an employee. This was simply a downsizing of personnel necessary for maximum efficiency in the restructuring of the newly merged companies.

"It's more polite than some firings I've had," Fitz said. "I didn't even know my last one was coming until I read in one of the trade papers that my character was about to be killed off. And it's not a bad severance deal, considering." He hadn't had that paper in his hands long, but those sharp eyes obviously hadn't missed a thing.

Having never been severed before, I was in no position to evaluate the deal, but I supposed it was fair enough. Not exactly one of those golden parachutes you hear about, but I'd get a lump-sum payment equal to four months' pay, and I could keep my company health insurance for six months. And—oh, happy day!—I'd also be receiving the company's quarterly newsletter, *Security and You*. If the company didn't see the irony in that, I did.

"You can get another job," Joella said. "You're hardworking and dependable, and you know a lot about insurance."

"So do the four hundred or so other people they're letting go. F&N is the second-largest employer in Vigland, right after the wood products mill. There'll be rioting in the streets when that many people start looking for work in a town this size."

"Lots of locals carpool and go into Olympia for jobs. Some even drive all the way up to Tacoma," Fitz said. "It could be a great new adventure. I wasn't too thrilled about moving up here from LA a few months ago, but it's turned out fine. I don't even get seasick anymore."

Just what I needed. *Two* sunnier-than-thou optimists. Couldn't either of them see that what I was most likely to wind up with was minimum wage at Greasy Burgers, Inc.?

"Yeah, but can I find something soon enough, or something that pays enough, to help Rachel with college?" I asked gloomily. Something that would also provide me with something more than a bread-and-water diet until I was old enough to qualify for Social Security?

"Who's Rachel? Not being nosy," Fitz added hastily. "Just interested."

"My granddaughter. She'll be starting college at the University of Florida this fall."

"Her parents can't afford to send her?" Fitz asked. "Or scholarships?"

"My daughter and her husband are divorced, and it's all Sarah can do to make ends meet. The ex-husband just re-married and has a new baby, so he's no help. But she's check-ing into scholarships and loans."

And why did I blurt all *that* out to Mr. Nosy?

"God can bring good out of the worst of situations," Joella said. "Maybe you'll find an even better job."

Joella P. Picault. The P was supposed to be for Pilar, but I suspected it really stood for Pollyanna. And yes, this was one of those times when I wanted to pick her up and shake her. And I could do it. Okay, I'm not exactly a powerhouse of lean muscle . . . there are those jiggly thighs. But I mow my own lawn, and I do it with a push-type mower, so my five-foot-six 134 pounds definitely outmuscles Joella's five-foot-one 120. With her blonde hair, blue eyes, and pink cheeks, she looks like the girl on top in a high-school cheerleader pyramid. Albeit a considerably pregnant one.

"God doesn't care about my situation," I informed her firmly.

"How do you know? Did you ever talk to Him about it?"

I waved a hand dismissively. Joella and I don't really argue about God. I kind of think He exists, out there somewhere, but I'm not on *Hi there, God, how're You doing?* terms with Him, the way Joella seems to be.

"What about Jerry?" she asked.

I wasn't surprised that Fitz immediately cut in with, "Who's Jerry?"

"When I have time, I'll send you a cast list of everyone in the program of my life," I snapped.

"I'd appreciate that."

"He's the boyfriend," Joella explained. "He works at F&N too."

At my level of sixtyish, *boyfriend* seems a much too adolescent term, but I suppose it's as accurate as any.

"I haven't talked to him yet." I glanced at the ceramic rooster clock on the wall of the shop. "He'll probably call later."

I needed some commiseration time with Jerry. The downsizing at F&N would surely hit him hard. He'd been in line for a position as head of the finance department, if Mr. Findley ever retired, but this corporate change would sink that possibility. He wouldn't have Joella and Fitz's rose-colored-glasses view of the situation.

"Look, how about if I buy you one of the great new peach smoothies, and we'll talk about the job problem?" Fitz suggested.

I wasn't interested in discussing my job problems with a stranger, but the peach smoothie sounded appealing. I was just about to accept when my cell phone played that hard rock thing Rachel programmed in when she was here at Christmas. It always gives me a little jolt, but I haven't changed it because it reminds me of my granddaughter.

As if just thinking about Jerry a minute earlier had made a connection, his voice on the phone said, "Hi, Andi. Hey, I've got a little time and thought I'd run over for a minute. I need to talk to you."

"I'm down at the Sweet Breeze rereading my you're-fired-have-a-nice-day letter. Want to join me?"

"This is kind of private. I'd rather come to your house."

"Sure. I'll head on home. Want to barbecue burgers later?"

"No, I have some things to do."

"See you in a few minutes, then."

"Jerry," I said to Joella as I returned the phone to my purse. And to Fitz too, of course, since he seemed as interested in my phone call as he was in my correspondence.

Joella looked mildly disapproving as I headed for the door. She doesn't actually say anything against Jerry, but she tends to avoid him, and once she said that he seemed "a bit insensitive." I hadn't asked her to elaborate, but I think it had to do with a mean crack he made about an overweight woman when we were all at a neighborhood barbecue. I'm sure he didn't really mean anything by it. It's just that Jerry runs and works out, and his lean physique shows it, and he hasn't much sympathy for those who don't take such care of themselves. And Joella is prejudiced toward some guy, Dean somebody, at her church that she wants me to meet.

"I'll see you at home later," she called. "And don't forget, we *are* going to celebrate your birthday this weekend. I'll bring the cake."

"With sixty candles?" Fitz looked interested, as if he might like to be invited to the blaze.

"We'll think about the birthday." Given my coming un-employment, even hitting the big six-o had dropped a notch on my worry list. Although age and employment status were probably a combination problem. No matter what Fitz said, sixty is not prime time for finding a new job. "See you later."

"Maybe we can have that peach smoothie some other time," Fitz called.

I gave him a noncommittal wave.

"We're heading out on a charter trip tomorrow, but when

we get back, I'll give you a tour of the *Miss Nora*, and you can meet my son."

Right. Like I'm going to rush over and give Nosy & Son, Inc., a chance to rummage around in more private details of my life.

2

Jerry's car wasn't parked at the duplex when I turned onto Secret View Lane. I felt a fresh thunder of panic when I pulled into the double driveway between the two units.

What if no job and a financial crunch forced me out of my home? I loved my little place. I loved my green grass and daisy flower beds. I loved my patio out behind the house and the huge cedars and forsythia and more daisies along the back line, and the squirrels that stole seed from my bird feeder. I loved my cozy kitchen with the sunny yellow curtains I'd made myself.

Maybe it wasn't much compared to the big house I'd had to give up after Richard pulled his wife-switcheroo act. No expansive lawn sweeping down to the tidewaters rushing through Hornsby Inlet, no expensive powerboat tied to a picturesque dock, no view of the shining waters of Vigland Bay in one direction and distant Mount Rainier shimmering in the other.

My only view here, in fact, was of the house across the street and the forested hillside above it. A house where, as usual, old Tom Bolton was parked in a lawn chair on his deck, keeping watch on the neighbors. I couldn't see his binoculars at the moment, but I knew they were there. Once I'd seen him jot something in a little notebook when Moose, the Sheersons' spotted dalmatian, was running down the street, and later the Sheersons had a stern visit from Animal Control.

But in spite of meddlesome old Tom, the potholes in the street, and the critters that kept mounding up piles of raw dirt on my lawn, I loved this quiet lane and my little duplex. But I repeat myself.

Inside, I changed to denim shorts, a pink shell top, and flip-flops. The late spring day was unusually warm, though I wasn't in a mood to appreciate blue skies and sunshine.

I made lemonade while waiting for Jerry. From fresh lemons, of course. Jerry doesn't like the frozen kind. I expected him any minute, but a half hour went by. An hour. Two.

I kept peering out the window, watching for him. Joella got home from work and waved as she struggled out of her old Subaru, looking tired after being on her feet all day.

Where could Jerry be? He runs a Web site–design business in addition to his position in the finance department at F&N— but if work was detaining him, he could have called. I bounced between annoyance and worry.

Finally, almost three hours after I'd gotten home, I heard his Trans Am pull into the driveway. He didn't look the way I felt, down and discouraged, as he slid out of the car and headed for the front door. In fact, he looked quite jaunty. His combination of jeans and black T-shirt molded his muscles, and he looked sophisticated and a bit dangerous. A combination that can tingle even an almost-sixty heart—even though, now that I saw he was okay, I was exasperated with him for not calling. I let him ring the bell before I opened the door.

"Hi, babe. Hey, you're looking good!" He grabbed my upper arms and gave me a quick kiss.

Jerry Norton is the guy I've been dating for almost four months now. Granddaughter Rachel shudders at the term. No one *dates* anymore, she says. But it still works for me. Anyway, Jerry is my first maybe-serious relationship in a long time. No spoken commitment here, but neither of us was dating anyone else. We like hiking together, and he has a little sailboat he keeps at a friend's dock. We take it out on the bay or inlet, sometimes out into the rougher waters of Puget Sound. He cooks up a mean slab of salmon on my barbecue, he loves my fried chicken, and we both enjoy finding new places to eat out. He's hardworking, ambitious, fun, and good-looking, with curly, dark hair and a smile and lean body that look especially good braced against the mast of the sailboat. I have that photo on the nightstand in my bedroom.

With the proper nudge, I think I could be in love with Jerry. Maybe I am anyway, but unwilling to admit it to myself just yet. Maybe just a wariness that comes with this time of life, combined with a bad marriage experience in my past. Plus the fact that Jerry is nine years and ten months younger than I am, and I've never been quite sure what he sees in me. Joella, bless her heart, says I sell myself short.

Now I said, "I thought you were coming right over."

"Sorry. I got tied up on some e-mail stuff."

"Sending out résumés already?"

He looked blank for a moment; then his expression sobered, as if the question reminded him this was a day of gloom. "Well, uh, like I said, we need to talk."

"Lemonade?"

"Sure."

I went on through to the kitchen, and he perched on one of the tall stools at the counter separating kitchen and dining room. I poured a glass of lemonade for him. The termination letter with the F&N letterhead lay on the counter. He didn't pick it up, but he apparently knew what it said.

"Tough break. You've been with F&N a long time."

"I guess everyone got the same letter." I knew because in my department we'd compared. Only my friend Letty Bishop was being kept on for the final days, after the department supervisor turned down the job. "You too?"

"Well, uh, no."

"No?"

"They've offered me a transfer to the San Diego office. Findley is going, and they've offered me a position as his assistant. That's what I wanted to talk to you about."

"A transfer?" What I really felt was a big flood of dismay, like the tide surging in over the mud flats of Vigland Bay, but I squelched my reaction. "Jerry, that's wonderful! You must be one of a very select few."

"Findley specifically asked for me, which is probably what did it."

"Are you taking the transfer?"

"I'm not wild about working with ol' Freaky Findley, that's for sure. He's lazy and self-important and . . . well, you know. But I don't see how I can turn it down. It's a promotion, actually, with more money. So it's really an awesome opportunity."

"Awesome," I echoed. I wanted to feel glad for him. And one nice part of me *did* feel glad. A transfer *and* a promotion. The problem was that the self-centered *what-about-me?* question loomed like a skyscraper on a desert island. I cast around for nice things to say, but all I came up with was a lame, "The weather should be great down there."

"Right. I've never been fond of western Washington's rain."

My world is falling apart, and we're discussing the climate. "How soon will you go?"

"Probably within the next couple weeks. I'll be going down ahead of Findley to get things set up."

I felt a peculiar hollowness inside. A strangely large hollow, which made me wonder if I wasn't in love with him.

"But it makes for a problem, of course," he added.

"The condo?"

Jerry's condo was in one of the newer complexes in town, and he'd owned it less than a year. It had what the real estate people called a "forever view" out over Vigland Bay and Hornsby Inlet. He could even see the jagged Olympic Mountains to the north.

"No, not the condo. All the F&N people out of work may depress local prices for a while, but I can hang on a few months before putting the condo on the market if I have to." He reached across the counter and pulled me around the end of it. "The problem isn't the condo. The problem is *us*."

I nodded as I stood within the circle of his arms and echoed the word. "Us."

"The thing is, I don't think it's practical to carry on a long-distance relationship, do you?"

I caught my breath. We'd talked around marriage in a generic way, but we'd never really discussed it on a you-and-me basis. Jerry had been married when he came to F&N five years ago, but they'd divorced, and his ex had taken the two kids and moved back east somewhere. I had the impression he wasn't totally disillusioned with marriage, but wary, which was about how I felt. Was now the time to let the past go and look at a future together?

Sure, I'd had some doubts about Jerry. Sometimes I had the feeling there were parts of his life he wasn't sharing with me. And sometimes that almost ten-year difference in our ages loomed higher than the Olympic Mountains. But did anyone, with our unhappy past experiences, go into marriage 100 percent sure?

"Yes," I agreed with a catch in my voice at the looming possibilities. "Long-distance relationships can be a problem. How do you think we should handle it?"

Quick ceremony before he left for San Diego? Or a settling-in time for him there, and then a trip to a wedding chapel in Reno or Vegas? Or maybe even a little church somewhere? Yes, a church. I'd like that.

"I'm thinking you'll agree that making a clean break would be best for both of us."

A jaw can drop. It really can. *"What?"*

"The thing is, I've been in contact on the Internet with a woman in the San Diego area for a while. In fact, she's looking for a nice apartment for me down there right now. She's a fitness instructor at a health club, and she loves sailing and surfing. And we just discovered we're both interested in skydiving too. It seems like we really click."

I was stunned. I'm thinking about the possibility of closing the long-distance gap between us with a wedding ring, and he's thinking skydiving with a fitness instructor. No doubt with thighs of steel.

But in case I was jumping to some unwarranted conclusion here, I backtracked and put it as a blunt question. "So what you're saying is, you and me, we're over?"

"I'm saying we've had great times together, Andi. Lots of fun. But I'm going to be down in San Diego, and you're going to be here. And I think we've both always recognized that our relationship has . . . certain limitations, and we both need to widen our horizons and pursue new interests."

"But we can still be friends."

He missed the sarcasm in that old line, because his face lit up in a relieved beam. "Exactly. Friends! I knew you'd understand. You're such a good sport, Andi. The best."

I didn't feel like a good sport. I didn't even want to *be* a good sport. What I wanted was to dump the glass of lemonade over Jerry's head.

"What about your sailboat?" It was a dumb, irrelevant question, but it was all I could think of to fill space while I tried to keep my hand off that glass.

"I'll sell it before I leave. I'll get a bigger and better one down there. Hey, maybe you'd like to buy it? I can give you a deal on it."

"I . . . I don't think so. Thanks anyway."

"If you hear of anyone who might be interested, let me know. We've had fun times in it, haven't we? You've turned out to be very good sailor." He leaned forward to give me an affectionate kiss on the nose. A good-sport kiss.

I backed out of his arms. Joella was right. The man had the sensitivity of a toadstool. Breaking up with me and telling me how wonderful this new woman was, trying to sell me his old sailboat. And then kissing me on the nose.

He kept on talking, telling me enthusiastically about how the company was going to pay his moving expenses, but I wasn't really listening. I was standing there feeling like the time I'd been dumped overboard from his sailboat. In over my head and floundering in deep water.

Downsized.

Dumped.

Depressed.

And the week was only half over. What next?

As if in ominous answer to my unspoken question, the doorbell rang. Given the way things were going, it could be anyone. IRS agent, terrorist, serial killer . . .

3

The young guy who stood on my doorstep was unfamiliar, but he looked harmless enough. Midtwenties, brick-red hair, freckles, baggy khaki pants with pockets down to the knees, sloppy gray T-shirt, scruffy running shoes of some indeterminate brand. But who knows what a serial killer looks like?

However, he was obviously at the wrong house. Probably even the wrong neighborhood. Because parked at the end of my walkway was the longest, sleekest, blackest vehicle I'd ever seen, the likes of which had surely never touched the potholed asphalt of Secret View Lane before. Across the street, Tom Bolton had left his deck and come out to his gate for a better look.

"You're driving *that*?" I said.

The guy gave the vehicle a disinterested glance. "Yeah. I drove it up from Texas."

"But it's a *limousine*." A stretch limousine. And he didn't look as if he could afford to drive a '79 Pinto, let alone tool around in a limo.

"I'm looking for Andalusia McConnell. Is that you?"

Andalusia. "Well, yes," I said, "but—"

Jerry was behind me, hands on my waist. "Is that your real

17

name? *Andalusia?* Sounds like some awful disease." He deepened his voice to somber newscaster tones. "We've just gotten the latest update, folks, and the Andalusian flu is going to be really bad this year."

The young guy gave Jerry an odd glance. "It has something to do with Spain, doesn't it?" he asked me.

I felt an unexpected rush of warmth toward him for knowing that much. "Yes, it does. And, yes, I am Andalusia McConnell." With a good reason for the name, although I didn't intend to explain it now.

"Okay, I have some papers for you." The guy thrust a big manila envelope at me. It looked as if it had been kicked around the floor at Burger King for a couple of days. "Sorry. I guess I dropped it a time or two."

Given the bad news that had already come my way today, I eyed the envelope suspiciously and kept my hands at my sides. "What kind of papers?"

"About the limousine. Or limou*zeen*, z-e-e-n, as old Uncle Ned called it in his will. His favorite possession, also according to the will. He left it to you."

"Andi, you had a rich relative who left you a *limousine?*" Jerry asked, his tone incredulous. "How come you never told me?"

I could hear in his voice that I'd just risen several notches in his estimation. Did becoming a limousine-inheriting heiress put me up there with the sailing/skydiving queen? Too late if it did. Jerry had already taken a fatal skydive in my estimation. About all I could give him credit for was that he had come over to dump me in person. I knew a couple of women at F&N who'd been dumped by e-mail.

"Who are you?" I asked the red-haired guy.

"Larry Noakes. I think we're cousins or something."

I ran the name through my limited knowledge of the family tree. Nothing clicked. No surprise, since I'd never met more than a couple of them. My mother hadn't bad-mouthed the family, but she'd never had much good to say about them either.

"I've heard of Ned," I said cautiously. He was the rich member of the family. I think my folks tried to borrow money from him one time, but he'd turned them down. "He's your uncle too?"

"Actually, my great-uncle. He and my grandmother were brother and sister. I guess your mother was another sister. You did know Uncle Ned was dead, didn't you?"

"No, I didn't. Look, you want to come in so we can talk about this?"

Jerry interrupted. "Let's go look at the limousine first."

"You go look if you want. I need to talk to Larry here."

Larry looked at the watch on his wrist. "I don't have much time. I have to catch a bus at 6:45. Can you believe that? Those cheapskate lawyers didn't even give me a plane ticket home. I got a *bus* ticket. To *Texas*. It'll take me a month to get there."

A slight exaggeration, but I couldn't blame him. A bus trip to Texas wouldn't be high on my list of fun things to do either.

"I was hoping you could drive me to the bus station," he added. "I don't even know where it is."

"Me? I can't drive a limousine."

He pointed out the obvious, which my rather dazed mind had missed. "You don't have to take me in the limo. You can use your own car."

He looked with interest toward Jerry's flashy Trans Am sitting in the driveway. My own little Corolla was out of sight in the garage.

"But sure, you can drive the limousine. Why not? It's long, but no different otherwise."

"Don't you have to have a special license or something?"

"I don't, and I was Uncle Ned's chauffeur for a year and a half before he died. That's why I got the job of delivering the limo to you. Anyway, I don't know why you'd need anything special. Look at all those old geezers barreling around in their dinosaur-sized motor homes. They're twice as big as a limo, and they don't need any special licenses."

Jerry cut in before I could decide whether to be insulted by the "old geezer" reference.

"So why didn't this Uncle Ned leave the limo to you?"

"Who knows why Uncle Ned did anything? He was eccentric. With a capital *E*."

"Did he leave you something else?" I asked.

"Oh, sure. Seven electric toothbrushes. Five of them were still in the boxes, unused."

I gaped at him in disbelief. "But Uncle Ned was rich. Who got all the money and oil wells and the mansion?"

"Most of it went to various Save-the-Blank organizations."

"Save the blank?" I repeated doubtfully.

"You fill it in. Whales. Whooping cranes. Chickadees. Depressed dolphins. Left-handed monkeys." He gave a shrug that expressed his frustration with Uncle Ned's charitable recipients. "The lawyers got a big chunk. None of the real heirs got any actual money."

With that, Jerry lost interest. He headed for the limousine. I still thought there must be some mistake here. A *limousine?*

"What caused Uncle Ned's death?"

"He was eighty-nine," Larry said, as if that were explanation enough. Then he added, "He had all kinds of stuff wrong with him. Including a mean, cold heart. But it was kidney failure that finally did him in."

"Okay, c'mon inside and start from the beginning. How about some lemonade?"

"Yeah, I could use some lemonade."

He sat on the same stool Jerry had occupied earlier, and I filled another glass. I set out some day-old peanut butter cookies Joella had brought home from the bakery. He grabbed a cookie, ate it in two bites, took a long swallow of lemonade, and swiped the back of his hand across his upper lip.

"It's like this: Uncle Ned kicked the bucket about a year and a half ago. He had a will, but it was handwritten. Holographic, I think is the fancy word. They're legal in Texas, if they're done right, and his was, even though he misspelled everything from *limousine* to *pencil sharpener*."

"There was a pencil sharpener in his will?"

"He left it to Aunt Jasmine. It wasn't even electric. Anyway, I think because the will was handwritten, it took longer than usual to probate. He didn't have any kids of his own, but there were something like twenty-six various other heirs in the family, and everybody got something. I guess that's the way to do it so no one can challenge the will by saying they were forgotten. You must have been his favorite, because you got the only inheritance worth anything."

"How could I be his favorite? I didn't even know him."

"Everyone figures that's why you were his favorite. He *knew* the rest of us and got even for every dinky little thing he thought we ever did to him."

"Did you do something to him?"

"I may have gotten a few traffic citations in the limo, that he had to pay," Larry said, his offhand tone suggesting this was hardly worthy of notice. "I guess Aunt Jasmine teed him off when she refused to name any of her kids after him. Although there's another theory on how he decided who got what."

"What's that?"

"That he put all the family names on slips of paper in one hat and the stuff he wanted to leave on slips of paper in another. Or, knowing Uncle Ned, he probably used something he considered more appropriate, like a couple of old chamber pots. Anyway, the speculation is that he drew a person's name out of one and an item out of the other, and however they matched up, that's what the person got."

"And I really got the limousine?"

"Yep. The limou*zeen*"—he emphasized the *z* sound—"is yours. I figure he threw in that one big prize to make everyone else envious and maybe get them fighting. He liked to do stuff like that. The papers you'll need to get the title transferred are all in there." He nodded toward the envelope that now lay on the counter. "And I put my two old chauffeur's uniforms in the trunk. There's a framed photo of Uncle Ned back there too. Everybody got one."

"What am I going to do with a limousine?" Or a framed photo of an eccentric uncle?

"I don't know. Drive around in it. Sell it. Take the neighbors for rides. Get in a parade. Start a limousine business. Turn it into a hot-dog stand."

"I'm . . . flabbergasted."

"Aren't we all," he muttered.

A thought occurred to me. "I wonder if he left anything to my daughter and granddaughter?"

"I don't remember. You can look for yourself. There's a photocopy of the will in the envelope. If you can read it. Uncle Ned's writing looks like something done by a schizophrenic pigeon practicing hieroglyphics."

"What have you been doing since Uncle Ned died?"

"Going to school part-time. Working at a pizza joint.

Watching my toenails grow. Got parts in a couple of local plays. I was Bo Decker in *Bus Stop*." He looked at his watch again, eyed the plate of cookies, grabbed a double handful, and stuffed them into his baggy pockets. "I've gotta get going. I don't want to miss that bus. Seems kind of ironic, doesn't it? Being in *Bus Stop*, and now I'm going to be *on* a bus. Oh, I'd better give you the keys."

He dug in a different pocket and tossed me a key ring. Attached was a chunk of leather cut in the shape of Texas.

"I'll take you to the depot," I said.

Outside, Jerry was down on his hands and knees, peering under the limo. I'd ridden in a limousine a few times, long ago when we had the store and Richard was trying to impress people, but it certainly wasn't a mode of transportation with which I was familiar. The long, sleek lines practically screamed money and power and glamour. Except that screaming, of course, would be much too gauche for something this elegant.

But at the same time I felt . . . *peculiar* about it. It was like seeing someone giving away kittens in the Wal-Mart parking lot. You know they're adorable, but you can't even stop and look. Because you know if you do, you'll surely fall in love and take one . . . or three . . . home with you. And what you don't need is kittens.

I sensed that same feeling with the limo. I did not need a limo. I had no use for a limo. It was surely an expense I couldn't afford. And it would hang out of my garage like a foot-long hot dog in a six-inch bun. But I had the awful feeling that if I ever sat in it and drove it, I'd never be able to part with it, no matter how impractical it was.

"I have to take Larry to the bus depot," I called to Jerry.

Jerry threw the driver's side door open as if the limo belonged to him. "C'mon. Get in and I'll drive."

I rushed over and shoved the door shut. "No."

Okay, it was petty, but the guy who had just dumped me was not going to be the first one to drive my limo. I wasn't about to admit to that pettiness, so a little lamely I added, "There's probably a . . . a manual or something about it I should read first."

"It's in the trunk. With the uniforms," Larry said. "All the scheduled maintenance work is up-to-date. It's in really good shape. Except the fridge is empty. Though all Uncle Ned ever kept in it was Snapple anyway."

"Okay, we'll go in my car," Jerry said. I had the feeling he was now trying to butter me up. He was good at that. *But no luck this time*, I warned him silently. *Because you are not driving my limo.*

Larry got in the front seat of the Trans Am with Jerry. I sat in back. They chatted about the car as we drove to the bus station: speed, power, gadgets, all that testosterone-type stuff. Then Jerry started asking similar questions about the limo. I wondered about the gas mileage, but they didn't discuss that. Perhaps, when you're into the high-powered world of limousines, mundane matters like mileage aren't a major consideration.

Vigland's bus station isn't really a depot. It's just a corner inside the Lumbermen's Café, which in turn occupies a street-level corner of the long-defunct Vigland Hotel. Larry got his suitcase out of the trunk, where Jerry had stashed it, and I went inside with him. The clerk checked over his ticket and said the bus should be coming within five minutes, right on schedule. He also warned that it only stopped for about two minutes.

"It's been nice meeting you, Larry," I said as we went outside. I felt a little awkward. I had a limousine, and Larry had seven electric toothbrushes, two of which were used. "I appreciate your bringing the limousine all the way up here."

"Sure. Actually, it was kind of a fun trip. In little towns you get lots of stares, and girls wave at you. If you ever get down to Texas, look us up. Mom said she's never met you. She still lives out at Dry Wells, though I've been in Dallas since I went to work for Uncle Ned."

I couldn't see me ever getting down to Texas, but I said, "I'll keep that in mind."

The bus pulled up to the curb, and Larry picked up his suitcase. The door whooshed open. The last thing Larry said before he stepped inside was, "Oh, by the way, the windows in the limo are bulletproof. You can't open them. Uncle Ned had it custom-built. So if you ever decide to rob a bank with it, you'll be safe."

"Bulletproof! Why would Uncle Ned need bulletproof windows?"

"He probably didn't. He was paranoid as well as eccentric." Larry paused, a thoughtful expression on his freckled face. "But then, Uncle Ned had made some enemies over the years. A lot of people thought he was an old shyster, and some of his business dealings were questionable. So who knows? He also had it customized with an oversized tank so he wouldn't have to stop for gas very often. He hated gas stations."

Larry took a seat halfway back in the bus. Only one other person, an older woman, got on. I waved as the bus pulled away. I realized I'd have rather liked to get to know Larry better.

Jerry already had the engine running when I returned to the Trans Am, and I knew he was eager to get back to the limo. I opened the door but didn't get in.

"I'm going to walk back to the house." It was almost three miles, but I didn't want any favors from Jerry. "I hope everything works out great for you in San Diego."

I'd try very hard, I promised myself, not to hope that his parachute failed on his first skydive.

"Oh, come on, get in. We're friends, aren't we? You can't walk all the way home in those." He nodded toward my feet.

Flip-flops. The cheap plastic kind. He was right. I'd have blisters to my knees if I walked three miles in them. Reluctantly I slid inside.

Back home, I thanked him for the ride. By then he'd apparently figured out he hadn't a worm's chance at a robins' convention of driving my limousine. He tried another tack as he pulled around the limo and parked in my driveway. "C'mon, Andi, one little spin in it, okay? For old times' sake."

Old times? We'd never had *any* times in a limousine together. "I don't think so."

I slid briskly out of the car. Jerry came around and draped his arm around my shoulders, and we looked at the limo together. I was momentarily too entranced even to object to the arm. The sun had slipped over the forested hillsides to the west, but the long metal hood gleamed as if lit with an inner fire, the tinted windows a dark contrast of mystery.

I won't drive it. There's no point in driving it. It would be like taking one nibble of a Godiva chocolate, knowing you can't have the whole box.

"Basically, it's just an overlength car, isn't it?" Jerry said, his head tilted and his tone uncharacteristically philosophical. "But there's something . . . *captivating* about that extra length."

Yes, there was indeed. Captivating.

4

I was just standing there, wanting to run and jump into the limo but unwilling to give Jerry a chance to ride in it, when Joella opened her door, did a double take, and dashed across the lawn. Well, maybe not *dashed*, considering her condition, but hurried.

"Andi, what's going on? What is a limousine doing here?"

"It's Andi's," Jerry said. "She inherited it from some rich uncle."

"You inherited it?" Joella gasped. "I lie down for a nap, and when I get up, you're an heiress with a limousine?"

"It's only temporary. A cousin drove it up from Texas. I'll have to sell it."

"Oh, can we take a ride in it first?" Joella clapped her hands, starry-eyed as a little girl looking at her first Christmas tree. "Does it have an intercom system and a TV?" She rushed over and pulled open the rear door.

I followed her and peered over her shoulder. A black leather sofa-type seat curved across the front and down one side. Another seat ran across the back, the long stretch from front to back carpeted in burgundy. The far side held a wine rack, a small fridge, and a TV and DVD player. And on the ceiling—

Joella and I looked up at it, dumbfounded. It was a painted scene of an oil field crowded with big derricks and heavy equipment and little stick men in yellow hard hats, all done on what looked like a piece of old tarp fastened to the ceiling. You could almost smell the oil fumes from the derricks. Or maybe that was the tarp. It was totally out of character with the luxuriousness of the limo.

"I don't believe I've ever ridden in one with a mural on the ceiling," Joella said tactfully.

Jerry was right there peering into the limo too. "You've ridden in a limo *without* a ceiling mural?" he asked skeptically.

Jerry didn't know anything about Joella's past, of course. To him, she was just the unmarried pregnant girl to whom I was renting the other half of the duplex at below the going rate, which he disapproved. I'd never thought about Joella and limousines, but now that I did, I realized they probably weren't all that unfamiliar to her.

She closed the door and stepped back, her hands now clasped behind her as if she were ashamed of her enthusiastic outburst. "I haven't ridden in one for a long time. They're, well, you know, *different*. But . . . no big deal."

"Would you like to go for a ride now?" I asked impulsively. "It might be fun."

For Jerry I wouldn't do this, but for Joella I would. There wasn't a whole lot of fun in her life. "Okay, let's go!"

I had the keys where I'd stuffed them in the pocket of my shorts. I opened the driver's door, then paused. More black leather seats that were oh-so-buttery soft, so rich smelling, a world apart from the discount-store seat covers that scratched my legs in my Corolla.

There were a few buttons and switches I didn't recognize, but the basic controls looked identifiable enough. I slid in and tried them. Lights, turn signals, windshield wipers, tachometer, gauges for gas and temperature and oil pressure. I was happy to see that the transmission was automatic. But the heating/air-conditioning system looked as if it might take a rocket scientist to operate. As did the radio and sound system.

Joella opened the rear door again. I hadn't invited him, but Jerry scooted in with her. I turned the key in the ignition. I was so accustomed to my noisy old vehicle that it took me a moment to realize that the limo's engine was running. A kitten's purr, sweet and low. Though when I cautiously revved the engine, it turned to a roar of tiger power.

I drove slowly up to the circle where Secret View Lane dead-ended, then carefully stopped and backed up to turn around, uncertain if the limo could make the circular turn in one sweep. All around the circle, doors opened and people stepped out to stare. It was like synchronized cuckoo clocks. Tom Bolton was at his gate, staring again as I drove by. At the corner, a teenager in a jacked-up pickup lost his cool long enough to brake and stare.

Hey, this was fun!

We cruised up through town. Limousines aren't unknown in Vigland, of course. Every once in a while you see one parked at the nearby casino or headed for one of the waterfront resorts, and a newspaper article about last year's senior prom had photos of several couples who'd hired limousines from a service over in Olympia. But neither were they commonplace, and we were definitely drawing second looks.

In the back, Joella and Jerry were playing with their own controls, turning on the TV, opening and shutting the privacy divider, pushing something that closed the curtains. Something buzzed beside me, and I didn't know what it was until Joella yelled at me to pick up the intercom.

When I did, her voice said, "Madam Chauffeur, this is fantastic!"

I wanted to open the window beside me, then remembered what Cousin Larry had said. By the time we got up near Wal-Mart, where traffic was heaviest, I knew how the long-tailed cat in a roomful of rocking chairs feels. The end of the limo as seen in the rearview mirror seemed miles back.

At the red light, a teenage girl in a denim miniskirt waved frantically. I couldn't make out her words, but it seemed clear she wanted to hire me.

I was just beginning to feel more confident with the driving when a beat-up Chevy zoomed through a yellow light and turned left in front of me, barely missing the front fender. I jammed on the brakes, and in back I heard a big thump.

"Jo, did I hurt you?" I yelled in a panic. "Are you all right?"

"I'm fine. Jerry's on the floor, but he's okay."

She sounded disappointed, and less clearly I could hear Jerry grumbling about my driving. Tough. Nobody invited him to come along.

"He's getting up now."

We cruised on down the hill beyond Wal-Mart, then back along the bay to the center of town, and finally on around the hill to Secret View Lane. I parked at the end of the walkway to the house. I'd move the limo into the safer area of the drive-way as soon as Jerry got his car out of there. Maybe I'd be all heartbroken about him in a few hours, but right now I just wanted him gone. Out of sight, out of my life.

Jerry stepped out of the rear door of the limo first, rubbing his neck and glaring at me as if he figured I'd knocked him down on purpose.

Joella rushed up and gave me a big hug. "Thanks, Andi. I don't miss stuff like that, but it really was fun." She grabbed my wrist and looked at my watch. Hers had stopped working, but she couldn't spare the money to buy another one. "Oh, hey, I'm late for Bible study."

A minute later she was backing her old Subaru down her half of the driveway. She'd had a Mustang convertible when she first moved in, but she'd sold it to help with expenses.

I turned to ask Jerry to move his Trans Am, but JoAnne Metzger, a neighbor from the end of the street, was running down the sidewalk and waving at me.

"Andi, got a minute for a nosy question?" she called.

"Sure."

JoAnne is the social organizer of Secret View Lane. She puts together neighborhood barbecues and recycling drives and organizes the annual garage sale for the whole street. I went down the sidewalk to meet her.

She patted her chest and puffed with the exertion. "My niece is getting married in a couple of weeks, and when I looked out and saw this limousine, I thought, oh, wouldn't it be great to give Tanya a ride in that as a wedding present? She'd love it. But I have no idea how much it costs to hire one, so if you don't mind my asking . . ."

She glanced around as if wondering why the limousine was here, since there didn't appear to be any special event going on. I had the feeling she was pointedly ignoring Jerry. The "fat slob" he'd disparaged at that barbecue had been her sister.

"I didn't realize you could rent one and then just drive it yourself," she added.

"Actually, I'm not renting it. I'm as surprised as anyone, but I seem to have inherited it from an uncle in Texas."

"It's *yours*?" Her interested look went wide-eyed. "Andi, that's fabulous! How *fun!* So maybe we can hire you *and* the limo for Tanya's wedding?"

"Well, uh, I don't think so. I don't see how I can keep it. I'll probably sell it as soon as possible."

"Couldn't you hang on to it just until the wedding? Tanya would be so thrilled. Dan could drive it, if you don't want to get in heavy traffic with it."

Cousin Larry had suggested that I start a limousine business. He was probably being facetious, same as with his hot-dog stand suggestion, but was a limousine service perhaps a real possibility? Even if it wasn't, if I could just make a few bucks with the limousine before I sold it . . . why not?

"Give me a day or two to see what I'm going to do with it, okay?"

Although I was pretty sure I wasn't going to let her husband drive. I didn't have acrimonious feelings toward him as I did toward Jerry, but I was feeling very proprietary about this long, black, magic chariot that had unexpectedly dropped into my possession.

"Sure, just let me know." She gave me a little wave as she started back toward her house at the end of the street.

Jerry had gone back to the limousine, though I doubted it was because he sensed vibrations of hostility from JoAnne. As I'd already concluded, he wasn't that aware. He was leaning over and running his hand around a hubcap now.

I suppressed an urge to stomp on his fingers as I walked over and said, "Could you move your car out of the driveway, please? I'd like to park the limo there so it can't get scraped or bumped out on the street."

I noted a little dust on a front fender and headed for the garage to get a rag to polish it off. Instead of going to move his car, Jerry followed me.

"Hey, babe, I'm thinking, why don't I run down to the store and pick up a couple steaks? It's a great evening for a barbecue."

I turned at the door to the garage and looked at him. He hadn't been interested in my suggestion about barbecuing burgers earlier. "It's getting late. I thought you had things to do."

"They can wait." Without looking at the Rolex he always wore to check the time, he stepped closer and draped his arms around me. "How about it? Maybe a bottle of champagne?"

"You want to *celebrate* our breakup?"

"Not celebrate it, Andi. Just give it the kind of conclusion it deserves. With a little celebration of your new limo thrown in."

I was about 99 percent inclined to tell him *no way*, but there was that one percent of mental foot dragging. Maybe because he was almost begging, and that was certainly a change. Maybe because I figured he owed me a steak. Or maybe because, deep down in some hope-never-dies part of me, I thought maybe there was still a chance for us?

And then he said, "I'm just thinking, I've never . . . you know . . . in the back of a limousine." He ran a fingertip across my eyebrow and down my temple. "We'll pull all those little curtains and light a couple of candles . . ."

I drew back and stared at him in astonishment. "We've never 'you know' anywhere!" I pointed out. Jerry had made some moves and hints before, but I thought he understood where I stood on this.

"And that's one of the problems with our relationship," he pointed out.

"One of its 'limitations'?"

"A definite limitation."

"So you're thinking that now, when our relationship is ending, that I'm going to . . . jump into something I wouldn't before?"

"It would put a beautiful end to the relationship. Give it—

what's it called?—closure. Yes, that's it. A beautiful closure. A beautiful memory for both of us."

And suddenly I was totally and completely furious. He had just dumped me, tried to sell me his old sailboat, blithely told me he was taking up with another woman, and now he wanted *closure* in the back of the limousine? *Toadstool* was way too generous.

I put both hands on his chest and shoved. He stumbled backward, looking baffled, as if he couldn't understand this uncooperative attitude.

"Andi, come on. What's the matter?"

"Out!" I yelled. "Get away from me! Get out of here, *now!*"

My old broom was still standing there from when I'd last swept the front steps. I grabbed for it blindly, intending . . . I don't know what. Maybe shake it in his face to let him know how I was feeling.

But suddenly I was even madder than that, and I was yelling a lot more things. "Jerk! Idiot!" I think I got *scumbag* in there too, and maybe even *slime bucket* and *sleazeball*.

I swung the broom back and forth . . . *whoosh, whoosh, whoosh!*

Jerry had a strange look on his face. He jumped like a kangaroo in reverse, then started running and stumbling backward. He crashed into a flower bed, scrambled to his feet, and crab-stepped sideways.

I had him on the run! It was an exhilarating thought. *Whoosh!* Sweep that man right out of my life! A little closer and I might even do a *wham*.

"C'mon, Andi, take it easy—"

Was that *fear* I heard in his voice? The man was afraid of a woman with a *broom*?

"Out! I never want to see you again!" *Whoosh!*

He jumped into the Trans Am, and my *whoosh* turned into

a *wham* on the door as he closed it. A wham that *boinged* and vibrated up my arms and across my shoulders and ricocheted around in my brain. I shook my head, trying to clear the shooting stars.

Which was when I suddenly realized it wasn't an old broom I was swinging. It was a *shovel*. The shovel with which I'd been flattening those dirt mounds in the lawn.

I stared at the dent in the car door, horrified at what I'd done. Bare metal showed through the glossy red paint. "Jerry, I'm sorry! I didn't mean to—"

He didn't give me a chance to finish. He gunned the engine and shot out of the driveway like a race driver in reverse. Out on the street, a scent of burned rubber sprayed the air like some macabre barbecue.

I stared after him. How could I have done such an incredible, ridiculous thing? Chasing a man down a driveway with a *shovel*, whacking the side of his car, all the time yelling and screaming like a banshee.

I looked at the shovel still hanging like a metallic appendage from my hand. Appalling. Bizarre. Unbelievable. And then I realized I had an audience. Tom Bolton from across the street was staring at me from his gate. Farther down the street, two doors had opened, and more people were gawking as if they thought I'd gone berserk.

Maybe I had, I thought guiltily. Never in my life had I behaved in such a way. I cringed, wishing I could dig a quick hole with the shovel and pull the dirt in over me. How would I ever live this down?

But it doesn't really matter, I told myself firmly as I straightened my shoulders and pretended to ignore the stares. It was humiliating, of course, to have witnesses to my ridiculous display. It was disturbing to realize I could do such an awful thing, with or without an audience. It was scary to know that in anger I couldn't differentiate between a broom and a shovel. What if I'd actually whammed Jerry?

But I hadn't, after all, done that. Except for some possible damage to his ego, I hadn't hurt Jerry at all. I'd drop him a polite note and tell him to send me the repair bill on the car. Not something I could afford, but the only decent thing to do.

With careful dignity, I walked to the garage and set the shovel next to the broom that I'd meant to pick up. No harm done, I assured myself firmly.

Wrong again. Although it would be a couple of days before I knew that.

5

Joella came over after she got home from Bible study. I knew she wouldn't have if Jerry's Trans Am had still been in the driveway. By then I'd moved the limo off the street and was morosely drowning my guilt and humiliation in lemonade and cookies.

She peered around cautiously. "He's gone?"

I nodded. "Permanently. We broke up. He's getting a transfer to the San Diego office."

I didn't give details about Jerry's suggestion on "closure" in the back of the limousine, but I did tell her about what I euphemistically termed an "unpleasant confrontation" and that the Trans Am had been the unfortunate victim of my fury. She sipped lemonade while she listened.

"Do you want me to be sympathetic or truthful?" she asked when I was finished.

"Whatever."

"Okay, if you want sympathy . . . there, there, sweetie, I know how you're hurting." She patted my shoulder solicitously. "But if you want what I really think . . ." She shot a fist of victory into the air. "Good riddance!"

She was probably right. When I looked at him clearly, there

were definitely rough spots on Jerry's luster. A lack of concern about being on time for dates, sometimes even forgetting them entirely. That snobbish attitude toward people who weren't as physically fit as he was. A tendency toward status symbols, including that overpriced condo and the pretentious decorator he'd hired to decorate it. And once the guy had actually cheated when we were playing a Sudoku board game, though I hadn't let myself acknowledge that at the time. Realistically, even if he hadn't gotten the transfer, we probably wouldn't have lasted much longer.

I had to wonder now if I hadn't overlooked some of Jerry's less-appealing personality traits because I was too dazzled that this very attractive guy, this ten-years-younger-than-me guy, was interested in *me*.

"I'm sorry," Joella said. "I'm sure he had his good points."

"No, that's okay. Although at the moment, *good riddance* is probably what he's thinking about me."

"It's his loss."

"I guess it's a wonder we lasted as long as we did." I shook my head. "The difference in our temperaments and values. To say nothing of our ages. I'm not sure what he ever saw in me. I'm a grandmother, for goodness' sake."

"Andi, don't sell yourself short." Joella's tone was almost severe. "*I* can certainly see what he saw in you. You're sweet and smart and fun. You have beautiful eyes and a great figure."

"I should lose at least twelve pounds. Gray hair—"

"I don't see any gray hair."

"That's because I cover it with 'Cinnamon Sunrise.'" Which, in less fanciful terms, was light brown with goldy glints.

"You look at least ten years younger than you are," Joella declared, ever my loyal supporter. "But even if you didn't, so what? It's no sin to look your age. And I have to give Jerry credit for one thing. He may be a jerk, but he had the good taste or good sense or whatever to be attracted to *you*."

"Whatever it was, he ran out of it."

"A jerk is a jerk is a jerk," Joella said. "A jerk can hide his jerkiness for only so long, and then it breaks through. Like a rotten egg exploding in a microwave."

"I didn't realize you were such a philosopher."

"I've known some jerks too. They come in all ages."

I sighed. "Jerk or not, I still can't believe I went after him with a shovel." I could still feel the tingle from that *boing* on his car door. "Maybe I need an anger management course or something."

"What you need is God."

"How does God feel about shovel-wielding women?"

"He's forgiven much worse. We were studying forgiveness in Ephesians just this evening at Bible study. You should come sometime."

Sure. I could take my shovel and do show-and-tell.

I got up and restlessly peered out the kitchen window. Joella came around to stand by me. We looked out at the limo.

"How do you figure on trying to sell it? Newspaper ad?"

"I have no idea what it's worth. Maybe I should contact some limousine services over in Olympia or Seattle and see if they'd like to buy it."

"Maybe you should think about starting your own limousine business."

"That's what my cousin said. Although he also said I might turn it into a hot-dog stand. One's probably as practical as the other."

Joella looked as if she were about to scold me, but then she giggled. "Why not? Limo-dogs! Great idea. You can drive around town with a big mustard-striped wiener mounted on top. I'll toss out flyers about the Limo Special of the Day. You'll cater exclusive private parties and feature Limo-dogs with caviar!"

Joella's silly scenario made me feel smiley in spite of my glum mood.

"We'll need a sound system blaring something lively," I said. "How about 'Itsy Bitsy Teenie Weenie, Yellow Polka Dot Bikini'?"

"What's that got to do with limousines or hot dogs?"

"Who cares?"

"Right! You'll add a second limo, then expand to a whole fleet. You'll sell franchises and become known nationwide as Queen of the Limo-dog Empire!"

"I'll attend society functions wearing a tiara of entwined hot dogs! Hot-dog jewelry will become the latest fad!"

The scheme collapsed under its own grandiose silliness. Joella giggled again, and so did I. She often had that effect on me. I put an arm around her slender shoulders and squeezed my thanks.

"Seriously, though, maybe you should think about the limousine-business idea. Look how excited that girl on the street was about getting a limo for some event. Kids have all kinds of money to spend these days."

And JoAnne Metzger had seemed thrilled with the idea of a limousine for her niece's wedding . . .

I shook my head. No. A fun idea, perhaps, but impractical on a daily basis. "What I need is a *job*. Steady, go-to-work-every-day, paycheck-paying employment. With benefits."

"I suppose."

"First thing Monday morning I'm job hunting." Hopefully before everyone else from F&N beat me to it.

BY THE NEXT day at the office, I realized Monday morning might be too late. At least a third of the employees didn't even show up for work, no doubt thinking, *What can they do to me now? I'm already fired.* Those early birds were probably out there snatching up whatever jobs might be available. I knew a lot of job hunting with big companies was done on the Internet these days, but I doubted that smaller business offices around Vigland worked that way, and it might well be the early birds who got the jobs.

Joining them was a tempting thought, but a persistent sense of responsibility and loyalty kept me glumly sitting at my desk. F&N had been good to me for the past eleven years, and I was getting paid through Friday, plus that four months' severance pay, so cheating on these final days wouldn't be right. Also, Letty Bishop, who was in charge now that the department supervisor had already cleared out, was frantically trying to operate with only half a crew, and I didn't want to let her down either.

Jerry worked in another wing of the building, and I didn't usually run into him. I was grateful for that now. I sent him a brief e-mail about paying for the damaged car door.

I'd barely gotten home from work when the phone rang. I steeled myself, thinking it was probably Jerry telling me he'd taken the Trans Am into the shop, and repairs were going to cost more than the total worth of my old Corolla.

But it was my daughter, Sarah, singing, "Happy birthday to you, happy birthday to you, happy birthday, dear Mother, happy birthday to you!"

"Thank you!"

"I'm calling a couple days early because I thought you might have big plans for Saturday. So, what are you going to do to celebrate?"

"Oh, the usual. Champagne party, catered dinner for five hundred, fireworks, etc."

"Yeah. That's what I usually do too. Am I catching you at a bad time?"

Sarah is a bright, intelligent woman, but even after all these years of living in Florida, she sometimes gets befuddled about which way the three-hour time difference works.

"No, I'm just getting home from work."

"Everything okay? You sound a little frazzled."

There was that downsized-dumped-depressed thing, of course, but I didn't want to unload my problems on her. "I'm fine."

"Mom, the strangest thing happened yesterday. Do you know someone named Ned Nicholson?"

"Uncle Ned, the family's token rich guy. I understand he died."

"He was rich?"

"Oil wells, mansion, who knows what else."

"Rachel and I both got registered packages from a law firm in Texas representing his estate. He left me a can of pistachios and a set of nut-cracking tools. Can you imagine? Pistachios! Why would anyone *bother*? Especially someone rich?"

"What did Rachel get?"

"A book on raising llamas. And we both got framed photos of the old guy. It's just weird. Did you get something?"

These inheritances proved one thing to me. I hadn't received the limousine because I was any favorite of Uncle Ned's. He'd never met either Sarah or Rachel, so he had no reason to hold any grudges against them either. Which meant he must have used the random, papers-in-a-pot system of asset distribution.

"Actually, I did. A cousin delivered it yesterday. I got a limousine."

There was a moment of stunned silence until Sarah squeaked, "A *limousine*?"

"A limousine. L-i-m-o-u-z-e-e-n, as Uncle Ned called it in his will."

"We're talking a real, life-size limousine, not a toy?"

"A real stretch limousine. It's sitting out in my driveway now. The cousin drove it up from Texas."

"What in the world are you going to do with a limousine?"

"Good question."

"It must be worth something. A whole lot more than a can of pistachios or a book on raising llamas."

For a moment I thought I detected a twinge of indignation or even envy in her voice. But then, with her usual generous good humor, she laughed.

"I know. You can drive down to visit us in it!"

"Unfortunately, I'm going to have to look for a job. F&N is closing down here, and everyone was terminated."

Well, almost everyone. There were the Jerry exceptions.

"Oh, Mom, I'm sorry to hear that. Finding another job may not be easy at—" She broke off, leaving unspoken the *at your age* we both knew was there.

"They're giving me a severance package that will help temporarily."

"Good. And you know, you're always welcome to come live with us. We'd love to have you. Just jump in that limousine and move on down here."

"Thanks, but I think I'll be fine here." Dearly as I loved my daughter and granddaughter, I liked my independent life.

"I wonder how the lawyers knew how to locate all of us."

"I have no idea. I didn't think to ask the cousin when he was here."

"Well, given how weird the old guy was, maybe he had

private detectives look us up or something. Doesn't matter, I suppose. Oh, in the excitement of birthdays and pistachios and limousines, I'm almost forgetting my news! I've decided to go back to college."

"Sarah, that's wonderful!"

Sarah had dropped out of college to marry and help The Sleaze-Bum, as I now thought of him, get his degree.

"I'm so glad to hear that."

"Finances will be tight with both Rachel and me in school, but I'm looking into loans and grants and scholarships, whatever's available. The counselor I talked to thought I should be able to fulfill the requirements for my degree in two years."

"I'll do whatever I can to help." Another reason to get a good, solid job *fast*.

We talked a few minutes more about her plans for a degree in business economics at the University of Florida, where Rachel would also be starting this fall. It would be a good deal for both of them, I thought, living at home together and sharing the expense of commuting to classes. And I was so pleased that Sarah was grabbing hold of her life, not drifting as she'd seemed to do since the divorce.

"Oh, here's Rachel. She wants to talk to you too."

"Hi, Grandma. Happy birthday!"

"Thanks, hon."

Some shuffling noises, as if she were doing something with the phone, then a frantic whisper. "Grandma, you've got to *do* something!"

I was startled. "About what?"

"About Mom. She's signed up to start college this fall—"

"I know. She just told me. I think it's a wonderful idea."

"Yeah, going to college is probably good. But she intends to go where *I'm* going. It'll be a disaster!"

"In what way?"

"Think about it, my mother right there on campus. Watching my every move. Doing . . . well, who knows what? We might even wind up having some class together. It's creepy. Like some back-to-the-future thing."

"Rachel, I think you're overreacting. The University of Florida has a huge number of students, and it's unlikely you and your mother will have any classes together. And even if you did, I'm sure she isn't going to humiliate or embarrass you."

"No? She was trying on jeans the other day. The kind that come to about four inches below your belly button. And one of those gauzy tops. Grandma, she's thirty-nine years old."

"Thirty-nine is not over the hill, Rachel. In fact, it's . . ." I searched for an appropriate word and chose Fitz's. "It's prime time, Rachel. Definitely prime time."

Small silence, as if Rachel was wondering whether that could possibly be true. "Actually, she looked pretty good in the jeans," she finally muttered grudgingly. "But still . . ."

"Did she buy any?"

"No. But she might. Okay, I gotta go now. She's coming back down the hall."

"Rachel, I think this is something you just have to live with. Your mother has a life to live too, and you need to be supportive."

Another moment of silence as she digested Grandma's tough-love stance. "I suppose."

In a you'll-be-sorry-when-I'm-dead tone she added, "I guess if it gets too bad, I can always go raise llamas. I have this book on how to do it, you know."

"There you go," I agreed cheerfully.

Although, after Rachel hung up, I had to wonder. Sometimes

women Sarah's age, and in a situation such as hers, did try the back-to-youth thing, with disastrous results. Something else to worry about.

I changed out of my office clothes and went to stare into the refrigerator, trying to spot something appealing for dinner. I was echoing Joella's *good riddance* about Jerry, but at the same time the evening stretched out long and empty without even the prospect of a phone call.

This is what life is going to be like from now on, I reminded myself dispiritedly. *Get used to it.*

6

I was just sitting down at the counter to eat leftover meat loaf and spinach when the phone rang again. Whatever worrisome news it was this time, it couldn't be any worse than the downsized, dumped, and granddaughter blues I'd already encountered.

"Hello?"

"Andi? Is that you? This is Fitz. From the coffee shop. Remember?"

"I remember. The guy who read my private letter."

"That's all you remember about me?" He sounded disappointed.

"There's more?"

"You could remember that I'm this handsome ex-TV detective, currently involved in glamorous charter sailboat trips, and I wanted to buy you a peach smoothie."

"Whatever."

"Come to think of it, if that Jerry guy doesn't have your evenings all sewed up, I might even spring for dinner."

I gasped dramatically and clutched my throat. "Be still my throbbing heart!"

"You going to hold some permanent grudge about the letter thing?"

Okay, it probably was petty. Nosy wasn't a capital offense. I changed the subject. "I thought you were taking a charter sailboat trip out today."

"We are. I'm on my cell phone. We're sailing by Seattle right now. I can see the Space Needle and the Seattle skyline. It's beautiful. Maybe you can come along sometime. You'd love it."

"Ummm," I said. How did he know what I'd love? For all he knew, I could be a shopping-mall addict without a drop of outdoorsy blood in my veins.

But he was right, of course. I probably would love it. I'd loved hiking and sailing with Jerry.

"The reason I called, I stopped in at the Sweet Breeze this morning before I picked up our guests, and Joella told me about your limousine. She said you're thinking about starting a limousine service."

"What I'm planning to do is sell it."

"Oh? Isn't this a great opportunity to have a business of your own? You wouldn't be stuck in an office. You'd be meeting interesting people and going places and being your own boss. All kinds of adventure and excitement."

He had some good points there, though adventure and excitement were not high on my list of occupational requirements.

I muttered another noncommittal "Ummm."

"The thing is, we have guests from New York arriving next Tuesday for a trip up around the San Juan Islands. They'll be coming in at Sea-Tac. I usually transport people in our SUV, but these people are arriving at a different time than they originally planned, and I have an appointment with a lawyer set up for that morning."

A lawyer? I wondered why, of course, but I hadn't the

nerve to come right out and ask. Though I suspected Fitz might have, if the situation were reversed.

"Anyway, I was thinking you could pick up these people with the limousine. In fact, we might turn it into a regular thing. It would add kind of a classy touch. We'll pay whatever the going rate for limo service is, of course."

I was still hung up on one word back there. Sea-Tac. The huge Seattle-Tacoma airport was situated on the other side of Puget Sound, up between the two cities, at least an hour and a half or two hours' drive. Maybe considerably more, if the traffic was bad, and it often was. Just the thought of putting my long-tailed limo out there for every eighteen-wheeler and oversized SUV to take aim at made me cringe. "Oh, I don't think so. It's quite a distance, and all that traffic . . ."

"Joella said you took her for a drive and did great in traffic. And you are unemployed, remember?"

Like I needed reminding. "What's the going rate for limousines?" I asked cautiously.

"The one time we used one, I think we paid something like $250 or $300 to a limousine service in Olympia. Call up some limousine outfits over there and find out their rates. Though we'd expect a break on price if we made it a regular deal."

Shrewd as well as nosy.

"I guess I could think about it."

"Except that we need to know right now. We won't be getting back into the marina until midday Monday, so I need to call now for a reservation with someone else if you aren't available."

"Tuesday morning, you said?"

"Right. Their flight comes in around eleven."

Three hundred dollars sounded pretty good. And by Tuesday, I'd be sixty. Maybe it was time to try something a bit adventurous. I could get the title change taken care of on Monday.

Insurance too, if I had time, though my policy allowed thirty days to add an additional vehicle. But that would be on liability only, of course, since that was all I carried on my old Toyota. But, feeling oddly exhilarated, I made the leap. "Okay, I'll do it."

"Good. I'll talk to you about details when we get back from this trip. And I still want to buy you that peach smoothie."

With no more phone calls, I finally got to my meatloaf and spinach. I read through the hieroglyphics of Uncle Ned's will while I ate. No surprise to see that he'd mangled the spelling of Sarah's pistachios. But he had gotten *lava lamp* spelled right. That went to someone named Candace.

IT WASN'T UNTIL the following day after work, Friday, when I officially became unemployed, that I remembered the chauffeur's uniforms Larry had said he'd left in the trunk. I got the limo keys from the spot I'd assigned them, a hook by the door that opened from the kitchen into the garage.

The trunk compartment was deep and roomy. It was on two levels, the second making a kind of platform at the back of the main compartment. The spare tire was fastened to the upper level, where it was easily accessible.

Inside the roomy compartment were cartons and sacks from some of Larry's on-the-road meals—grease seemed to be his main food group—and a cardboard box. A maintenance book lay on top of the box. I set it aside to take into the house. I unfolded a black jacket from the box, and at the same time something fell to the ground with a glass-shattering crash.

Uncle Ned's photo. He stared up at me from the gravel driveway, a sour-looking face topped with a shiny, coal-black toupee, as if he'd just had a midair collision with a disoriented crow. And mean little eyes that said *I know what you did—you dropped me—and I'm gonna get you for it.*

I assured myself that dead people can't get even and hastily scooped what was left of Uncle Ned into a Kentucky Fried Chicken sack. But just in case, I added a conciliatory thought. *I'll get you a nice new frame.*

I don't know what chauffeur uniforms usually look like, but I was favorably impressed with these. A sophisticated black with two rows of gleaming silver buttons up the front of the jacket, a snug-fitting collar, two more silver buttons on the sleeves, and pants with a narrow, black-satin stripe running down the side.

Joella knocked on the kitchen door while I was trying on a uniform in my bedroom, and I yelled at her to come on in.

"Hey, wow, classy!" she said when she saw me. The jacket was overlarge, but wearable. Both jacket and pants had nice silky linings. "You can cinch in the waist of the pants with a belt. It'll be under the jacket, and no one will see."

There was a neat cap, too, also black with a silver pin in the shape of Texas above the visor. I stuck it on my head at a snappy angle, clicked my heels, and saluted my image in the mirror.

"Right this way, sir," I told an imaginary client as I made a grand sweep of the arm. "Your chariot awaits."

Joella applauded.

I told her about Fitz's call and asked, "Should I wear this on Tuesday when I go to Sea-Tac?"

"Oh, yes. You'll probably get a fifty-dollar tip."

"Limousine drivers get tips?"

"My father always tipped the driver when he rented one."

This was looking better all the time.

"Hey, is my birthday celebration still on for tomorrow?" I was suddenly feeling more upbeat about a birthday too.

"The cake is in the oven. I just came over to see what time would be good. Anyone you want to invite?"

Oddly, the face that popped into my head was Fitz's. But he was off sailing. Not that I'd invite Mr. Nosy anyway.

"No, I don't think so . . . Hey, I know what let's do. Let's make it a picnic out at that park on the other side of Hornsby Inlet. We'll go in the limousine!"

Joella clapped her hands. "We can build a fire and roast limo-dogs!"

We decided to leave about noon the next day. My first-ever birthday celebration with a limousine. Maybe sixty really *was* prime time!

I WOKE SOMETIME in the night. No, closer to morning, I realized as I peered at the red numbers on my clock radio. I had the feeling something had wakened me.

Moose, the Sheersons' Dalmatian, was barking, but that wasn't out of the ordinary. The early-morning garbage-collection guys always set him off, as did anyone taking a stroll too early or late for his strict time standards.

But the thing was, Moose usually barked *at* something. He also sometimes got out of his yard, and what he especially liked to do when he got out was rush over and dig in my flower beds.

I listened another minute. No, he wasn't in my yard now. His bark was too far away. So what had set him off? Crime certainly wasn't rampant on Secret View Lane, and traffic wasn't heavy because it was a dead-end street. But last fall someone had managed to dig up and steal an expensive Japanese lace maple JoAnne Metzger had newly planted in her yard.

The limo. What if teenagers were hot-wiring it for a joyride? Or getting their kicks vandalizing it! Slashed seats, obnoxious graffiti, key-scratched paint, flattened tires—

I jumped out of bed and raced to the kitchen window. A heavy fog blanketed everything, blocking out stars above and turning the houses across the street into mist-shrouded blobs. No streetlights on our little lane, though JoAnne was nagging the powers-that-be about it.

But I could make out the long, sleek shape of the limo and my little Corolla, which I'd parked behind the limo when I got home from work. Nothing going on there. Moose was still barking, but sometimes he got excited about a stray cat wandering by.

Then I glanced at the hook by the back door. No limo keys! And now I realized with even more dismay that I couldn't remember locking the limo after I brought the uniforms in last night. Had I left the keys sitting right out there, readily available to any thief or vandal?

I flicked on the outside light, released the chain across the front door, and stepped outside. The cool, misty air hit me, and an unexpected prickle of apprehension stopped me on the top step. If I really *had* heard something . . . if Moose was barking at something more than a stray cat . . . was rushing out there in my bare feet and pajamas really a smart thing to do?

I peered at the dark shapes of the limo and the Corolla in the driveway. With the light over the front steps on, the night seemed darker, the mist more ghostly, the tinted limo windows more mysterious. Was that a movement? A flicker of something on the far side of the hood?

I watched for a long, breath-held minute. No, no movement, just my imagination doing a 4 AM tango with nerves. But still, I decided, I'd feel better if the limo were properly locked.

The shaggy grass between the concrete walkway and gravel driveway reminded me it was time to get the mower out again, and my bare feet squishing through the night-damp grass told me I should have taken time to put on some shoes.

But this would just take a minute. Moose had resumed barking, but he was barking at me now, of course.

I opened the driver's side door. The dome light came on, casting a reassuring rectangle of light across the grass.

But no, the keys *weren't* on the front seat. I frowned. Had I used the keys rather than the button to open the trunk, and then left them in the lock?

I turned to go around to the back of the limo and look.

And plunged headlong into an explosion of silvery stars and then a pit of darkness . . .

7

There is no awareness of time when you're out cold, but I knew minutes or hours had passed, because I was now looking up at a pale dawn sky, not foggy darkness. I also had a different view of the world now, a very peculiar view. The limousine loomed over me, the door open. Beside me, the underside stretched out in a gray maze of pipes and springs and un-identifiable car stuff.

I was, it appeared, flat on my back.

I felt groggy and stiff . . . and why was my right leg bent under me, and driveway gravel digging into my backside?

And my head, I realized with a sudden groan, oh, my head . . .

I reached up to touch it gingerly, and something moved to block the pale sky overhead. Tom Bolton's frowning face. What was he doing here?

I felt a strange sense of disorientation, as if I'd plunged into a time warp in one of those science fiction books Rachel likes to read.

"You okay?" Tom asked.

"I don't know. What happened?" I wiggled my lips. They'd gone puttyish, slow moving and sluggish.

"I noticed the limousine door standing open. I came over to see what was going on and found you lying here unconscious."

I sat up hastily. Mistake. Limousine, Tom, and pale sky whirled as if we'd just been engulfed in some cosmic readjustment. I waited until the whirling stopped, then winced as I fingered the back of my head and found a lump that felt like the shape and size of Texas.

I offered the only explanation that seemed plausible. "I must have stumbled and bumped my head on the door when I fell."

"What were you doing out here in the middle of the night?" Tom's tone oozed disapproval, as if he figured I had to have been up to something nefarious.

I hadn't been, but why *was* I out here? And in my pajamas too. Straining to think back, I remembered trying on that chauffeur's uniform. Yes, and waking up in the night, being worried about the limousine. Coming outside, opening the limo door . . .

Then that big, dark pit.

I got my hands under me and tried to lever myself to my feet. Tom pushed me down.

"You'd better stay right there. I called 911. An ambulance and someone from the sheriff's department will be here in a few minutes."

Alarm joined the foggy mist in my head. Police? Ambulance? I knew I should thank Tom for coming over to check on the open door of the limo, but at the moment I didn't feel too appreciative. Would they charge some huge fee just for coming out with the ambulance, even if I didn't need it?

Again I tried to rise; again he pushed me back. I looked at his scowl and had the peculiar feeling he wasn't so much concerned with my welfare as he was with keeping me immobilized until someone from the sheriff's department arrived.

"Perhaps you could call back and tell them everything is okay here," I suggested.

He didn't move. "Soon as I saw that limousine in the neighborhood, I knew we were in for trouble," he said darkly.

His logic escaped me. "Why?"

"Mafia. Crooks. Drug dealers. Hookers. It's people like that who use limousines." He nodded sagely.

"All kinds of ordinary people use limousines," I said, with as much indignation as I could muster with chunks of gravel digging into my bottom and Texas throbbing on the back of my head. "They use them to go to the airport or get married or celebrate an anniversary! Kids even go to the prom in them."

"Emma and I never rode in any limousine."

I could hear sirens approaching. I was still sitting beside the limousine door, Tom watching me suspiciously, when a blue-and-white car bearing the insignia of the county sheriff's department pulled to the curb.

We were outside the city limits here, so it was the sheriff's department rather than the city police who'd responded to Tom's call. Two middle-aged officers in brown uniforms stepped out. When Tom wasn't looking, I struggled to my feet.

"Got a problem here?" the shorter of the two officers inquired pleasantly.

He introduced himself as Deputy Somebody and the other officer as Deputy Somebody-else, but by now I was so rattled that the names slid by me like fried eggs on Teflon. Down the street, I saw a front door fly open, then another.

"Nothing's wrong." I yanked my pajama top down, feeling uncomfortably exposed even though everything was modestly covered. At the same time I was halfway wishing I'd worn something more stylish than these daisy-flowered things that were more Old Mother Hubbard than Victoria's Secret.

"Everything's fine. I just came out to check on the limo and stumbled and hit my head on the door. My kind neighbor here found me and was concerned for my welfare and called you."

I gestured toward my kind neighbor. I realized I was babbling, but there's something about police officers looking you over that makes you feel you have to explain yourself. It gives you a guilty feeling, as if you've probably done something illegal even if you can't remember what. "But I'm fine, so if you could just radio the ambulance not to come—"

Too late. The ambulance skidded to a stop behind the deputy's car. The paramedics rushed to Tom, who, with rubbery folds of flesh above his thick neck, gray stubble on his jaws, and the expression of a man who's just eaten a raw squid, apparently looked as if he needed medical attention more than I did. He was also dressed in pajamas, a wild plaid like the pants he usually wore, but he did have a blue terry-cloth robe on over them.

"Hey, get away from me!" Tom backed away and waved his hands as the paramedics approached him. By now Moose was in a full frenzy of barking in the Sheersons' backyard, and I remembered he'd been barking in the night too.

I stepped forward. "I guess it's me you came for," I said reluctantly. "But I'm fine, just fine." I smiled brightly and bounced on my bare feet to reinforce that claim.

"And you are?" the shorter officer inquired.

"Andi McConnell. I live here." I pointed to the house. "And that's my limousine—"

"Your limousine?"

"I inherited it a few days ago. Long story," I said. "Everything's fine."

After some discussion with the officers, with me trying my best to look both physically and mentally robust, the ambulance finally departed. By this time Joella had come out, and other neighbors had clustered and were milling around on the sidewalk.

"What's going on?" Jo was in a robe too, with a wispy nightgown trailing around her bare feet. She reached up to touch my sticky hair. "Andi, you're hurt!"

I repeated my mantra. "I'm fine, just fine. This is all just a misunderstanding."

Short Deputy was examining the door of the limousine, Tall Deputy circling the vehicle, both of them being very careful not to touch anything.

"We don't find anything that suggests you had contact with either the door or doorframe," Short Deputy commented. "No hair or blood."

I fingered my head. I didn't feel any stream of blood, but my hair was sticky and matted over Texas. "What do you mean?"

Tall Deputy: "It doesn't appear you hit your head on the door. Or anywhere else on the vehicle."

"Then I must have just fallen and hit my head on the gravel."

"Are you sure you weren't struck?"

"Struck by what?"

"You didn't see anyone?"

"No. Just Tom here, when I came to."

"She was out cold when I found her."

He sounded defensive, and I was startled to realize that under the circumstances the deputies might think he was involved in my injury. Okay, Tom and I have our differences. Most people in the neighborhood have differences with Tom. He's pointed those binoculars in my direction more than once, and he called in a complaint when Rachel was playing "Rudolph, the Red-Nosed Reindeer" too loudly to suit him one Christmas. But I'd never suspect him of clunking me on the head.

Short Officer pulled out a notebook and looked at Tom. "Your name is?"

"Tom Bolton, 413 Secret View Lane." He pointed across the street. "Lived right there for the past twenty-four years. I'm up by five or five thirty every morning. I like to get an early start on the day."

An early start on spying on the neighbors, is what I thought, but what I said was, "Tom is my good neighbor. He didn't have anything to do with this."

"About what time did you look out and discover the door of the limousine open?" the officer asked Tom.

"Five fifteen, five thirty, somewhere around there. I hadn't had breakfast yet. Still haven't had it."

His sour glance in my direction suggested this was definitely my fault.

"Did you see anything else?"

"Like what?"

"Strange persons, vehicles, anything?"

"No."

"Okay, thanks." Short Officer turned back to me as he put the notebook away. "Have you checked the interior of the vehicle?"

I'd looked over the interior of the limo when I moved it from the street into the driveway, but I hadn't checked inside it since I'd found myself stretched out beside it in my pajamas. "No, I didn't even think about it."

"Mind if we have a look inside?" Tall Officer asked.

"Help yourself."

The officers briefly inspected the interior of the limo, front and back; then Tall Officer motioned me over.

"Everything look okay to you? Don't touch anything," he warned, as I leaned inside to look.

I peered around. Nothing looked wrong or different, and yet, oddly, something didn't feel quite right. The door of the little fridge hung open. Had I left it that way? Had the tarp mural always sagged like that? Had the curtains all been pulled shut?

"I guess it's all the same," I said finally.

"You still think you fell, you weren't struck with something?" Tall Officer asked.

I hesitated, a smidgen of doubt surfacing. Could someone have clobbered me? I couldn't actually remember stumbling. "Why would anyone hit me?"

"We'll check the house. Someone could have gone inside while you were unconscious."

It was an alarming thought. Had I been knocked out by someone for the specific purpose of burglarizing the house?

"I'd appreciate that. Thank you."

"We'll take a look around, then you can come inside and see if anything's missing." Short Officer turned to the crowd. "Okay, folks, fun's over. Nothing's happening here." He waved an arm, gesturing them to disperse.

The small crowd, with some reluctance, I thought, headed back toward their homes. Except for Tom, who apparently felt he had a proprietary interest because he'd found me. Joella wanted to stay too, but I squeezed her hand and told her to go back inside. Standing out here in the wet grass in her bare feet, looking worried and scared, didn't strike me as the best situation for a pregnant young woman.

The officers went inside, moving cautiously as they shoved the door open, guns drawn. By now I was more jittery than when I'd first found myself stretched out on the driveway.

Now that I thought about it, my head felt as if it *could* have been struck, walloped by anything from a baseball bat to that shovel I'd been waving at Jerry. The officers were inside for several minutes before Tall Officer stepped up to the open door and motioned me inside.

"All this look normal?"

Inside, looking at the rooms through the officers' eyes, I could see that it might appear someone had pawed through the place. Mail and magazines scattered around the swivel rocker where I usually watched TV or read. A couple of kitchen drawers open. Cornflakes box fallen over on the counter. My purse on the coffee table, contents scattered because I'd been looking for spare change in the bottom. Clothes piled around the bedroom because I'd started a get-rid-of-old-stuff project a few days ago. Medicine chest in the bathroom open, contents strewn across the counter.

I almost wished I could claim an intruder had ransacked the house, to explain the disarray, but the truth was, this was just my level of live-alone housekeeping. I kept my desk at F&N scrupulously neat and organized, but at home my inner slob seemed to take over. I peered in my jewelry box, where I kept the only good jewelry I owned, a pair of diamond-stud earrings. They glittered up at me, and my mother's old Hamilton watch was there too.

"I don't see anything missing."

"Good." Short Officer pulled out a notebook. He asked a few questions, the exact spelling of my name, my marital status, did I own the house or rent, how long I'd lived here, where I was employed.

He nodded sympathetically when I told him I'd just been laid off at F&N. "My sister-in-law just lost her job there too."

He scribbled my answers in the notebook, then snapped it

shut. "We'll be on our way, then. Take a flashlight if you go chasing around out there in the dark again. Avoid any bumps or falls."

"Right. Thanks for coming. I appreciate your quick response."

Outside, the officers paused to admire the limousine gleaming in the rising sun. "Quite an inheritance. What are you planning to do with it?" Short Officer asked.

"I haven't decided yet." I thought about my Tuesday deal picking up the charter sailboat clients. "People are telling me I should start a limousine service."

"Good idea. Vigland could use something like that. I might even impress my wife on our anniversary and take her out in it."

I gave my best chauffeur's bow and click of heels. Neither of which were particularly impressive since I was still in pajamas and bare feet. "Your chariot awaits, sir."

The officers headed for their patrol car; then one of them stopped. A ray of rising sun glinted on something in the gravel at the rear of the limousine.

"It's just shards of glass," I called. "I dropped a photo there yesterday, and the glass in the frame broke."

The two officers glanced at each other. "Maybe we should have a look in the trunk," Tall Officer said.

"There's nothing in there. I cleaned it out just yesterday."

"We'll take a look anyway, if you don't mind."

The driver's door was still open. I went to it, intending to pop the trunk button, but Short Officer smoothly intercepted me.

"We'll use the keys. They're in the trunk lock."

I followed him around to the trunk, and I saw the keys now too, dangling from the lock. I couldn't remember using the keys to open the trunk to get the uniforms, but I must have. The officer didn't instantly open the trunk, however. Pulling latex gloves from a pocket, he donned them and carefully touched only the metal part of the key ring.

For the first time I realized that even though the officers were being polite and considerate and helpful, they hadn't dismissed the possibility that I wasn't being on the up-and-up with them. But what could they think was going on here? Drugs in the trunk? And my clunk on the head was part of some drug-deal skirmish? Was that what all these don't-touch-anything precautions were about—fingerprints?

"Really, the trunk's emp—"

I'm not sure just how it happened, but both officers, Tom, and I were all congregated around the trunk when Tall Officer lifted the lid with a gloved hand.

We gave a collective gasp as we all saw what lay inside.

8

That's the guy you were chasing around with the shovel!" Tom yelped.

I couldn't speak. I just stared, shocked, astonished, horrified, sickened. My head and stomach reeled. Jerry lay on his side with his knees bent, his neck twisted so his face was looking upward. One arm was under him, the other draped across his body.

I grabbed for something, anything, to steady myself. That happened to be Tom. He gave me a dirty look and shoved my arm away. The taller officer reached inside the trunk and felt for a pulse at Jerry's throat. He didn't say anything, but he didn't need to. I think all of us already knew. Jerry's eyes were partly open, glazed with that awful unfocus of death.

After one petrified moment, the shorter officer ran for the patrol car, and in another moment I heard the squawk of the police radio. It came like something from another planet, loud and yet incomprehensible. Or maybe the incomprehensible part was because everything in my brain seemed stalled. Tall Officer looked at me.

"You know this person?"

I touched my throat. "No . . ." I whispered.

But I didn't mean no, I didn't know him. I meant *No, no, no! This can't be!* I'd been furious with Jerry. I'd wanted to dump lemonade over his head. I'd wanted to wham him with what I thought was a broom. But I hadn't wished death on him. How could he be dead? How could he be here, dead?

"Do you know him?" the officer repeated.

"It . . . it's Jerry Norton."

"A friend of yours?"

"She was chasing him all over the yard a couple of days ago! Yelling like a wild woman! She banged a shovel right into his car door trying to get to him!"

Tall Officer's eyebrows lifted questioningly at me.

"We, uh, had a disagreement," I admitted. "I was . . . encouraging him to leave. But the shovel was a mistake. I thought it was a broom—" I broke off. Even I could hear how lame that sounded. Surely a person could distinguish between a broom and a shovel. "I sent him an e-mail offering to pay for damage to the car door."

"There's the shovel!" Tom sounded gleeful. He made a dramatic fling of outstretched arm toward the rusty old shovel, now lying in the gravel on the far side of the limo, where I hadn't seen it until now.

He started toward the shovel, but the officer commanded sharply, "Don't touch it!"

Tom looked startled, then stuffed his hands into the pockets of his robe with a pretended nonchalance, as if he'd never intended picking it up.

"I use it to flatten those mounds of dirt that keep showing up on the grass. Moles or gophers or something. Like those." I pointed to a couple of new mounds over on Joella's side of the lawn. "I didn't hit Jerry with it!"

I broke off again. No one had accused me of hitting Jerry.

Why was I so frantically denying it? "I mean, someone hit *me*. Maybe they used the shovel!"

"A few minutes ago you said you'd stumbled and fallen."

"I . . . I thought I must have, but maybe . . . I don't know!"

I've never fainted in my life, but I felt on the edge of it right then. Jerry dead . . . *dead*. In the trunk of my limousine. The officer looking at me with an oddly speculative expression. My head doing a loop-the-loop carnival spin.

"He was murdered, wasn't he?" Tom said. "Clobbered with that shovel and then dumped in the trunk! I knew it. I knew something like this was gonna happen soon as I saw that limousine!"

"I don't understand . . ." I shook my head, too bewildered to be more than distantly aware of pain caused by the movement. "How did he die? How did he get in there?"

"He didn't crawl in by himself," Tom said. "That's for sure. Looks to me like—"

"Cause of death will have to be determined by the medical examiner," the officer cut in. "Deputy Cardoff is calling the station now."

"I don't understand!" I repeated. "Everything was okay when I came out to lock the limo—"

"What time was that?"

I thought back, and my mind tossed up those red letters on my clock radio. "It was 4:03 AM. I looked at the clock," I explained quickly, because I thought the officer might think it odd I knew the exact time. "I heard Moose—that's the Sheersons' dalmatian—barking. And I realized the limo wasn't locked, so I came out to do it. It was all foggy then."

"Did you look in the trunk at that time?"

"No, I just opened the door on the driver's side, and the light went on and . . . something happened. I don't remember anything after that until Tom found me lying on the ground."

"Had Mr. Norton been a visitor in the house earlier last night?"

"No. We'd . . . broken up," I said reluctantly. "I hadn't seen him since Wednesday."

"You'd had a personal relationship?"

"For the last four months or so. He also worked at F&N."

"But you don't know why he was here on your property, or how he got here?"

"I have no idea."

"But it's no wonder she didn't want you guys looking in the trunk of the limousine," helpful Tom put in.

The officer joined his buddy over at the patrol car. I couldn't hear their discussion, but I doubted they were talking about what an exemplary citizen I was.

I couldn't look at Jerry. And yet I couldn't *not* look at him. He was wearing jeans and a dark blue sweatshirt. Dark socks. His loafers were around behind his body, as if they'd been tossed in after him. I couldn't see any wound, but there was a dark blotch of something around his head and shoulders.

Oh, Jerry, Jerry, I'm so sorry! Who did this? Because somebody had. Tom might be acting like a pea brain, but he was right about one thing: Jerry hadn't crawled into the trunk by himself. He was put there by someone. But by whom? Why? And how come *here*?

Murder.

Both officers returned to where I was still standing by the trunk. I sensed a change in atmosphere now. Before, the officers had been interested and sympathetic, concerned that I may have been hit by some unknown assailant and not realized it. Now there was a ground shift, invisible vibes changing channels, and I felt myself helplessly slipping from victim to suspect.

Neither officer said anything to me, but I found myself almost frantic to convince them of what really was true. "I . . . I don't know anything about any of this!"

Together the two men went over and bent to examine the shovel without touching it. One of them pointed to the blade. The other one nodded. I could see something red on it. Bits of paint from the Trans Am? Or blood?

Tall Officer returned. "When did you last use the shovel?"

"I . . . I guess when I was chasing Jerry with it."

The notebook came out again. "And this was?"

"Wednesday evening. We had a disagreement, and I wanted him to leave. But, like I told you, I didn't realize I was chasing him with the *shovel*—honestly I didn't! I thought I'd grabbed the broom. That one over there by the garage." I pointed to the broom.

"Did you leave the shovel where it is now?"

"I think I put it back there by the broom." But I wasn't certain. At this point I wasn't certain of anything.

And this could look bad for me, very bad, I realized with an apprehension that made my palms go icy-sweaty. I'd chased Jerry with that shovel. With Tom and half of Secret View Lane as witnesses. To add to it, Jerry's body now lay in my vehicle. And I'd been out here in the middle of the night under what even *I* could see looked like odd and suspicious circumstances.

"But someone hit *me*. That's why I was unconscious. It must have been the same person who killed Jerry." I touched the back of my head again, wishing now I'd let the paramedics at least look at the bump.

Tom's face lit up as if a lightbulb had just gone on in his head. "Hey, I saw it on TV just last week. This guy shot himself in the leg to make it look like he'd been attacked, and he was really the killer!"

I planted my fists on my hips, annoyance with Tom finally crashing through my combination of numbness and panic. "Tom, for heaven's sake, I couldn't hit myself on the back of the head."

Tom looked at me as if sizing up my potential for an anatomical pretzel twist that would enable me to accomplish such a blow.

I pushed the point. "And how do you think I could have gotten him into the trunk? I weigh 130—" I guiltily amended it. "Around 134, and Jerry weighs at least 190."

"The trunk was open. You whacked him with the shovel, and he fell forward into the trunk. Then all you had to do was lift his feet inside. Which was when his shoes fell off!" Tom added triumphantly. He turned to the officers again. "And then she was going to haul him off to the woods somewhere and dump him."

"So why would I knock myself in the head instead of just *doing* that? Why would I let you find me and call the police?"

"Well . . . maybe you didn't hit yourself," Tom conceded. "Maybe you were getting in the limousine to drive away, and you did slip and fall."

"I was going to drive off in my pajamas?"

"Women wear all kind of strange things these days."

This was ridiculous! And yet Tom's scenario wasn't totally unbelievable, I realized, appalled. It hadn't happened, but it could have. Were the officers thinking that too? "But—"

Tom turned to the officers with a sage nod. "I always figured those two could be up to something. A flashy sports car and a limousine. They could be dealing in heroin, cocaine, meth, who knows? Or maybe some of those—what d'ya call 'em? Decorator drugs."

"Designer drugs," I corrected, then groaned at myself. My

kind, good neighbor is trying to railroad me into a drug and/or murder charge, and I'm helping him with vocabulary.

All three men were looking me over.

Sometimes Tom puzzles me. His wife, Emma, had been meddlesome and cranky, always complaining or making trouble about something. Before her death Tom had seemed like a quiet, easygoing sort of guy, sometimes even a little embarrassed by his wife's troublemaking. But after Emma was gone, it was as if he felt obligated to take up where she'd left off, and he'd turned into this grouchy curmudgeon, exactly like her.

I looked sideways at the officers. Surely they weren't buying into Tom's wacko theories . . . were they? I decided to ignore Tom, as I hoped the officers would do also.

"Was he murdered?" I asked.

"That's for the medical examiner to determine, ma'am," the officer said, as he had earlier. "Now we're going to need more information here."

He was in the process of asking me Jerry's full name, his address, occupation, what kind of car he drove, and next of kin, when two more sheriff's department cars arrived.

Then everything turned chaotic. Neighbors returning to crane their necks and mill around. A crime-scene van arriving. Yellow crime-scene tape going up. One officer photographing everything. He didn't suggest it, but I pulled my hair aside and asked him to photograph the back of my head. If they were going to document everything, I wanted it documented that I'd been clobbered.

To explain the Texas license, I had to show the officers the papers concerning the limo, one officer going inside with me while I located the envelope Cousin Larry had left. I asked at the same time if I could get dressed, and the officer allowed that.

Outside, I discovered I'd put on mismatched shoes, one a Nike from a pair Sarah and Rachel had given me at Christmas, one a cheapie from a pair I'd bought myself. I hoped the officers wouldn't notice. Maybe mismatched shoes were some secret psychological mark of a killer.

Joella came out, also dressed now, in shorts and a loose maternity blouse. One of the recently arrived officers told her to keep back.

"No!" She rushed over, put her arms around me, and glared at him. "My friend is hurt, and I'm going to take care of her!"

I felt a quick rush of affection for her, grateful that she was concerned about *me*—unlike all the other curious gawkers.

The officer, not one of the original two who'd seen me on the ground, came over too. "You're hurt?"

I skipped the *I'm fine* and turned around to let him see the back of my head. I really was feeling quite shaky by now. He had a discussion with Short Officer, then waved me off.

"But don't leave the premises," he warned. "We'll need to talk to you again."

With a protective arm around my waist, Joella led me over to her side of the duplex. Inside, she sat me down at the counter that was a duplicate of my own and made a cup of strong instant coffee in the microwave. Joella didn't even own a coffeemaker, cautious about any possible adverse effects of coffee on the baby.

I knew she had to be curious about what was going on out there, but when I started to tell her, she said firmly, "Let's see what's with your head first."

She put a hot washcloth on the back of my head and soaked away the messy ooze. Then, using a wide-toothed comb, she carefully worked through the hair until she could pull it away and expose the wound.

"What's back there? Does it look as if I was hit with the shovel?"

"It isn't a slash type wound, but the skin is broken and there's a big bump. I don't think you need stitches, but you were sure hit with something. Maybe the flat side of the shovel?"

I was glad to hear she didn't think I needed stitches. I'd been a little afraid resourceful Joella might whip out needle and thread and start sewing. She cleaned the wound with hydrogen peroxide, then finished up with antibacterial ointment. She settled me on the sofa in the living room with a blanket. I lay on my side to keep from putting pressure on the wound.

"Now do you want to know what happened?" I asked.

"Only if you feel up to telling me. At first I figured Tom was just causing trouble again, calling the police to complain about something, but now—?"

"Jerry is dead. The officers opened the trunk of the limo and found him in there. I . . . I think he was murdered."

"Oh, no . . ." She touched her fingertips to her lips.

I knew she was thinking not only of the horror of his death, but also her earlier "good riddance" about him. But she hadn't been thinking *dead* then, any more than I was.

She swallowed. "You saw him?"

I told her everything I knew then, from waking up in the night to the almost certainty that I was now a suspect in Jerry's murder, especially with Tom supplying appropriate scenarios.

"How did he die?"

"I couldn't tell, and the deputies aren't saying. But maybe with my shovel."

"Oh, surely they'll realize you couldn't have done anything like that!"

"If I was them, I guess I'd be suspicious of me too."

I really expected her to say something soothing. *They won't listen to Tom's wild ideas. They won't accuse you of something you didn't do.* But instead she had a strange, worried look on her pale face, and the thought occurred to me that after what had happened to her, perhaps she hadn't a lot of faith in the criminal justice system.

But she did have faith in her God, because she squeezed my arm and said, "God is in control." She was standing by the window, and now she said in a choked voice, "I think they're taking Jerry's body away now."

I rose up . . . carefully . . . and looked out. More vehicles had arrived since I'd come inside, one with a TV station's letters on the side and electronic equipment on top, another a van with a county insignia on the side. Two men were carrying a covered figure on a stretcher from the back of the limousine to the van. A professional-looking man in a dark suit walked beside them.

Jerry. Jerry dead on that stretcher. It was so hard to believe. *Jerry murdered.*

"Was he murdered somewhere else and then put in the limousine? Or murdered here?" Joella asked.

"I don't know." Either thought was horrifying . . . and puzzling. Why would a killer bring Jerry's body here? But if he'd been here when he was killed . . . why? What was he doing here? Was the noise that had wakened me the sound of the trunk slamming on his body?

When the van drove away, Short Officer came around the limo and headed for Joella's door. She opened it before he knocked. My hands did that peculiar icy-sweat thing again. All I could think was that he was here to take me away in handcuffs.

9

I need to talk to Mrs. McConnell again."

Joella let him in, but she watched him with wary vigilance.

I started to swing my legs from the sofa to the floor, but he said, "No, that's okay. Don't get up. How's the head?"

"Feeling better. I'm sorry, I didn't catch your name earlier?"

I figured I needed to start thinking of him in terms more dignified than simply Short Officer. He had a stocky build, ruddy face, wedding ring, and hands that looked as if he'd done hard physical labor at some time.

"Deputy Cardoff. The medical examiner is removing the body now. If you're up to it, we'd like you to come in to the station this afternoon. We need further information."

"But I've already told you all I know."

"We'd like to have you talk to one of the detectives on the force, Detective Sergeant Molino. He'll be heading up the investigation. He's out there now."

They still weren't confirming that Jerry's death was murder, but having a detective "heading up the investigation" gave a strong clue to their thinking.

"Okay, I can do that." I found myself nervously twisting a thread on the blanket. "Do I need a lawyer?"

"At this time we're simply interviewing everyone who may have knowledge or information about the case. You can have a lawyer present if you like, but it isn't necessary. We'll also be talking to Mr. Norton's coworkers and people here in the neighborhood."

"I was here all night. I didn't hear or see anything," Joella volunteered.

"Someone will interview you later. And there'll be a tow truck here shortly to pick up the limousine."

"You're taking my limousine?" I asked, dismayed.

"You'll get it back when the lab is finished with it. I'd guess ten days to two weeks. Unless it turns out we need to hold it as evidence for a trial. In that case the time could be considerably longer."

I tried not to think about *whose* trial. "Okay. Thank you."

"We need to move the Corolla so the tow truck can have access to the limousine," he added.

I started to struggle to my feet, but Joella put a protective hand on my shoulder. "I'll do it."

"We'll move it ourselves." His authoritative tone suggested they didn't want either of us meddling around in the crime-scene area. "We just need keys."

The officer went back outside. Joella cut through our joined garage space to get my car keys. Looking out the window, I saw her hand them to an officer. She came back inside, and together we watched him move the Corolla over onto the grass, out of the way.

Within a few minutes only the original patrol car and the crime-scene van remained. An hour or so later a tow truck showed up, and away went my limousine. Even strung up like a junkyard reject, it still looked sleek and elegant, an aristocrat even in shabby circumstances.

"I guess we won't be going to the park to make limo-dogs for your birthday after all," Joella said glumly as we watched it go.

My birthday. Yes, that's what today was. I hadn't even thought about it. A birthday seemed trivial and irrelevant now. So I was sixty. Big deal. Jerry was *dead*.

I was unexpectedly overcome with memory of all his good points and why I'd been so close to falling in love with him. The fun we had sailing together. The way he told slyly impudent knock-knock and lightbulb jokes. The way he made me feel young and lighthearted. His eagerness to try anything new—restaurants, food, movies. His deep, contagious laugh.

I swallowed. "I don't feel much like celebrating anyway."

"Me neither."

"We'll do it some other time," I promised.

"Is what happened going to make the limo feel forever . . ." Her voice trailed off as if she couldn't think of the right word.

"Tainted?" I suggested.

She nodded. "Tainted."

"I'm not sure." Would I ever be able to look at it without also seeing Jerry's body in the trunk? Did I really want it back? "We'll see."

"Do you have any idea who could have killed him?" Joella asked. "Did he ever mention enemies?"

"I think most people at F&N liked him."

It was true. Jerry was great at hitting it off with almost anyone. When the company had foreign visitors, he was usually chosen to shepherd them around because he was so good at making people feel comfortable and welcome. But I knew he could also be impatient and abrasive.

"He had a run-in not long ago with one of the other condo owners, something about their cat digging in the flowerpots on his balcony. They had to get rid of the cat. And over in Olympia he got some waiter who spilled coffee on him fired."

I'd felt he'd overreacted in both instances. And there was

also the unpleasant scene he'd made at a car wash when an attendant stumbled and accidentally put a minuscule scratch on the Trans Am. But surely none of those incidents would have driven someone to murder. He could be good-hearted too. I once watched him spend a half hour helping a little boy lost in the Wal-Mart parking lot find his folks' car.

"Didn't he have some business outside F&N?"

"His Web site–design business. Some of his clients were a little strange. One woman was indignant about what she said was an unfair prejudice against vampires, and she wanted a Web site to correct that. Jerry told her that image upgrading for vampires wasn't in his line of work, and she'd have to get someone else."

"Good for him."

"He did set up a Web site for some rabid group that sold all kinds of anti-everything literature over the Internet. He called them 'weekend commandos' who were into paintball wars and looking for conspiracies or cover-ups in everything from Barbie dolls to movie-theater popcorn."

"Nuts can be nutty, but they can be dangerous too."

"He shut off their Web site when they didn't pay their bill."

But the uneasy thought occurred to me that even though Jerry had laughed at the group, he'd said there were a couple of guys in it he thought could actually be dangerous. Then a totally unrelated thought jumped into my head.

"Fitz!"

"Fitz killed Jerry?" Joella sounded both startled and bewildered.

"No. I just remembered, I have to get hold of him and tell him I can't pick up their guests at Sea-Tac. Do you have his cell phone number?"

She didn't. We found a listing for MATT'S SAILBOAT CHARTERS in the phone book, but it was an office that handled information and reservations for several local businesses. The woman couldn't or wouldn't give me Fitz's private cell phone number, but she could give Matt a message. I asked her to have him call me.

An irrelevant thought struck me. "Jo, has Fitz ever asked you about your pregnancy?"

She shook her head and smiled. "Fitz is incorrigibly nosy . . . 'interested,' as he puts it . . . but he's never ungentlemanly."

"How come you don't have him going to your church?"

"I'm working on it."

"Same as you work on me?" I teased lightly.

"I try to open the door, but you have to step through yourself. Though God may give you a good shove, like He did me."

A shove from God. I wondered what that would feel like. Would I know it if I had one, or would I just ignore it?

I went back to my side of the duplex for a shower. I felt dirty from toes to head wound, although it wasn't just a physical feeling, and water didn't eradicate it. Murder left an invisible scum of its own.

Joella offered to drive me to the sheriff's station, and I took her up on it. My headache was down to a dull throb, but I felt too jittery for safe driving.

A few neighbors were still watching the activities in my yard as we drove out. Tom, wearing his usual plaid pants and with binoculars glued to his eyes, was gazing from his deck. I sometimes wondered where he got his strange wardrobe. Was there some Plaids-R-Us store I didn't know about?

Joella turned the corner, but about a quarter mile down the road, in an area where there were no houses, she suddenly braked. "Look!"

79

"Where? What?" My mind was fixed on the coming interview. Being singled out to appear at the station, when neighbors would be interviewed in their own homes, felt ominous.

"There. In the parking lot." She pulled over to the edge of the lot.

It wasn't really a parking lot, just a vacant lot where local carpoolers sometimes left their vehicles. On this Saturday, only a half dozen cars were lined up in the lot.

One of them was Jerry's Trans Am.

"Why would he park way out here if he was coming to your house?"

"I have no idea."

The thought hit me again that what I knew about Jerry was like the blurb on the back cover of a book: enough to intrigue, not enough to give away the whole story.

10

At the station, a woman officer led me down a hallway to a small, windowless room holding one table, two chairs, and a tape recorder. She introduced me to Detective Sergeant Molino. He was small and wiry, with carefully styled dark hair, a narrow mustache, and blue eyes sharp enough to split ice cubes.

We shook hands, his movements quick, his handshake not exactly intimidating but brief and intense, a guy who probably had a black belt in something I'd never heard of. He was also giving me a quick once-over—not in any smarmy way, but I had the feeling he knew all about the ticket I'd gotten for no taillights a couple years ago and that I was late getting my property taxes paid this spring. I also had the uneasy feeling he could outthink me, like I was a kid still struggling with multiplication tables and he was into calculus.

The woman officer departed, leaving the two of us alone in the dismal room. He politely reiterated that I wasn't under arrest and was free to leave at any time. I didn't hear a *yet* when he said I wasn't under arrest, but I figured it was there.

Before he could start asking questions, I jumped in and told him about spotting Jerry's Trans Am in that vacant lot parking area. I wanted him to know I was eager to cooperate and find Jerry's killer.

"You're certain it's his car?"

"I could see the dent in the door, although I'd have recognized it anyway."

He consulted some notes in front of him. "The dent you put there."

"Well . . . uh . . . yes. But it was an accident." Then I realized that was not necessarily a point I should emphasize. It reminded the detective that I'd really been trying to bash Jerry and got the car by mistake.

"Did Mr. Norton often park there?"

"Never, that I know of. I can't imagine why he'd park out there and then walk all the way to my place. There's plenty of parking space right on the street by my house."

"We'll check it out." He made a note on the lined tablet in front of him.

"One more thing—"

He looked up. "Yes?"

"Jerry had a Rolex watch. I . . . I was pretty shaken up when I saw him there in the trunk of the limousine and didn't think about it at the time, but I'm almost certain now that the watch wasn't on his wrist. I'm wondering if it may have been stolen."

"You mean you think someone killed him for the watch?"

In fact, what I was thinking was that whoever killed Jerry had seen the watch and simply decided to grab it, but maybe he had been killed for the watch. "That's possible, isn't it?"

"Murder has been done for less," Detective Molino agreed, although he sounded skeptical. "We can check the pawnshops. He usually wore the watch?"

"Always."

I remembered when he first showed it to me, a month or

so after we'd started seeing each other. I was impressed, but also a bit appalled. Sixteen thousand dollars, for a watch? I'd wondered how he could afford it. He made a lot more than I did at F&N, and he had the Web site–design business too. But still, sixteen *thousand*? I'd decided the Web site business must be more lucrative than I realized. Although several times he'd also hinted that his family came from "old money," so perhaps he had income I didn't know about.

"You're being very helpful, Mrs. McConnell. We appreciate that." Detective Molino again spoke politely as he made more notes, yet I thought I heard an edge of cynicism behind the politeness. *Trying to kiss up to us, lady? Don't bother. We're gonna nail you.*

But maybe nerves make you hear things that aren't there.

The remainder of the interview repeated questions I'd answered earlier, but went into more detail on everything. Questions about what had awakened me, what I'd done outside, my injury, my relationship with Jerry, did we go out alone or with others, did we work together at F&N. Eventually I realized Detective Sergeant Molino—who was intimidating enough that I couldn't think of him with anything less than his full title—was approaching the same subjects from a variety of angles, which might indicate he was simply an expert at digging out information. Or was he trying to trap me into a giveaway contradiction about something I'd said earlier?

"Have you seen a doctor about this injury to your head?"

"My neighbor cleaned it up and put salve on it, and it seems okay. Though there's still a bump. When one of the deputies was photographing everything, he took a picture of it." I wondered if they were buying into neighbor Tom's accusation that I'd somehow deliberately whacked myself on the head. "Would you like to see it?"

He looked mildly alarmed, the first time I'd seen him a bit off center. Not a man who liked personal contact, I suspected.

"I'd prefer a medical report, if one is available."

I watched him write something, but his handwriting rivaled Uncle Ned's hieroglyphics.

"And this breakup you mentioned," he went on briskly when he'd stopped writing. "Was this at Mr. Norton's instigation or yours?"

"His." I swallowed, trying to keep it from being an audible gulp. Now it was out. The woman scorned. One of the oldest motives in the world for revenge. "But it was mostly because he'd be moving to San Diego soon. He was offered a transfer rather than being let go, as most of the employees at F&N were."

We went into more details about the relationship, how long we'd been seeing each other, etc.

Finally he said, "Thank you. I know this must be difficult for you. Do you know if Mr. Norton had other personal relationships?"

I was startled. Another woman? I'd thought all along that our relationship was exclusive, but had I been incredibly naive? Was Jerry in fact working on his Web site business all those evenings he wasn't with me, as he'd said? Maybe there *was* another woman, one who'd just found out Jerry was also seeing me. One who felt betrayed and angry enough to commit murder?

"I wasn't aware of any other current relationships, but it's possible one . . . or more . . . could have existed that I didn't know about."

What I did know right now was that from Detective Sergeant Molino's viewpoint, jealousy about another woman was another potential motive to tie me to the murder.

"What about previous relationships?"

"There was his ex-wife, of course, but I don't know that he had any contact with her. And once he got a phone call when we were barbecuing on the balcony at his condo. The call annoyed him, and he said something about 'ex-girlfriends who won't give up,' but I don't know any details." I'd heard that Jerry had dated a couple of other women at F&N before we met, but he hadn't volunteered any information, and I hadn't had the nerve to quiz him.

Detective Sergeant Molino moved on to ask about Jerry's family.

"He has a brother, Ryan, I think his name is, but I don't know where he lives. And there's the ex-wife and two children and the rest of his family back east."

"Back east where?"

"I'm sorry. I don't know."

More notes. I wondered if he didn't trust the tape recorder, or if he was one of those obsessive-compulsive types who double-do everything. Like save files on the computer but then print it all out too. Or maybe he liked to make comments in the notes that went beyond what would show up on the tape. *Subject exhibiting excessive nervousness during questioning. Crossing and uncrossing legs. Twisting fingers. Excessive blinking.* There was an intensity about him that I found disconcerting.

I gritted my teeth and willed my legs to stop crossing and my fingers to stop twisting, but my eyelids had a blinky life of their own. Then I couldn't help but wonder what other giveaway movements I was making that I wasn't even aware of. So I tried to hold myself rigidly motionless, not a muscle twitching.

Detective Molino added something to his notes. *Subject*

now exhibiting unusual body rigidity indicative of extreme anxiety, my nervous imagination supplied.

"You don't seem to know a great deal about Mr. Norton, considering that you'd had a four months' relationship with him," he observed.

True, as was becoming more obvious all the time. Murder-sized gaps in what I knew about Jerry. There didn't seem any right response to this last observation, so I remained silent.

Detective Sergeant Molino gave me a minute, no doubt hoping I'd blurt something incriminating into the silence. When I didn't, he went on to ask about possible enemies. I dutifully mentioned the run-ins I knew about, although I felt squeamish doing so, as if I were maligning Jerry when he had no chance to defend himself.

More as an afterthought, I also mentioned Jerry's Web site business, and I was surprised by an unexpected uptick in the detective's interest. He leaned forward, his ballpoint pen poised over the notepad. If he'd had antennae, they'd have been quivering.

"Did you help him with this business?

"No, I didn't have anything to do with it."

"Were you familiar with any of his clients?"

"Not by name, no. Though I'm sure there must be a complete record of them on his computer."

"Did he ever meet with any of the clients personally?"

"I was under the impression all his dealings were done over the Internet. But I don't know that for certain."

He went on to ask numerous other questions about the business, most of which I couldn't answer—no doubt emphasizing again that I seemed to know suspiciously little about Jerry. Or wasn't telling all I knew.

The interview ended when Detective Molino thanked me

and we shook hands again. I tried to make my shake firm and confident, but it's hard to feel confident with nervous sweat rivering down your ribs and your mouth feeling as if it's stuffed full of old socks.

"We'll be in touch if we need any further information," he said. "You may notice deputies in the area, interviewing your neighbors during the next few days. And if you think of anything else, give me a call."

He handed me a business card. Detective Sergeant Anton Molino. I wondered if kids ever called him Ant when he was a kid. Probably not without risk to life and limb.

"I'll do whatever I can to help." Then, thinking maybe that had too much of a kiss-up sound, I took a deep breath and asked bluntly, "Am I a suspect?"

"At this point we're looking at the circumstances of Mr. Norton's death as suspicious," he said. "The medical examiner will determine cause and manner of death after the autopsy."

"When will the autopsy be done?"

"Monday morning, I believe."

"Should I locate a lawyer . . . just in case?"

He gave me a calculated look that to me said, *Yes! Get a lawyer. You're going to need a good one.* Although what he said out loud was, "That's up to you, of course." Followed by a smooth segue into, "You aren't anticipating leaving town anytime in the near future, are you?"

"Are you saying I can't leave?"

"I'd think it advisable if you stay here in town. We may want to talk to you again. Or we may need you to come in for fingerprinting." He paused. "Although, come to think of it, if you don't mind, we could just take care of that now. We'll need your prints for elimination purposes because they'll be in the limousine."

I couldn't tell if this truly was an afterthought on his part, or if he was just trying to make me think that. Not an afterthought, I decided as we went down a hallway to a room where the equipment was kept. Detective Sergeant Molino was a man who planned ahead.

I expected a messy process, with my fingers rolled in ink, because I remembered that from an old detective show I used to like, but the county had recently upgraded to electronic equipment. I just had to fill out a form, scrub my hands with antibacterial soap, and roll my fingertips across a scanner surface.

I think I'd have preferred the ink. There's something extra-scary about feeling as if an all-knowing computer is probing your deepest, darkest secrets.

I had to wait around a few more minutes until my statement was typed up and I could sign it. When I finally staggered out to the car, where Joella was patiently waiting, I felt drained, sucked dry as an old shell on the beach.

"Everything go okay?"

"I'm not under arrest, so I guess that's about as okay as it gets at the moment. But they took my fingerprints."

It wasn't until we were driving away that another thought hit me. The other woman.

If she'd killed Jerry, she must also have hit me over the head. Had she done it because I'd interrupted the murder? Or had she been angry enough to kill both of us? Had she perhaps thought she *had* killed me with the blow?

Would she try again?

11

A few days ago the big looming crisis in life was my sixtieth birthday. I should have realized when I was well off. Even dumped and downsized had paled. Now I could worry about whether I was soon to be accused of murder . . . or soon to become the next murder victim.

I half turned in the seat. "Jo, do you think Jerry was seeing another woman?"

She didn't seem surprised by the question. Sounding as if she were choosing her words carefully, she said, "Neil at the bakery sent me over to Olympia one time to pick up some special decorations for a wedding cake, and I saw Jerry coming out of a restaurant with someone. But I don't know that he was *seeing* her."

"An attractive someone?"

"Yes, quite attractive." She sounded reluctant.

"Attractive how?"

"Oh, you know. Tall and slender and graceful."

"How old?"

"Maybe twenty-eight or thirty. Long, dark hair. Not messy, but . . ."

"One of those styles that looks like you just got out of bed?"

"Just kind of . . . tousled."

"And you never told me?"

"Andi, it was lunchtime. They seemed engrossed in each other, but they weren't pawing or climbing all over each other. I heard him call her Elena, but she could have been a business associate. His stockbroker. His guru."

"That's really what you thought?"

Joella hesitated. "I thought it looked . . . suspicious. You know how you just kind of get vibes sometimes? But I also thought it wouldn't be fair for me to jump to conclusions and tattle about something that could be perfectly innocent. You hadn't been seeing him very long then. He could have been breaking up with her."

"Did she look as if she could clobber me with a shovel?" I muttered, but I didn't repeat the question when Joella said, "What?"

Back at the house, she told me to come over about six for dinner. "We won't celebrate, considering the circumstances. But a birthday is a birthday. Neil gave me a recipe for a special frosting with pecans and coconut, and the cake's all ready."

I called Sarah before I went over to Joella's, and she was appropriately horrified by my news.

"Mom, I think you should get out of there *now*. Who knows what kind of psycho nut is running around and might come after you again? Come down here. Just get on a plane and come."

"I'm not sure I can leave."

"If they need you as a witness, they can fly you back."

"Actually, I think they may be looking at me as something other than a witness."

"What?"

"A suspect."

When I told her why, she scoffed, but I'd heard her gasp and knew she was worried.

By six o'clock, when I slipped through the garage to Joella's side of the duplex, the patrol car and crime-scene van were gone, leaving only the yellow tape around the driveway. Inside, Joella had pulled the drapes across the windows to shut out the grim reminder of what had taken place out there. She had the radio tuned to Garth Brooks singing cheerfully about his friends in low places.

She offered a prayer, and we ate her great dinner of lasagna and broccoli and salad, determinedly keeping the conversation small-talky upbeat. Neil's new berry strudels that were selling great at the coffee shop, a rummage sale at the church, the odd inheritances Uncle Ned had left Sarah and Rachel, and how Rachel was upset about Sarah going back to college. At the end of the meal, Joella brought out the cake, three tall layers with a rich, brown-sugar frosting jumbled with pecans and coconut.

"Jo, it's gorgeous!"

There was no blaze of sixty flames, just one oversized candle. Joella lit it and sang a sweet "Happy Birthday" to me.

"One candle because you were afraid the right number would bring the fire department?"

"One candle because this is the first day of the rest of your life."

We both contemplated that statement until she gave a sheepish smile and said, "I guess that's kind of corny, isn't it?"

"I didn't know your generation even knew what corny was."

"Corny is intergenerational. Probably nondenominational too." She giggled, that infectious laugh that so often got me going too. "But the first day of the rest of your life is true even if it is corny."

"And I love it!" I really did. The first day of the rest of my life. For a few moments the awfulness of the past twenty-four hours faded, and I felt a burst of jubilation. I could do anything, be anything, no matter what my age! I leaned over and gave her a big hug. "Thanks, Jo."

Then I blew out my candle and dug in and ate enough cake with nutty frosting to add a half dozen new jiggles to my thighs.

JOELLA CAME OVER the next morning to ask if I wanted to go to church with her. I'd gone a couple of times, but this was the first time I felt as if I really needed to go. Though when I examined my reasons, I was embarrassed.

What did I think, that going would earn me enough brownie points with God to keep the police from deciding they had evidence enough to arrest me? I didn't figure I had enough standing to ask for anything during prayer time, but I found myself more caught up in the sermon than I'd expected. All about Job and his problems, which did something toward putting my own in perspective.

Afterward Joella dragged me over to introduce me to the man she'd been wanting me to meet, but he turned out to have an attractive older woman tethered to his elbow. Even eager Joella could see her matchmaking plan was down the drain. I was relieved.

MONDAY MORNING I waved to Joella when she left for work, then tried to get a résumé started. I was on chatting terms with people at several insurance offices around town, and I could contact them. Maybe the school system or county government?

But it was no use. I couldn't keep my mind on this. All I could think about was what was happening to Jerry right now. An autopsy.

Joella had said reports of the death in a limousine had been on the TV news both Saturday and Sunday, but I'd deliberately avoided watching. I'd had numerous phone calls from reporters, and I'd tried to be polite and explain to the first one why I didn't want to be interviewed, but I'd finally just had to hang up on him. After that I'd opted for the handy "No comment" and hung up right away.

Just after noon—not lunch, because with my thoughts on Jerry, lunch just wouldn't go down—the phone rang. An unfamiliar male voice said, "Is this Andi McConnell?" and I felt every muscle from scalp to toenails electrify.

Surely they wouldn't be calling to give *me* results of the autopsy . . . or would they? Maybe they figured it would jolt me into a confession?

I tried to keep my voice from squeaking when I said, "Yes, this is Andi."

Apparently I was unsuccessful, because after a short pause the voice said warily, "Are you all right?"

"Just a little catch in my throat." I cleared my throat . . . *hrrumph* . . . to fortify that position.

"This is Matt Fitzpatrick, MATT'S SAILBOAT CHARTERS," he continued briskly. Apparently if I wasn't actually strangling, he wasn't going to concern himself.

"Oh, Fitz's son."

"He's running some errands, and I just wanted to let you know that the clients we're expecting tomorrow will be arriving at Sea-Tac at 11:12 on Continental Airlines. There are three couples—"

"I'm afraid there's a problem," I broke in. "I tried to get hold of Fitz over the weekend, but I couldn't reach him."

"What do you mean, a problem?" The ominous edge to his tone suggested he was not a man who tolerated problems of anything below the nuclear level.

"I can't use the limousine to go over to Sea-Tac tomorrow."

"But you assured my father—"

"I'm sorry, but something has come up. I know it's inconvenient for you—"

"Yes, it is. Extremely inconvenient," he agreed in a voice that suggested I'd knocked the universe's time-space equilibrium out of kilter. "I told my father we'd be better off contacting a reliable limousine service, but he was quite insistent."

In one sentence Matt Fitzpatrick had managed to castigate both his father and me: I was unreliable, and Fitz made lousy decisions.

I sputtered and then snapped, "I'm sorry, but I didn't know at the time I talked to Fitz that the police were going to find a body in the trunk of the limousine. It isn't something you plan ahead for."

"A . . . dead body?"

"Yes. Dead. The sheriff's department towed the limo away to . . . do whatever it is they do to look for clues."

"I see." He sounded more wary than convinced.

"Okay, look. I think Fitz said he usually picked up people in your SUV, but he couldn't tomorrow because he has an appointment with a lawyer?"

"That's right."

"How about if I drive the SUV over to Sea-Tac to do it? And I won't charge you anything for my time. I'll just do it. So you won't be inconvenienced."

If he heard my sarcastic emphasis on *inconvenienced*, he ignored it. "Yes, well, okay. That should work out. You have a driver's license and everything?"

"Yes."

"Okay, fine then. And we will pay you, of course."

"I'll be at the marina about eight. That should give me plenty of time to get up to Sea-Tac. You can give me further details then."

"Okay. Well . . . thanks. I'll tell my father. I'm sorry if I sounded a bit abrupt. We had engine trouble on this last charter trip."

Too bad. I had a murder.

The tone of Matt Fitzpatrick's call annoyed me to the point that I felt a sudden burst of energy. I changed to my usual mowing outfit: faded old denim shorts, grass-stained T-shirt, and sneakers with holes in both toes. I dragged the push mower out of the garage and blasted across the lawn as if the grass were an enemy I was mowing down. But by the time I was halfway through my side of the yard, I was sweating and feeling swirly in the head, and the thought occurred to me that this exertion might not be the most appropriate activity for someone who's recently been whacked on the head.

I was leaning against the handle, head down, resting for a minute, when two cars from the sheriff's department whipped around the corner at the end of Secret View Lane and pulled to the curb in front of my house. Three officers I didn't recognize, plus Detective Sergeant Molino, jumped out.

I straightened uneasily. Tom was right out there on his deck. The binoculars appeared to have taken root on his face. Had he called the police again? What now?

Detective Sergeant Molino came to me, official-looking paper in hand. "We have a search warrant for your house and vehicle, Ms. McConnell. I'm here to serve the warrant and conduct the search."

"A search warrant?" I repeated blankly. "Why?"

He handed me several pages stapled together. "It's all in there."

I had the feeling I should inspect the warrant line by line

and not let him intimidate me, but the words were a blur of legalese. I was also suddenly aware that I was standing there with bare toes poking through the holes in my sneakers and bits of grass plastered to my legs. Not exactly your basic power outfit.

"The warrant, as you can see, has been properly signed and authorized by Judge Adkins." He pointed to the scrawl of an unreadable signature. "You may come inside to watch the search if you wish, but you will be required to remain in one place and not interfere."

"I . . . I think I'll just stay out here."

He took the paper back. "When the search is completed, you will be furnished with a copy of the warrant along with an itemized list of any items seized."

Two officers headed for my Corolla. Detective Sergeant Molino and the other officer advanced to the house.

"The door's unlocked," I called, so they wouldn't think they had to kick it down. I had the feeling Detective Sergeant Molino would have been delighted if he'd had to do exactly that.

With the arrival of the sheriff's department cars, neighbors rushed out to their yards to watch, of course. Tom and his binoculars had moved to the gate for a closer look. Moose gave a few desultory barks.

I swallowed, suddenly feeling so alone and vulnerable. Like the many times we'd moved when I was a girl, facing yet another new school as the outsider, lonely, uncertain, and scared.

I thought I'd just continue mowing, trying to act as if nothing out of the ordinary was happening, but after one length of the yard, my leg and arm muscles felt as if they'd gone through a shredder, and the mower seemed as unwieldy as a tank.

I gave up, parked the mower under the big maple on

Joella's side of the yard, and plopped down on the white metal bench in the shade. Then, wouldn't you know it, ol' Moose got out of the Sheersons' yard and headed right for my daisies. I grabbed him by the collar and dragged him home, but I couldn't be too mad. He was such a goofy, loving creature.

By the time I got back to the bench, the two officers were taking the floor mats out of the Corolla, emptying the glove compartment, and digging into the spare tire area under the floor of the trunk.

I tried to comfort myself with the thought that there couldn't be anything that tied me to Jerry's murder. Because I *wasn't* tied to it. And yet, could they find something that would look as if I were connected, something they could use as evidence against me?

I was thinking maybe I should go inside to observe the search, when another car pulled in behind the deputies' parked vehicles. I was astonished to see Fitz jump out. He spotted me and dodged around the crime-scene tape to get to where I was sitting under the maple.

"Hey, Matt told me some strange story about your limo and a dead body. I tried to call, but I didn't get any answer, so—"

I wasn't sure if I was glad to see him or not, considering his son's grumpy attitude on the phone. "How'd you know where I live?" I cut in.

"I'm a detective, remember?"

"A TV detective."

"Yeah, well, I solved a murder once. Mr. Bolivar, who lived right next door to me down in LA, was poisoned, and the police were getting nowhere finding out who did it till I solved the case for them."

I was impressed, though I didn't intend to show it. "So how'd you know where I live?" I repeated. My phone book listing, like that of many women living alone, doesn't show an address.

"I went by the Sweet Breeze and asked Joella."

He sounded a little sheepish, but I figured that was pretty quick-thinking detective work.

"Anyway, I decided I'd come over and see if I could help. I thought maybe Matt had things mixed up, but it looks as if something did happen here."

Fitz eyed the patrol cars, crime-scene tape, and two officers burrowing through my Corolla. I was embarrassed to see them set out a squashed McDonald's coffee cup, a pair of tangled pantyhose, half a mummified doughnut, and a book on growing daisies that was long overdue at the library. I couldn't believe there was so much trash tucked away in the nooks and crannies of the car. But it was good to see the library book. I'd been try-ing to find it for two weeks.

They laid everything out on the grass like finds from an archeological dig. The artifacts of Andi McConnell's life. Not pretty, but surely nothing there that could connect me with murder.

"So what did happen?" Fitz peered at me more closely. "Are you all right?"

It was a question I seemed to be getting a lot lately. "I'm not sure," I admitted.

"Can I get you something? Water? Soda?"

"No, that's okay. You probably can't go in the house. They're searching in there too."

He sat on the bench beside me. "Why?"

"The dead body in the limo. I . . . I think they think I killed him."

"Who is it they think you killed?"

"Jerry Norton."

"Boyfriend Jerry Norton?"

"That'd be the one."

"I'm not going to ask if you did it, because I know you didn't. But tell me what happened."

Once more I ran through my tale of hearing something in the night, coming out to lock the limo, getting hit on the head, Tom finding me and calling 911, and the deputies discovering the body in the trunk of the limo.

"Did they have a search warrant then?"

"No, I told them they could do it. The trunk was empty the last time I looked. They'd looked in the house too, before that, but they were looking for a possible intruder then, not evidence."

"And you have no idea how the body got there?"

"All I know is I didn't kill him and . . . I'm scared."

Unexpectedly he slid over and put his arms around me, and just as unexpectedly I was so glad he'd come. I leaned my head against his shoulder. I wasn't alone now. Fitz was here. Here not just because he was nosy, but because he wanted to help.

12

Have you been questioned?" Fitz asked.

"A deputy asked a few questions here, and then I had to go to the sheriff's station, where a detective asked a lot more questions and took my fingerprints. They said I didn't need a lawyer and didn't read me those . . . what are they called? Miranda rights."

"They don't need to do that unless they're arresting you. What are they looking for here?"

"I have no idea."

"They can't just barge in on a generalized fishing-and-snooping expedition. They're required to name what they're looking for in order to get a search warrant. Did they show you the warrant?"

"They did, but I was too shook-up to make any sense out of it. And I don't understand what there is to search for. The deputies or crime-scene people already took the shovel. And the limo, too, of course."

"The shovel? What does a shovel have to do with it?"

So again I had to explain my chase and assault on Jerry's car. It was not a story that improved with repetition, but Fitz made no comment.

"The shovel was lying out in the driveway right by the limousine, so I think it was probably the murder weapon. And maybe what someone hit me with, too."

"Let me see where you were hit."

If it had just been nosiness, I'd have told him to take a flying leap into the Bay, but I heard real concern in his voice. I slid around on the bench and parted my hair with my fingers.

"Joella cleaned it up and put some salve on it. It feels kind of goopy."

He peered and then fingered the lump gently. "There's still a fair-sized bump, but the break appears to be scabbing over. I'm no expert, but it doesn't look like the kind of wound a shovel would make. The edge of a shovel with any force behind it would probably make a pretty deep gash. This looks as if it was done with something more blunt."

"Joella suggested the flat part of the shovel rather than the edge."

"Could be. But why would the cops suspect you of anything if you were attacked too?"

"Would they be searching my house and car if they didn't suspect me?"

"Good point."

"Your son was upset with me. I told him I'd pick up your clients in the SUV since I can't do it in the limousine."

"Matt's a great guy, and I love him dearly, but sometimes he can be a pain in the you-know-where. He's a nitty-gritty perfectionist and likes everything to run according to schedule. *His* schedule. But I don't want you driving all the way over to Sea-Tac if you don't feel up to it."

"Mowing the lawn today probably wasn't such a bright idea, but I think I'll be okay by tomorrow. I don't want you to have to do it and miss your appointment."

In spite of all my other worries, I was still curious about

Fitz's meeting with a lawyer. My fishing trip didn't produce any results, however. Instead he grabbed the mower and attacked the lawn, pausing a couple of times to kick aside fresh mounds of dirt the lawn critters had pushed up. He used special care around my daisy beds, lifting the drooping stems so he could mow under them and not take off the blooming heads. With his energetic style, he also finished the mowing in about half the time it usually took me to do it.

By that time the two officers had finished with the Corolla and gone inside the house. They'd added several more items to the lineup of artifacts from the car: a box of macaroni and cheese, various scraps of paper, and a broken comb.

All four men exited the house at the same time, a flying wedge of them, Detective Sergeant Molino in the lead. He started to hand me the official-looking papers, but Fitz stuck out his hand.

"I'd like to see those, please."

Detective Sergeant Molino gave me a questioning look.

"This is my friend—" I broke off, and it took me a moment to come up with Fitz's real first name. "My friend, Keegan Fitzpatrick. And I would like him to see the search warrant," I added firmly.

"Then you may show it to him at your leisure," the detective said, stubbornly thrusting the papers at me. "The list of items seized is attached."

For the first time I noticed one of the other officers was carrying a baggie with a small jar of white tablets.

"Why do you want my calcium pills?" I asked, astonished. Another baggie in his other hand.

"And my basil. What are you doing with that? And my thyme!" I added indignantly. "My friend Letty at F&N gave me those. She raises her own herbs."

Detective Sergeant Molino looked uncharacteristically nonplussed. "Calcium? Basil? They weren't labeled—" He recovered quickly and added smoothly, "The lab will make proper identification of the materials." With the definite hint that just because I said they were calcium and basil and thyme didn't make them so.

The officers removed the crime-scene tape on their way out and drove away. Fitz was still studying the search warrant.

"What does it say they took?"

"One bottle of unidentified white tablets, two plastic bags of unidentified crushed green organic substances. Maybe they're making spaghetti down at the station."

"But I don't understand. Surely this isn't what they came to look for."

"No—" Fitz flipped to an earlier page. "They were looking for drugs. Apparently they thought your unlabeled calcium pills and spices could fit in that category."

"Drugs!"

Then I remembered. Tom and his wild suggestion that Jerry and I could have been involved in drug trafficking. Would they do a search based on that? Or had they suspicions of their own? Police had busted several home-based meth labs around Vigland in the past year.

"But the big search was probably for what's right up here at the top of the list. A handgun, .38 caliber."

"A gun! I don't have a gun. I've never had a gun! And why would it matter if I did? Jerry was killed with a shovel."

"Are you sure?"

I reconsidered. "No, I guess not. There was supposed to be an autopsy this morning."

"They were also looking for ammunition and a silencer. And a Rolex watch."

"But I'm the one who told them Jerry's Rolex might be missing! Would I tell them that if I'd hidden it in my own house?"

"And then they also did what the police usually do, which is make a catchall list of small items: papers and records connected with drug deals, drug paraphernalia, etc. That way they can look in all the small spaces they couldn't look in if they listed only larger items."

"You know a lot about this."

"I did a fair amount of research and worked with the police on situations we were using on the show to be sure we got them right."

"I'm glad you were here today. And thanks for mowing my lawn too."

"Glad to do it."

"Well, I guess I should go in and get cleaned up." That green shadow of cut grass sprayed by the mower still clung to my legs and ankles. And there were my bare toes, of course, peeking through the holes in the sneakers.

"Maybe I should come in with you. It may be a mess in there."

"A mess?"

"Police aren't noted for leaving everything neat and tidy after a search. We used that situation a couple of times on the detective show."

I realized now that I didn't know what TV detective show he'd been on. Crime and detective shows are not high on my list of TV preferences, so I'd probably never heard of it, but to be polite I thought I should ask.

"It was called *Ed Montrose, P.I.E.* The initials were for Private Investigator Extraordinaire. It wasn't any huge hit, but it ran for about four years. Though that was almost twenty years ago. A couple of older guys on the city police force remember it, but I don't suppose anyone else does."

I was astonished. "But I remember it! It's the only crime

show I've ever really liked. They're usually so grim and gory."
I peered more closely at him, a little doubtful. "You were Ed
Montrose?"

"In person. I still have my old slouch hat back on the boat."

I tried to subtract twenty years and then remembered a difference. "Ed Montrose had a mustache."

Fitz leaned over and grabbed a handful of cut grass. He
plastered it between upper lip and nose, leaning his head back
to hold it in place. "That help?" he asked.

In spite of all the tension of the day, I giggled, à la Joella.
"It's a little green, but yes, that helps. Hey, you really are Ed
Montrose!"

He wiped the grass mustache away and grinned at me.
"You really did like the show?"

"Oh, yes. Ed was kind of droll, and he had this wry sense
of humor, and he was always willing to admit when he made a
mistake. And I liked the way he'd sit down with his stubby old
pencil and make lists and think things through intellectually. It
wasn't all just high-tech stuff. He used his brains. And I loved
that slouchy old hat he always wore . . . and he put alfalfa
sprouts on everything."

"Hey, you do remember the show, don't you?" Fitz
sounded both surprised and pleased.

He was right about a mess inside. The house wasn't trashed,
but kitchen drawers had been searched right down to removing
the liners, the contents scattered on the counter. In the bedroom, bureau drawers had been emptied and turned over.

"Looking to see if anything was taped to the underside,"
Fitz explained.

Sofa cushions removed, bedding tossed aside, nightstand
contents dumped on the bed, clothes jumbled in piles on a
chair. Even the cover on the toilet tank was awry.

"A more common place to hide something than many people realize," Fitz commented. "One of our shows had a murderer who put the leftover rat poison he'd killed his wife with in a plastic bag and hid it in there."

They'd rummaged through my canister set, spilling flour and sugar and tea. They'd looked in my spice jars and an open box of Bisquick. They'd found the place in the hallway where you could push aside a panel in the ceiling and get up to the attic. Fitz had to climb up on a chair to get it scooted back into place.

Although it wasn't all the searchers' mess, I had to admit. Herds of dust bunnies from under the sofa, where they'd moved it aside. Circular marks in the bathroom cabinet, where bottles had stood. And I'd never realized how the gunk on the inside of a toilet tank can accumulate. I could see marks on the side where someone's fingers had slid down to reach the bottom. I wondered who got that fun job. Not Detective Sergeant Molino, I'd bet.

I also wondered if they joked about these things after they got back to the station. *Hey, you wouldn't believe that McConnell place. Looked like she hadn't cleaned house since she hit menopause.*

I didn't expect Fitz to stay and help straighten it all up, but he did, including getting out the vacuum to suck up the dust bunnies and other debris on the carpet. After doing the house, we went out to the Corolla, replaced the floor mats, and picked up the items scattered on the grass.

It was close to six o'clock by the time everything was back in order. By then I was embarrassed that Fitz knew so much about my personal life. Including the fact that I had two cartons of "Cinnamon Sunrise" hair coloring in my bathroom. It must look as if I had to put it on industrial strength, although it was actually a buy-one, get-one-free special.

Afterward I peered in the refrigerator. "I really appreciate the help. Can I fix you a hamburger? And there's some deli coleslaw and leftover birthday cake Joella made."

"I was thinking maybe I'd spring for that dinner we talked about. How about the new steak house out by the highway?"

"That's really nice of you, but I don't know . . . I guess I just don't feel up to going out. I'm kind of frazzled. Thanks anyway."

He didn't lack persistence. "How about if I go pick up a couple of steaks and cook them here?"

"You've already done so much."

He grinned. "I figure I have to do quite a lot to make up for my big social gaffe in reading your letter at the Sweet Breeze."

"Hey, I remember Ed Montrose was always reading other people's stuff! He'd go through trash in garbage cans, and he could read a letter upside down on a desk or in someone's hand. And when he went into an office, he'd pick up anything on the counter and just start reading it."

"Try it sometime. You may be surprised at what it does to speed up service. Someone always rushes over to see what you're doing. And you find out all sorts of interesting things. Did you know the shoe store in the shopping center sent around a memo telling employees that too much soap was being wasted in staff restrooms?"

"What fascinating information."

He grinned again. "The quality of data acquired in this manner does tend to be a bit uneven."

I showered and changed to jeans while he went to pick up the steaks. He returned with two T-bones plus deli Caesar salad, garlic bread, and a carton of alfalfa sprouts. All I had to do was make coffee and set the table. I watched, curious, as he expertly did the steaks under the broiler.

"Where did you learn to cook well enough to handle all the cooking for guests on the sailboat charter trips?"

"My wife was ill with cancer for quite a while before she passed away. She hadn't much appetite, so I did the best I could to make meals appetizing for her. Then, after she was gone, I was on my own, of course, with both the cooking and cleaning. For the sailboat trips, I keep buying cookbooks, or sometimes I just expand my old recipes. So far, no one's come down with food poisoning."

"How long ago did your wife pass away?"

"Seven years." He swallowed. "Emily died on our thirty-fourth anniversary."

"Oh . . . I'm so sorry."

"I try to keep the happy memories and let the rest go. How about you?"

"Divorced. About a dozen years ago. I was just glad my daughter was all grown up and married before it happened. Although her marriage also broke up not long ago. I hope it isn't turning into a family tradition. There's my granddaughter, Rachel."

"These are hard times for marriages." He turned the steaks with tongs, careful not to puncture the surface and let juices escape. "You never remarried?"

"At first I was so disillusioned with marriage I wouldn't have noticed Mr. Right if he thundered through the front door on a white horse. Then, after a while, I don't know . . . I was never into the singles scene, and life just kind of drifted along."

"Is your ex-husband around?"

"No, he and his new wife took off for the wilds of South America within a couple months of our divorce. He had a midlife crisis, I guess you'd call it, and decided he had to save the world and the environment before it was too late. I didn't fit into his plans."

"A hard way to find out."

"I didn't know until after he'd gone how he'd gutted the finances on the furniture store business we'd been building up for years. He borrowed money I didn't know about. Second-mortgaged the house. Business bills unpaid. All things I should have known about, but didn't."

"Because you trusted him."

I nodded. "I couldn't keep the business going, and wound up going to work for F&N." And paying off all the debts he'd run up, which took several years.

"He's still down in South America?"

"As far as I know. He's never kept in touch with Sarah or Rachel." I was more bitter about that than the divorce. Sarah never said anything about it, but I knew how hurt she was. Rachel didn't remember him.

I had the radio tuned to an oldies station while we ate— nice, mellow background music—and Fitz told funny stories about working on the Ed Montrose set and other shows he'd done since then. But he stopped talking and we both stopped eating, my fork halfway to my mouth, when the words, "A spokesman for the local county sheriff's department said today—" came on.

The report went on to say that an autopsy done on the body discovered in a limousine just outside Vigland on Saturday morning had revealed death was caused by a gunshot. The sheriff's department had several leads, and numerous tips had come in, but no arrests had been made yet.

"Now we know why they were searching for a gun," Fitz said.

The silencer listed on the search warrant also made sense. Apparently no one on Secret View Lane had heard a shot in the night, so they must figure a silencer had been used.

"They must have asked for the search warrant as soon as

the medical examiner told them the cause of death. They really do think I killed him."

"Did Jerry himself own a gun?"

"I have no idea." I found the possibility startling at first, but it took no more than a few seconds to realize it was the macho kind of thing Jerry would do. "Though I doubt it was registered if he did have one. Jerry didn't always . . . play by the rules."

He'd hinted he had somehow dodged paying the big state sales tax on the Trans Am, although I'd never been clear how he'd done it.

"Was he a hunter?"

"I don't think so. At least he never mentioned it. But I don't really know. I'm only now realizing how little I knew him."

We had leftover birthday cake, and then, after dinner, Fitz helped clean up and put things into the dishwasher.

"Well, I'd better be getting back to the boat," he said. "I have that appointment at the lawyer's office in the morning, and I have to stock up on supplies for the next trip too."

"I'll be over about eight o'clock to pick up the SUV." I walked with him to the door and turned on the outside light. "I'm really glad you came over. It's nice to have someone around who knows about such things as search warrants."

"Everything's going to turn out okay." He gave my arm a reassuring squeeze. "The police sometimes give people a hard time, but most of them are pretty good at their jobs."

"But sometimes they make mistakes. Sometimes innocent people get accused, even convicted. I almost feel as if *I* need to do something to find out who the real killer is before they decide it's me."

He'd started down the three steps to the sidewalk, but he came back a step, a sudden gleam in his eyes. "So let's do it."

"Do it? Investigate the murder, you mean? You and me?"

"Do you have anything to go on?"

"Maybe a few little things, but not much. And there may not be much time before they make it official and arrest me."

"Then we'd better get going."

"I don't think this is something that can be figured out the way Ed Montrose did it, always in a half hour."

"It may take us a little longer, but let's do it."

"Us? You and me?" I repeated doubtfully.

"Why not? Ed Montrose, P.I.E., sleuths again! I was always telling the producer Ed needed a good-looking sidekick. Now he has one."

"Who says the sleuth is male and the sidekick is female?"

"Well, uh, that's just the way it is."

We'll see.

13

We settled at the kitchen table with paper, pens, and fresh cups of coffee. We made notes about every person I could think of who might be involved, although I couldn't supply names for most of them. Fitz called them "persons of interest" since their involvement wasn't necessarily strong enough to make them suspects. On that list were:

— a dark-haired, attractive woman named Elena in Olympia, possibly a girlfriend, about thirty years old
— other unknown current or former girlfriends, including the one who had called the condo while I was there
— neighbors in his condo who'd had to get rid of their cat because of Jerry's complaints
— a waiter who'd been fired because he spilled coffee on Jerry
— a car-wash attendant who'd been angry and belligerent after Jerry chewed him out about the minuscule scratch on the Trans Am

Then there were the Web site people, more viable suspects in my opinion, than those with petty grudges: the "weekend commando" people who may have, for whatever warped reason, lumped Jerry in with other dangerous "conspirators" and decided he had to be eliminated. The vampire lady who may have been angry enough to do something because of Jerry's cavalier attitude toward the status of vampires.

Other Web site clients that I didn't know about. This was where I figured the real possibilities lurked. Who knew what kind of people Jerry may have been dealing with?

"Although there's another possibility," I added as I cut fresh helpings of birthday cake to go with the fresh pot of coffee. "Maybe the killing didn't really have anything to do with Jerry or anything he'd done. Maybe he just stumbled into something he shouldn't have."

"And got killed by accident or mistake?"

"Possibly."

I gave Fitz details on how I'd inherited the limou*zeen*, as it was called in Uncle Ned's will, and that it had bulletproof glass because Uncle Ned apparently thought he was in danger. "Cousin Larry said Uncle Ned had been involved in various questionable business dealings. He may have had serious enemies."

"He sounds like a strange one, all right."

"But if there *was* something to his fears, maybe someone connected with his shyster activities came here because the limo was somehow involved . . ." The thought, fizzled because I couldn't think where to go with it, but Fitz jumped on it.

"You mean someone associated with your Uncle Ned either as an accomplice or a victim of his questionable activities came here to look for something hidden in the limousine, and Jerry happened to get in the way, so he got killed?"

"Yes! When I looked inside the limo shortly after the deputies got here the first time, I had the impression someone *had* been in there. Nothing was torn up or damaged, but things seemed . . . not quite right."

"Did you say anything about this to the deputies?"

"No. I guess I should have, shouldn't I? But at the time I was just so shook-up by the murder itself."

"But getting killed by someone connected to your Uncle Ned wouldn't explain why Jerry was here at your place to begin with. What was he doing snooping around your limo in the middle of the night?"

"Good question."

"It's still an interesting thought," Fitz said. "Too bad we don't have a couple of Ed Montrose's writers. They were the real brains of the show. But we're on our own."

It was almost midnight by the time Fitz left. By then we'd added another interesting possibility: someone at F&N who may have had an unknown grudge against Jerry or been angry and vengeful because Jerry had been chosen for promotion and transfer, and he hadn't.

"Or *she*," Fitz cautioned. "Murder is an equal-opportunity crime, remember."

I WAS UP earlier than usual the next morning. I didn't want to be late getting to the marina and give Matt Fitzpatrick something else to nitpick about. Along the way I detoured through the vacant lot. Numerous cars were parked there on this weekday, but the Trans Am wasn't among them, so the police had apparently towed it also.

I hadn't been to the marina for a long time. Jerry kept his little sailboat at a friend's dock, so we never had occasion to use the marina. But I spotted the *Miss Nora* right away. She was the largest and by far the most impressive boat at the small marina. I left my Toyota in the parking lot, descended the steep steps to the wooden dock, and walked out to the end where the sail-boat was moored. Some marinas have locked gates, but Vigland's wasn't like that.

Here in port the boat's sails were not unfurled, but the tall mast rose to an impressive height, lines jingling in the breeze, and the boat was quite dazzling in its glistening whiteness. The silhouette was low and sleek and racy looking, with a railed area up front with lounge chairs. I didn't see anyone around, although the door to the cabin stood open.

"Hello," I called. "Anyone here?"

A man in grease-stained khakis and wrench in hand filled the door—a taller, heavier version of Fitz.

"Are you Matt Fitzpatrick?"

"Yes. You must be Andi McConnell. You're early."

He didn't sound overjoyed to see me. The unexpected thought occurred to me that he might be thinking I was out to snare his father in some matrimonial trap. Or perhaps I was older than he'd anticipated, and he was trying to decide if I was too senile to drive his SUV.

I'd been going to ask for Fitz, but instead I just said, "I've been to Sea-Tac, but not recently. If you could tell me where your clients will be arriving and how I can recognize them—"

"We have a sign with MATT'S SAILBOAT CHARTERS on it. Dad just holds it up and lets the clients come to him. It's in the SUV."

"Okay, I'll use it too."

"There are three couples. They'll be coming in on Continental. You'll have to ask Fitz for full directions. There are a lot more security regulations now than there used to be."

"Young couples? Old?"

"Thirtyish, I think. Erickson is the name of the guy who made the reservations."

"I'll need the keys to the SUV. Is it up in the parking lot?"

"Not at the moment. Dad's car wouldn't start this morning, so he took the SUV to go pick up supplies at Wal-Mart. He thought he'd be back before you got here, but you're early," he repeated. Apparently this was not an admirable trait in Matt Fitzpatrick's estimation.

"I'll go up to the parking lot and wait, then."

I'd taken a few steps, but then he called, "Would you like to take a look around the boat?"

The invitation didn't sound overly enthusiastic, but he was apparently trying to be nice, and I took him up on it. I'd never been on anything larger than Jerry's little sailboat.

He motioned me to step onto the rear platform of the boat, which, unlike most sailboats I'd seen, was built with an opening with steps so passengers could walk on directly and not have to climb over a railing.

"It's called a walk-through stern," Matt explained. "This is the cockpit area. And that's the helm." He pointed to an oblong pedestal with steering wheel attached.

There was a tall chair by the helm and padded bench seats on either side for passengers. Inside, a panel in the flooring was raised to expose an enormous chunk of machinery. Matt dropped the panel back into place.

"Diesel engine, 100 horsepower," he said. "I was just doing a little work on it. Fortunately it's not a big enough problem to have to call in a mechanic." He wiped his hands on a greasy rag.

"Does Fitz help with engine work too?"

Matt laughed. "Dad's a great cook. And a great guy, and I'm really glad he's here with me now. But he can't tell a diesel engine from a generator."

Which was no doubt important, although I didn't know

the difference either, and I figured Fitz knew plenty of important things that full-of-himself Matt didn't.

Matt showed me through the boat, two bedrooms in the rear, two up front. The room he and Fitz shared had narrow twin beds, the others doubles with nautically themed bedspreads, polished woodwork, and brass lighting fixtures. There were two bathrooms, "heads," as Matt called them, a small but well-equipped kitchen—galley, that is—and a kind of living room he called a *salon*, very elegant, with a dining area and comfortable seats, a TV, and more polished teak and mirrors. Also, off in a corner, a navigation center with a wood desk and gauges and equipment that looked capable of launching a spaceship.

"It's beautiful," I said honestly. I could tell Matt was proud of his boat, with good reason. "You've been handling sailboats all your life, I suppose?"

"Oh, no. Up until about four years ago, I was running the rat race down in LA, with a long-term game plan that I figured would make me CEO of the company in ten years."

"You were downsized?" I asked, thinking of my own predicament.

"No. In fact, I was up for a promotion. I'd been aware for some time that things weren't quite right with the company, but I'd always looked the other way. Until a big deal in the Middle East came up about the same time as the promotion, and I had to face the fact that it was more than things being 'not quite right.' The company was up to its corporate ears in unethical deals and deceiving investors. Moving money around all over the world. Juggling the accounting records and setting up subsidiaries to conceal what they were doing. And if I took that promotion, I'd be in it up to my ears, too, which was way over my conscience level. So I got out."

"You just . . . chucked it all?"

"I just chucked it all," he agreed, as if he liked the phrase. "I'd been up here sailing on vacations several times, and I came up and went to work for the old guy who owned this boat. So when he wanted to sell the boat a couple years ago, I jumped at the chance to buy it." He frowned. "Why am I telling you all this?"

Because I'm such a sweet, understanding, easy-to-talk-to person? I doubted he'd agree. So all I said was, "I admire your ethics," and changed the subject. "Did you name the boat the *Miss Nora?*"

"No, the old guy who owned it before me named her." He laughed. "Not some love of his life, if that's what you're thinking. Miss Nora was his cat. Meanest, worst-tempered cat you ever saw. She'd growl when you fed her. Had a rigid no-purr policy."

"Maybe the cat was named Miss Nora because she reminded him of some woman in his past."

"Hmmm. I never thought of that." He gave me a glance that suggested my thought had earned me a bit of unexpected respect.

"What happened to the cat?"

"She refused to live anywhere but here on the boat. So I kept her until she died of old age last year." His smile was a little sheepish. "I got kind of fond of the cranky old gal."

I liked him better for that admission. "What happened to the company after you left?"

"Collapsed," he said laconically. "Taking the pension I was supposed to get someday with it. Three top execs now in prison."

"Hey, daisies!" I said suddenly, spying a window box of them behind a little wooden barricade in the kitchen. They were a dwarf variety, only a few inches tall, blue with yellow centers. "I love daisies. I have several flower beds of them at home. They're so real and . . . you know, unpretentious. Not like big, ostentatious dahlias and other show-offy flowers. Are these Cape Town Blue?"

"I have no idea." He looked at me as if he were wary of anyone attributing personalities to flowers. "Dad's the daisy grower, not me."

Matt Fitzpatrick obviously didn't place much value on daisy growing, but I did. I'd tried a few fancy varieties, but mostly I grew the ordinary White Shastas because they tolerated my sometimes haphazard gardening habits.

Fitz came in, carrying a couple of big plastic bags of groceries. He set them on the counter in the galley. "Hey, you're here already. Good. I guess Matt told you about my car not starting?"

"That's too bad. Nothing serious, I hope?"

"Nah, just a run-down battery. I'll put the charger on it, and it'll be fine."

"Dad, I keep telling you, you should get a new battery. One of these days you're going to be out in the middle of nowhere, and it'll go dead and you'll be stuck."

"You're probably right," Fitz agreed, a cheerful Mr. Congeniality but obviously without any intention of heeding his son's warnings. "Oh, by the way," he added to me, "I talked to one of the guys I know on the city police force. He said that Molino detective who's heading up the investigation is a real gung-ho kind of guy, with ambitions of being sheriff himself one of these days. But he's a good, very thorough detective. He won't leave any stones unturned."

"I'm glad to hear that."

"What investigation? What detective?" Matt inserted in that same frowning voice I'd heard on the phone.

"Murder at Andi's place. The body in her limousine."

"You're not getting involved in that, are you, Dad?"

"Andi and I thought we'd see what we could find out before they try to pin it on her."

"Dad, you're not a real detective. I wish you'd remember that. And the real stuff can be dangerous."

"He solved Mr. Bolivar's murder down in LA," I put in defensively. "I'm sure it took real detective work to do that."

"Right. And did he tell you how many legs Mr. Bolivar had?"

"Legs?" I repeated uncertainly.

"Okay, so Mr. Bolivar had four legs," Fitz muttered. "He was a German shepherd. But he *was* poisoned, and I figured out it was that snooty couple down the street who did it."

"And have you told her about the big crime wave of flower thefts you also solved?" Matt asked.

"I'm sure you're going to if I don't."

"Flowers kept disappearing out of yards in Dad's neighborhood in LA. He figured out who did it."

I was still feeling defensive. "I'm sure the neighbors appreciated that."

"Captured the wild and dangerous Daisy Thief, who was all of nine years old. Picking the flowers to take to a teacher he had a crush on."

"Well, it was something he shouldn't be doing. And who knows? Maybe the talking-to I gave him deterred him from a life of crime. At least I never went *ker-chunk* off my sailboat into the water in front of six guests, like someone I could name."

"It was rough water. An exceptionally large wave hit the side of the boat—"

"You were giving a demonstration on sailing safety at the time!"

The two men glowered at each other, and for a moment I thought a family crisis was about to erupt. But then I saw the teasing twinkle in Fitz's eyes and an echoing twinkle of affection in Matt's, and I knew this was just chatter between two guys who probably never could manage to come right out and say they loved each other, so this was how they did it.

Then Matt eyed me, not so twinkly eyed, as if he suspected I was leading Fitz astray with this detective nonsense.

"And you, what about you? I suppose you're some kind of detective too?"

With me, his tone and look said if I was a detective, he was captain of the Battlestar *Galactica*.

I named the only credential I had as a detective. "I used to watch *Ed Montrose, P.I.E.* all the time."

Matt didn't physically roll his eyes, but I could see them practically doing a somersault on a mental level.

"Figures," he muttered. Then he went over and yanked up the floor panel to expose the engine again.

Fitz just looked at me and winked. I winked back. Then I edged around the hole in the floor to get outside and back up on the dock.

"I'm sorry I didn't have time to find out anything more. But after we get back from this trip on Saturday, I'll see what else I can turn up. The Vigland police and county sheriff's department work pretty closely together, so the guys I know may know something. Especially since Jerry lived within the city limits. The lot where his car was parked was in the city limits too."

"I think while you're gone I'll see if I can find out anything about Jerry's girlfriends. And contact some relatives in Texas to see what I can learn about Uncle Ned's shyster dealings and enemies down there."

"Good places to start. Just don't put yourself in any danger.

People who murder once may not be reluctant to do it again. I'll walk up to the SUV with you. I need to get the battery charger hooked up on my car so I can get to the lawyer's office on time." He paused. "Hopefully I'll get the connections right this time."

Fitz gave me the keys to the SUV, then showed me the controls and where the registration and insurance papers were located in case I needed them. He also gave me good directions about parking and connecting with the clients.

As I was getting into the SUV, I asked, "Has Matt ever been married?"

"He gave it a try back in his twenties. Lasted about a year, I think. He's forty now, but he seems to prefer his boat to the ladies."

I nodded. "Figures."

"Although his ol' Dad here doesn't necessarily feel the same way," Fitz said and winked again.

Again, no clue as to why he was seeing a lawyer. As I pulled out of the parking lot, my imagination busily supplied everything from lady-friend complications to drinking-and-driving problems.

The trip to Sea-Tac turned out to be easier than I expected. Traffic was heavy, but there weren't any bad accidents or big snarls. I parked, followed Fitz's directions, and held up my sign. Three chattering couples rushed over. They retrieved their luggage while I went out to get the SUV, and then I picked them up right outside the door. They asked a lot of questions about the boat and the San Juan Islands, some of which I could answer. Their enthusiasm was catching, and I found myself wishing I were going along.

Back at the marina, I dropped them off, collected a generous check from Matt, and picked up my Toyota. Fitz wasn't around. I'd spend the afternoon getting that résumé whipped into shape, I decided.

But an unfamiliar car was parked at the end of my walkway when I got home, and an unfamiliar man stood at my front door.

14

He was stocky, brown haired, plain looking, wearing tan slacks, a pale blue knit shirt, and sunglasses. Nothing threatening looking about him, but considering all that happened lately, I felt wary. Rather than jumping out to meet him as I might have a few days ago, I cautiously rolled the window down partway.

"Are you looking for someone?" I called.

"Andi McConnell, I think. I'd like to talk to her."

I was tempted to say, "She moved away," and burn rubber getting out of there. But I didn't, of course. I may be paranoid, but I seem to be stuck with a built-in politeness to strangers. So I said warily, "I'm Andi McConnell."

He took off his sunglasses as he walked up to the car. Without them I could see the forty-fiveish lines around his blue eyes. Studious looking. Crime investigator? Intellectual murderer?

"I hope you don't mind my coming here. I'm Ryan Norton, Jerry's brother."

I peered at him in surprise as I rolled the window on down. "No, of course not. I . . . I'm so sorry about Jerry."

"Could I talk to you for a minute? Ask a few questions?"

"How did you know to come here?"

He grimaced lightly. "The police haven't been eager to tell me much, but I did get out of them that this was where his body was found. In a limousine belonging to you?"

It came out a question rather than a statement, his doubt about the limousine obvious. His quick, surreptitious glance took in the non-limousine-status neighborhood. Moose was barking again, his black-on-white spots bouncing up and down behind the fence.

"Yes. In the trunk of my limousine. Long story about the limo and me," I added, figuring he didn't need to know all about Uncle Ned.

I made a quick decision. Ryan Norton didn't look like this year's serial murderer. In fact, he looked tired and sad and harried. I wasn't trusting enough to invite him inside, but I said, "Would you like to sit over there on the bench in the shade? We can have some sodas or lemonade while we talk."

"That's very nice of you. Thank you. It's been a difficult couple of days."

I opened the door and slid out of the car. "Except there's one thing you should know—it may change your mind about talking to me. The police haven't arrested me yet, but I'm pretty sure I'm at the top of their suspect list. I was, though I hate to use the rather juvenile term, Jerry's girlfriend."

I thought he'd be surprised. Fitz might consider my age "prime time," but I doubted someone Ryan's age would.

Jerry, in one of his more playful moods, had once told me I could make it as the Playmate-Grandma-of-the-Month, but I figured then—and now—that he was just trying to flatter me into a more cooperative attitude. Looking back, I'd also decided he'd probably viewed my resistance to his masculine charms as a challenge. Maybe that was part of what had kept him interested in me. In any case, all irrelevant now.

But, for whatever reasons, Ryan apparently wasn't surprised by the nature of our relationship. "I assumed that."

"Although neither were we—" I stopped, brought up short by the only word I could think of, which wasn't really a normal part of my vocabulary. Then I just braced myself and said it. "We were dating, but we weren't lovers. It wasn't that kind of relationship." I don't know why, but it seemed important to me that he know this.

Ryan looked as embarrassed as I felt. The only way I could have been more embarrassed was if I'd had to admit we were lovers.

"They think you killed Jerry?"

"They have their reasons for thinking it. Pretty good ones," I admitted. "But if you still want to talk . . ."

A smile crossed his plain face, and in it I saw a tiny hint of a brotherly connection to Jerry's roguish good looks. "The bench looks safe enough. I'm willing to take my chances."

"Have you seen Jerry's Trans Am? There's a good-sized dent in the door. I put it there. With a shovel."

"Perhaps that's one of the things I should ask questions about." He sounded curious, but in a good-humored, nonhostile way.

Except that once we were sitting on the bench to talk, a Pepsi in his hand and a 7UP in mine, I asked the first question. "Where are you from?"

"Jerry never mentioned me?"

"Your name, and that you were a younger brother, but that's about all."

"I guess I'm not surprised. We weren't exactly close. I live in Denver. Wife, Marilyn, and three kids, Cory, Jeff, and Kristin. I teach junior-high science. None of which Jerry ever mentioned either, I suppose."

"No."

"Somebody in the sheriff's department called me about his death, and I flew in on Sunday and rented the car."

I glanced at the car parked out on the street. A Honda Civic, gray, the boring kind of vehicle Jerry wouldn't be caught dead in. Then I choked on my soda over that thought, the truth slamming me afresh. Jerry had been caught dead in a vehicle, my limousine.

"Are you staying in Jerry's condo?"

He looked surprised. "No, of course not. The police are still—You do know the condo was broken into, don't you?"

"No! I had no idea."

"The police must be keeping it quiet. Maybe it's one of those situations you hear about where the police don't tell everything because they figure it will help them catch the perp." He smiled self-consciously. "My son is big on crime shows. There's often a 'perp.'"

I couldn't recall Ed Montrose ever talking about perps. "Was anything damaged or taken?"

"The place was ransacked. The police took me in for a few minutes just to look around. I couldn't touch anything. Jerry's computer and printer, everything was gone."

Was that why Detective Sergeant Molino had snapped to attention when I mentioned Jerry's Web site–design business? They must already have known his computer was missing, but probably hadn't known about the business.

"What about his CDs? He had a lot of them he'd burned on the computer."

"I don't know. I didn't see any. Even his filing cabinet and desk drawers had been emptied. And apparently the burglars did it all without arousing any neighbors in the building."

"It's one of those places that's big on privacy," I said,

remembering the few times I'd been there. "How'd the burglars get in?"

"Either a key or a very clever lock picker. The door and lock didn't appear to be damaged. Although that's strictly an amateur assessment, of course." He frowned, ridges wrinkling his high brow and slightly receding hairline. "What I can't figure out is why they wanted all the computer stuff. It was a lot more bulky to haul off, and certainly not as valuable as a pile of cash the police said they found hidden in a bag in the toilet tank."

"Maybe the burglars didn't look there, so they just took what was available. His equipment was all expensive, top-of-the-line stuff."

"Could be. Although I got the impression the police thought the computer equipment was the main target."

I thought so too.

Tom Bolton was on his deck, making no secret that he was watching us through his binoculars. I resisted the impulse to stick out my tongue at him and waved instead. "My busybody neighbor," I explained.

"I thought he was going to fall off his deck watching me when I arrived," Ryan agreed. He lifted a hand and waved too.

Tom was not fazed. He kept right on watching.

"Anyway, maybe taking the computer had something to do with his Web site–design business," I suggested. "I've been thinking Jerry may have been dealing with some rather shady characters. How was the break-in discovered?"

"According to the police, Jerry had a cleaning lady who came in once a week, usually on Wednesdays."

"Right. Consuela. She could get more housecleaning done in a morning than I could in three days."

"She had a key to the condo. She usually came on a weekday, but she'd been down with a stomach flu and came on Saturday instead. When she let herself in and saw what had happened, she called the police."

"Saturday morning. And he was killed sometime late Friday night or very early Saturday morning," I mused.

I was thinking, a bit guiltily, that a break-in at the condo had probably been fortunate for me. It might be the main reason I hadn't been arrested yet. Surely it was connected with the murder, and the police hadn't figured out how I could have broken in and hauled all the stuff off when I was lying out there unconscious by the limo.

"It must have been the killer who broke into the condo," Ryan said, his words echoing my thoughts. "The timing surely wasn't just a coincidence."

"Right. I wonder if he was killed first and the condo then broken into? Or if the condo was ransacked and the computer stuff taken *before* he was killed. And then he was killed because of something they found in the computer files."

"I'm guessing he was killed first, and then they got into the condo. If they'd entered the condo first, it seems as if they'd have just stayed there and waited for him to come home and killed him then."

"Sounds reasonable. The thing is, I've never been able to figure out why he was here—and here in the middle of the night—without my knowing it. So I've wondered if he was killed somewhere else, and his body then brought here and put in the limousine."

"But why would the killer do that? If they wanted to get rid of his body, why not take it out in the woods somewhere? It looks as if there's plenty of wild country around here where it might not be found for years. Why risk coming here?"

"Unless they were trying to involve me some way."

"Strange." He twisted the can of Pepsi on the thigh of his tan pants and gave me a sideways glance. "You, uh, want to tell me about the dent you put in his car?"

So I did. Although I left out the part about Jerry's sleazy attempt at "closure" and just said we'd broken up, and I was encouraging him to leave.

Ryan smiled at "encouraging."

"I e-mailed Jerry to tell him I'd pay for the damage, but I never heard back. But if you'll tell me what the repair bill is, I'll pay it or reimburse you."

"The police still have the car. So, we'll see. Don't worry about it."

"I keep telling the police, I really didn't intend to chase him with a shovel. I thought it was a broom. But I don't think they're convinced."

Ryan smiled again. "I rather think quite a few women would have liked to chase my brother with a shovel, or perhaps something even larger and more deadly. I love Jerry, but loyalty and faithfulness and sensitive breakups were not his strong points."

"Do you know anything about any other girlfriends?"

Ryan shook his head. "No. I didn't even know about the Web site business until you mentioned it. I hadn't talked to him in . . . oh, well over a year, I suppose."

I gave him what skimpy information I had about the business and added, "Do *you* have any idea at all who might want to murder him?"

"Living so far apart . . ." He shook his head again, then lifted his left hand and massaged his temple. "And as I said, we weren't close."

I was curious about that, but he didn't seem inclined to elaborate, and I felt uncomfortable probing into their relationship.

Although I was thinking, if I was going to get anywhere figuring out who the killer was, maybe I'd better try to cultivate more of Fitz's nosiness.

"Although, when the authorities told me on Monday that he'd definitely been murdered—before that, on the phone, they were just saying he'd died under 'suspicious circumstances'—one thought did immediately come to mind."

"What's that?"

"That it might have something to do with his gambling."

"Gambling! Jerry was a gambler?"

"You didn't know?"

One more thing I hadn't known about Jerry. Definitely the tip-of-the-iceberg kind of situation, what I knew about Jerry. "No, I didn't know anything about that."

"Well, maybe he'd kicked the habit. But a few years back, he was really into it. He wouldn't admit it was an addiction, but it was. Sports, horses, anything, he'd bet on it. And when I saw the Indian casinos around here . . ."

"They're very strictly operated. Nothing shady going on there."

"Maybe I'm mistaken, then."

And maybe he wasn't. If Jerry was into gambling outside the casinos, something illegal, there was no telling what kind of unscrupulous characters he'd gotten tangled up with. Could his computer have held incriminating gambling records and names? Could he have owed some big gambling debt? But that didn't seem compatible with the fact that he'd had money hidden in his toilet tank.

Now Ryan returned my question. "Do you have any idea who could have killed him?"

"Just some wild speculations. How long are you going to be here?"

"I'm not sure yet. The medical examiner's office released Jerry's body after the autopsy yesterday, and it's in a funeral home now. I'm trying to get arrangements made. At this point I still can't get into the condo to look for a will and all the other information that will be needed to settle his estate." The harried expression was back. "This has hit our folks pretty hard."

"Would you . . . I mean, I know it's a lot to ask under the circumstances, since I'm a more-or-less suspect . . . but could I come with you when you are allowed into the condo?"

He surprised me with an enthusiastic response. "Could you come? Yes! It'll be a relief to have someone there with me. And you'll surely be able to tell more than I can about anything that's missing."

I gave him my phone number, and he said he'd call as soon as he heard from the police that they were through with the condo.

It wasn't until after he'd gone, and I was looking through Uncle Ned's will to find names of relatives back in Texas to call, that I thought of something else connected to Jerry's computer equipment, and I wondered if it was also missing.

15

That evening I called information and asked for a number for Lucille Noakes in Dry Wells, Texas. I'd found her name in the will and figured she must be Cousin Larry's mother.

"I'd like to speak to Lucille Noakes, please," I said when a perky, Southern-accented voice drawled, "Hello."

"This is Lucy," she responded. "What can I do for you, hon?" She sounded ready to settle in for a juicy chat even before she knew who I was, the kind of person who asked a telemarketer about his wife and kids.

I explained my identity, but before I could even get into the reason for my call, she squealed with delight.

"Why, bless your heart, darlin', it's just fantastic to hear from you! Aunt Claudine's daughter, I do declare! She just dropped out of our lives all those years ago, but Mama never forgot her. Larry told me all about how nice you were to him when he delivered the limousine. Or the *limouzeen*, as Uncle Ned put it."

"I've been afraid the relatives might be unhappy with me because I got the limousine, and they got . . . other things."

Lucille, as I'd noticed in the will, had inherited a set of Tupperware containers.

Her laugh tinkled like a silver spoon clinking in a mint julep glass on a hot Southern day. "Now, don't you go worryin' about that. Everyone knows how peculiar old Ned was. You just enjoy that big ol' limo."

Enjoyment was not what the limo had provided so far, but I was still hoping.

"Actually, Uncle Ned is the reason I called. Somewhere"—I was careful not to identify my source by name—"somewhere I got the impression he'd been involved in some business dealings of a, oh, questionable nature and may have acquired some enemies along the way. The bulletproof glass in the limousine, you know."

"Well, yes, he was an old crook," Lucy said cheerfully. "But a lot of those old-time Texans got rich in ways that weren't exactly on the up-and-up. Though you don't need to be spreadin' that kind of talk around, of course. I figure Ned tried to make up for some of his misdeeds there at the end, leaving everything to all those charitable organizations."

I'd been under the impression he'd left his wealth to the charitable organizations mostly to keep it away from his relatives, but I didn't say that. Lucy didn't sound bitter. Maybe she needed Tupperware.

"Do you know anyone in particular who might have been angry enough at him to do something . . . drastic?"

"What are you sayin', darlin'?" She sounded alarmed. "What kind of drastic? So far as I know, there's never been any question about Uncle Ned's death being anything other than natural."

"Oh, no, I didn't mean that." I gave her a quick rundown on Jerry's murder and how I thought the limousine could have been searched.

"His body was in the trunk?"

I had no mental framework for Lucy Noakes, but I could picture a plump feminine hand touching a plump throat in distress.

"Oh, my heavens."

"I'm wondering if the killer's real motive was to find something he thought was hidden in the limousine, something someone back in Texas put there. And killed Jerry just because he happened to be in the wrong place at the wrong time."

"Well, it's true Uncle Ned was involved in one lawsuit after another. People were always suin' him. Although Jasmine—that's my sister, Jasmine Arquette—always said she thought he enjoyed those lawsuits. And he usually won, of course. Those lawyers of his could chew up a courtroom and spit it out before breakfast."

"I've wondered why Uncle Ned wrote his will himself instead of having his lawyers do it."

"Oh, well, he was a stubborn old coot. I doubt he trusted his lawyers any more'n he trusted anyone else. I especially remember one lawsuit, a big argument over some land Uncle Ned bought, and this guy came to the house with a shotgun. Of course Ned blasted back at him, and there was quite a ruckus. Though nobody got hurt, as I recall. But I can't imagine why anybody'd put something in the limo, or who it would be. Or what it could be. It'd have to be something really valuable, wouldn't it, for someone to traipse all the way from here out there to look for it?"

Given Uncle Ned's peculiarities, the possibilities seemed as numerous as the heirs in his will. "What was the shotgun man's name?"

"Oh my, let me think. Jones. Yes, that was it. Something Jones."

Great. That narrowed it down to a zillion or so people.

Although her next words removed any concern about zeroing in on this particular Jones.

"But he's dead now, I'm sure. Actually, I think most of Ned's enemies are dead. Larry said it was one of the joys of Ned's life that he'd outlived 'em all."

Mr. Nice Guy.

"Well, it was just a long shot. Probably my friend's death had no connection with Uncle Ned."

"That'd be my thought too. But I'll ask Jasmine and some of the others and see if anyone has any ideas. We don't want any murderers runnin' around loose, here or there."

I gave her my number so she could call if she wanted. "Did Larry get home okay on the bus?"

"Oh, yes, he's fine. Though I don't know what's going to become of that boy if he doesn't settle down. Would you believe he's traipsed off to New York—New York, can you fancy that?—on some wild-hare scheme to get into actin'?"

No doubt a worry, I agreed silently. But perhaps preferable to sitting around watching his toenails grow. "Tell him hi from me, if you talk to him."

"I'll do that. And you keep in touch now, hear? Everybody'd just love to meet you."

So much for a Texas connection, I decided. Like Uncle Ned's enemies, a dead end. This killer was probably homegrown, with roots right here in Vigland. Which was not exactly reassuring.

THE PHONE RANG after Lucy and I hung up. Sarah, calling to check on me. I told her that, no, I hadn't been arrested or murdered yet, and she chastised me for my facetiousness. I prudently decided I wouldn't tell her Fitz and I were into detective work of our own. She again urged me to come down there. I again declined.

Fitz called on his cell phone Wednesday evening. They were anchored off one of the smaller San Juan Islands, the weather was fantastic, and he'd fixed chicken marsala for dinner. I told him about calling Lucille and deciding we could eliminate any traveling murderer from Texas. Also about my meeting with Ryan, the break-in at Jerry's condo, and that I might have a chance to look around inside the condo in a day or two.

"This Ryan invited you?"

"I kind of invited myself."

"Good for you! Just don't forget one point."

"What's that?"

"Nosiness is good. Don't be shy. Look for anything with names or phone numbers or addresses. Peer into cubbyholes. Look in pockets. Investigate cans and bottles. Sometimes they're phony, hollowed out to keep something inside."

"I'm sure the police already did all that."

"They might not have recognized the relevance of something, and you will. Take advantage of opportunities. Ask questions. Pry."

"I'll try to do that."

"Okay. But above all, be careful. I'll see you when we get back. I miss you."

He missed me? We hardly knew each other. Although, to be honest, I kind of missed him too.

RYAN CALLED MIDMORNING on Thursday and said the police were finished with the condo. We agreed to meet a half hour later in the parking lot behind the condo complex.

I changed into faded jeans and an old, long-tailed blue shirt. Prowling through a dead man's condo didn't strike me as a dress-up occasion.

Ryan was in slacks and a short-sleeved sports shirt when he stepped out of his rental car. He looked off toward the bay, sparkling in the sunshine, and I had the impression he'd rather be anywhere than here. A tug pulling a huge container of wood chips was headed toward Hornsby Inlet on the outgoing tide.

"Well, I guess we might as well get at it," he said as if he were psyching himself up for an ordeal.

I also steeled myself when he opened the condo door, not certain what I'd feel. An overwhelming sense of Jerry's presence? An eerie echo of his absence? But the first thing that struck me wasn't a feeling, but simply the sight of a gray powder everywhere. On every hard surface of furniture, windowsills, counters, even on a coffee cup on the dining room table.

"What is that stuff?"

"That's what I asked the officer when I was here before. Fingerprint powder. For picking up—what do they call them?—latent prints, I think it is."

Of course. I should have remembered fingerprint powder from those old Ed Montrose shows. The next thing I noticed was the empty desk where Jerry had his office set up in a corner of the big living room. As Ryan had said, everything was gone. Computer, printer, scanner. And empty drawers, like multistoried, gaping mouths, hung open on the metal file cabinet.

"The CDs he'd burned are gone too. He kept them in a tall container over there." I pointed to an empty spot beside the sleek, black metal desk. "I wonder about his laptop."

"I don't know. If it was here, the burglars undoubtedly took it too. Do you notice anything other than computer equipment missing?"

I glanced around. Shaded by the covering of gray powder, the black-and-white décor looked less sophisticated now. In spite of all the expense Jerry had gone to, to have the place decorated, it somehow felt almost . . . shabby. Or perhaps death brings a hint of shabbiness with it.

The big abstract painting over the sofa lurched at an angle. Had police or burglars thought a safe might be hidden behind it? Stuffing spilled from a slash in a black pillow on the white leather sofa. Flowers in a vase on the coffee table were drooping and dead. Beyond the living room, cupboard doors in the kitchen hung open.

It didn't seem as if Jerry had been dead long enough for the condo to have acquired a musty, unused scent, but it had. Overlaid with something vaguely chemical smelling. Did fingerprint powder have a scent?

I didn't see anything else missing. The sculpture of some Greek god and that awful abstract painting, probably the most valuable items in the room, were still there. Although a burglar, unless fairly knowledgeable, may not have known how valuable they were.

"No, I don't notice anything else missing. Oh, but I remembered something the other night. He had a little gadget called a flash drive. It was only about this big." I measured off a small, oblong space with my fingers. "He always carried it on a keychain in his pocket."

"Yeah, I know what they are. I've never used one, but I know you can plug it into your computer. Works like a backup system to store important files in case something happens with the computer, or you can use it to move information from one computer to another. He kept information from his Web site–design business on it?"

"I assume so." Although it had always struck me as a little egotistical that he considered his Web site stuff so valuable he had to carry it with him every minute. "He misplaced the thing one time and had a fit about it until he found where it had dropped out of his pants pocket and fallen under a nightstand. I wonder what's happened to it now?"

"It apparently wasn't in his pocket when he was killed. The police kept his clothing as part of the evidence, but after the autopsy they gave me the personal items that were on the body. Just his wallet, some loose change, and a roll of breath-freshener mints."

"Where did you get the key to get in here today?"

"The police. They got it from the cleaning lady when they came to investigate her call."

Ryan jingled the key against coins in his pocket. It made an oddly empty, lonely sound in the silent apartment. *Echoes of the dead*, I thought, squelching a shiver. Jerry used to jingle his keys like that. Where were those keys now?

"No cell phone?" I hadn't thought of that either until now, but Jerry's cell phone would have been a gold mine of information. It was one of those do-everything-but-prophesy-the-future kind of phones, and I knew he kept a lot of information on it. "He always had it clipped to his belt."

"No. And I think the police would have told me if they'd kept anything like that. They gave me a list of a few items they removed from the condo. So the cell phone and flash drive must simply be missing."

Stolen off Jerry's body, no doubt. Along with the keys. Which solidified the thought that the break-in at the condo had come after the murder. They'd used the stolen keys to enter. This time I couldn't squelch the shiver. "What about a watch? Jerry had an expensive Rolex."

"He did?" Ryan sounded surprised. I had the feeling he didn't know Jerry'd had that kind of money. "No, they didn't return a watch to me."

"What did the police take from the condo?"

"Various papers they thought might provide information. Bank records that hadn't been in the filing cabinet. Some unidentified white pills."

I had to smile at that. I could identify them. Jerry had decided he should be taking calcium, and I'd given him some of my supply. That was when I'd thrown out the economy-size plastic container and put both his and my pills in small, unmarked jars. The Great Calcium Conspiracy.

"And they took all that cash he had hidden in a plastic bag in the toilet tank," Ryan added. "They said it would be returned if it hadn't come from criminal activity."

Once I'd have scoffed and said no way to Jerry being involved in any criminal activity. Now I wasn't so certain. "How much cash?"

"Over ten thousand dollars."

That was definitely enough to startle me. Jerry liked to flash an impressive roll of cash, true, but ten thousand dollars' worth? Why would he be dealing in that amount of cash? Where had he gotten it? Some unknown criminal activity now sounded like an even more likely possibility. Could he have been doing something illegal with his Web site business and gotten paid in cash?

"So, I guess we might as well start looking around." Ryan sounded uncertain, and I again felt his reluctance to poke around in his brother's belongings.

"If he kept a copy of the will here, it was probably in the filing cabinet and was taken along with everything else," I said. I was reluctant too. The eeriness of the place was starting to get to me. Being here with Jerry dead felt . . . spooky.

"Maybe his lawyer would have a copy of a will," Ryan said. "Do you know if he had a regular lawyer? Or a safe deposit box?"

I shook my head.

"Actually, I doubt if Jerry ever made a will," Ryan said, his tone gloomy. "He pretty much thought he was invincible."

True. "Well, we can hope we find something." But I had to doubt now that I was going to find anything helpful regarding his murder. It looked as if, between the burglars and the police, anything useful had been removed. Or was I, too, just trying to find reasons to avoid an unpleasant task?

"Maybe I should see if I could get that cleaning lady to come in first, before we go poking around." Ryan swiped a finger across a film of fingerprint powder.

Much as I wanted to jump at that escape, I doubted I'd ever get back in the condo if we walked away now.

"Well, we're here," I said, trying to sound more upbeat than I felt. "Might as well see what we can find."

16

Ryan decided to tackle the bedroom. Remembering Fitz's admonition about phony cans, I headed for the kitchen. I wanted to help Ryan find a will or important papers, but I was also looking for something else, although I had no idea what. Anything that might give a clue to Jerry's murder.

I checked cans in the cupboard. Not many of them, since Jerry mostly disdained canned food. The few that were there all appeared authentic. And more exotic than anything in my cupboards. Canned truffled goose foie gras. Had he been saving that for some special occasion for us? Or was foie gras reserved for tousle-haired Elena?

Then I mentally kicked myself. The man was dead, and my goal was to find out who killed him. This was no time for snide or petty thoughts.

I looked below the sink and prowled through containers of air freshener, dishwasher detergent, floor polish, and various cleaners, all of which appeared bona fide and were no doubt used by Consuela rather than Jerry himself. I poked through the freezer compartment of the fridge and again found the contents more upscale than my own: filet mignon, chicken cordon bleu, Canadian bacon, two lobster tails, and a frozen cheesecake.

In the bathroom, I got an in-depth view of various aspects of Jerry with which I was not familiar. He apparently had stomach problems I hadn't known about, given the bottles and cartons of antacids and other stomach remedies. And at some time he'd had a definite athlete's foot problem.

By that time I was beginning to feel uncomfortably like a voyeur. I doubted the identity of the murderer was going to be found among his four different brands of whitening toothpaste or his dandruff shampoo, so I went to the bedroom to see how Ryan was doing. He was down on his knees, looking through the bottom drawer of a chest of drawers.

"Find anything?"

"A box of old income tax and insurance papers on the top shelf of the closet. I'm not sure they'll be any help, but maybe."

Remembering what Fitz had said about pockets, I started going through clothing in the closet. Deep in the pocket of a pair of tan Dockers I found a scrap of paper with a phone number. I dutifully passed it along to Ryan, but not before surreptitiously copying the number for myself. Fitz would be proud of me!

Then I remembered something else I wanted to ask about. "What about Jerry's sailboat? Have you been to see it yet?"

"I didn't know he had a sailboat." Ryan leaned back on his heels, his tone dismayed, as if this was one more unpleasant surprise he had to cope with.

I wrote down the name and address of the friend, Griff Northcutt, who owned the private dock where Jerry kept the boat. I also made a mental note to add this name to the "persons of interest" list. He and Jerry'd once had an unpleasant disagreement about the rental fee, I remembered.

We gave up after about three hours. By then it was almost two o'clock. We were both smudged with fingerprint powder.

Ryan offered to buy lunch, but I said I just wanted to go home and clean up.

"Me too," he agreed. Unhappily he added, "But I can't leave for another day or two. I made arrangements yesterday to have the body shipped back to Lancaster for burial. Tomorrow I'll try to find a lawyer here and see what to do about the estate, since I can't come up with a will. I'm sorry, but there won't be any funeral or memorial service here."

"That's okay. I'll send flowers. That's Lancaster what? Georgia? Virginia?"

"Lancaster, Colorado. It's about fifty miles outside Denver. The small town where we grew up. Dad's a retired teacher, and it's an inexpensive place to live."

I was surprised. "I thought Jerry's family lived back east or down south somewhere." And had Rolex-level money.

"No, that would be his wife's family. They live in Augusta, Georgia. Where she and the kids now live also, of course."

He spoke as if I surely knew that, but I didn't. Then something ominous struck me about the way he'd said "his wife."

"You mean his ex-wife." Otherwise known as Cara the Crazy, in Jerry's unkind words.

"Well, no. They weren't divorced."

"They *weren't*?"

"He told you they were divorced?"

"He certainly did!" I suddenly felt crawly with more than fingerprint powder. All the time I'd been seeing him, Jerry had been married. If I'd known that, I'd have taken after him with a shovel long ago. "He said he'd been single for almost two years!"

"No. It was a . . . big, ugly mess."

"She wouldn't give him a divorce?"

"The other way around, actually. Cara's family is quite

wealthy, and he's been holding out, using the kids as a bargaining chip."

"He was trying to get custody of the kids?" In spite of all I now knew about Jerry, I was reluctant to give up the mental picture of Cara as a shrieking schemer with the temperament of a witch on a broomstick, with Jerry the long-suffering ex-husband. But painting Jerry as some wronged saint, I was beginning to see, was a losing proposition.

"No way. His deal was, they put up enough money and he'd cooperate on the divorce and give up all parental rights. Otherwise, he'd drag it out until you-know-where freezes over."

Family money, he'd hinted to me. But it was his wife's family money, not his. And I'd thought what he'd tried to do to me was sleazy.

"I wonder why the police didn't notify her instead of you, since she's still Jerry's wife."

"They did, but she referred them to me. We talk every once in a while. I've tried to keep in touch with the kids, and Cara's always been cooperative. She's a very nice, level-headed woman."

"How did she take the news about Jerry?"

"She was shocked, I'm sure, but I didn't hear any open weeping."

Hardly surprising, considering. I hadn't been weeping either. I'd had some moments of guilt about that, all wrapped up in my own problems with Jerry's death rather than mourning that he was dead. But I was feeling even less tearful now that I realized how he'd lied to me.

"I don't like to think it," Ryan began, his tone reluctant, "because I've always liked Cara, but . . ."

"But what?"

"I'm sure Cara herself wouldn't do anything. She's much too sweet and gentle a person. But her father, he's a rich old tycoon in a Southern timber business, the kind of guy who'd really like to be dictator of some small country, and he's been furious with Jerry's manipulations."

"And?"

"And I'm not so sure he wouldn't . . . do something."

"Her father might come out here and shoot Jerry to get him out of the way?" I gasped.

"No, no, not personally." Ryan waved a dismissive hand. "But I'm not so sure but what he might . . . get someone to do it for him."

"You mean hire a hit man to get Jerry out of the way?"

Ryan scowled. "Sounds pretty preposterous, doesn't it? I mean, that's the stuff of Mafia movies, not people we know. No, surely not," he added emphatically.

An emphasis that somehow did the opposite and made Cara's father's involvement ominously possible. None of which explained, of course, a basic problem with the murder. Why had it happened at my place? Had the murderer stealthily followed Jerry there? But what had Jerry been doing around my limo that night?

Ryan said he'd talk to me again before he left, and I made my way out to the car, feeling dazed.

Jerry . . . married.

I'd always wondered how any woman could be so dumb as to get mixed up with a married man. Now I knew.

17

Back home, I showered and was out weeding the daisy beds when Joella got home from work. She was carrying a big plastic bag from the bakery. Neil always kept her supplied with day-old goodies. The birds got what we couldn't eat.

She waved the bag at me as she got out of the car. "Hey, come on over later. I have some of Neil's new blueberry strudels. They're luscious." She sounded cheerful, but she looked as if she could barely drag one foot in front of the other. She was a little over seven months along now and, as she put it, "expanding like your average hot air balloon."

"You look beat. How about if I bring over some leftover chicken casserole from the freezer, and you can just put your feet up and relax? I'll tell you all about A Day in the Life of a Lady Sleuth. And then we'll have blueberry strudel for dessert."

Joella smiled. She reached down to rub a swollen ankle. "My guardian angel. Thank you."

By the time I went over an hour or so later, she'd showered and perked up a little. While I nuked the casserole, I told her about our search in Jerry's condo, the ugly details I'd learned about his personal life, and that I had this phone number.

"Who do you think it might be?"

"Who knows? Maybe a girlfriend. Maybe somebody he's dealt with on the Web site business. Maybe some bookie he placed bets with. Maybe the murderer, saying, 'We are unable to come to the phone right now, but please leave a message and we'll get back to you as soon as possible. Your call is important to Murder-by-Phone, Inc.'"

Joella wrinkled her nose. "Ugh. But what if it really is the murderer? And he or she has caller ID, and it shows that person your number?"

That jolted me. "But if I don't bring up the subject and ask, 'Did you murder Jerry?' they won't know why I'm calling, will they?"

"If it's an unlisted number, they might be curious about how you got it."

The possibility of caller ID was enough to give me second thoughts. Okay, this called for a change in tactics. Do cell phone numbers show up on caller ID? Could someone knowledgeable trace that number back to a name and address?

I didn't know, but it wasn't something I wanted to risk.

Joella had news of her own. Detective Sergeant Molino had come to the coffee shop that afternoon to question her.

"One of the questions he asked was whether I'd ever been in the limo, and when I said yes, he asked me to come in so they could take my fingerprints. So I'm going to do that tomorrow."

"Oh, Jo, I'm sorry. I hate having you dragged into this."

"I don't mind. Actually, he seemed very nice. He had a strawberry smoothie and said it was really good. He was on his way to pick up his cat at the vet's. It has some kind of skin problem."

The man had a cat? If I'd speculated about a pet for Detective Sergeant Molino, it would be something slithery or scaly.

"What kind of questions did he ask?"

"You were the main topic, of course. But he also asked a few questions about Tom Bolton. And about me, too. I think he'd have liked to know about my pregnancy sans husband, but he was too polite to ask."

Polite? Okay, I had to admit Detective Sergeant Molino hadn't been truly rude to me. But I figured it was a pit bull kind of politeness, with big teeth behind it.

When I went to set the table for dinner, Joella's mail was sitting on one of the place mats. I started to push it aside, then looked more closely.

"Hey, this is a birthday card! You're having a birthday and you never even told me?"

She jumped up with surprising alacrity and snatched the card out of my hand. "And you accused Fitz of being nosy when he read your letter," she said indignantly. "Now look what you're doing!"

Point well taken. I ignored it. "When is this birthday?"

"Sunday," she said reluctantly.

"And you'll be twenty-one."

"That's what my birth certificate indicates."

Something in her tone made me ask, "But?"

"But sometimes I feel about ten. Other times closer to ninety."

Oddly enough, I knew the feeling. Sometimes my sixty seemed impossible. How could I be sixty when I felt seventeen inside? Other times, sixty seemed impossible from the other direction. How could I be only sixty when I looked at younger people around me and realized I had clothes—and wrinkles— older than they were?

"Why were you hiding this from me?" I said severely.

"I wasn't hiding it. I just didn't want a big fuss."

"But you made a big fuss over *my* birthday."

"That's different."

Since I'd already been duly charged with nosiness, I grabbed the card again and looked to see who it was from. "Hey, this is from your mother! Have they changed their attitude?"

"Does ol' Moose change his black-on-white spots? Does the broken toaster heal itself? Does the woman in the exercise-machine ads on TV ever admit she was always skinny and didn't get that way using that machine?"

I wasn't sure all those references were relevant, but I saw what she was getting at. No change in the Picault parents.

"There was one small change," she conceded. "But if you're thinking maybe they sent a gift certificate to buy cute baby clothes or fuzzy toys, think again."

"Oh, Jo, I'm so sorry." I went over and put my arms around her. Joella covered her feelings with these tart comments, but I knew how much her parents' attitude hurt her.

I didn't understand her wealthy parents, so smug and righteous over in their big house in Seattle. By Joella's own admission she hadn't been an ideal daughter. She'd kept her grades up, but she'd been into smoking pot in high school and had dabbled in stronger drugs when she was in college down in California.

But had they been there to offer support or comfort or help when the worst that could happen to a girl *had* happened? No. All they'd offered were demands and ultimatums.

She'd told me her story. She'd had a fight and broken up with her boyfriend one Friday night, then defiantly gone to an off-campus party alone. She met people there, friends of friends of friends. Things got fuzzy.

She didn't recall leaving the party, much less who she'd left it with. But hours later she'd returned to consciousness alone in her own car with ugly physical proof of what had happened, but no memory of it. She figured out later that she'd probably been given Rohypnol in a drink, a favorite "date-rape" drug because it not only knocks the girl out; it destroys short-term memory of whatever happened. She hadn't gone to the police immediately, guiltily blaming herself because there had been warnings on campus about the drug, and she knew she'd acted foolishly. Then, by the time she did go to the authorities, when she knew she was pregnant, the event was several weeks in the past, and there was no evidence of the rape or of the drug in her system.

She'd given the police names of several people at the party, but nothing had ever come of it. Perhaps because Don and Scott and Mike weren't all that definitive. Or perhaps, she'd added when telling me, because the police suspected she was just making up a wild story to cover something she'd done willingly. In any case, nothing had ever come of her report to the police.

Her parents' reaction when she told them was a scathing blast of scorn and anger for letting it happen, and the demand that she have an immediate abortion. When she resisted, they were adamant. No abortion, no help. No comfort, no support, nothing.

"I'm not even sure why I refused at first," Joella had told me the only time we talked about it. She hadn't been a Christian then. But in exploring her inner feelings and looking for answers, what she'd done, she said, was "find myself . . . and God." She also found the inner conviction that she couldn't kill this unborn baby. No matter what its origins, it was still one of God's precious creations.

None of this mattered to her parents. They didn't care about her spiritual awakening. They had their ultimatum: have an abortion, or you're on your own. Which was when Joella pulled out and came to Vigland, intending to room with a friend. That fell through when the friend got an unexpected job offer in Portland and took it. Joella stayed on, even though she knew no one else in Vigland and had never even been in the town before.

"Where else did I have to go?" she'd said wryly.

She'd answered my ad to rent the duplex, sold her snappy little Mustang, bought the old Subaru, and got a job in the coffee shop. When I found out what her real situation was, I lowered the rent so she wouldn't be skimping so much on food or medical care.

"So what is this change?" I asked as I set the bottle of ranch dressing beside the salad on the table.

"I can come home, or they'll send money to help me out here. On one condition."

"Which is?"

"That I give the baby up for adoption as soon as she's born. That I not only promise to give her up, but that I make all the arrangements now, so it's a sure thing."

Another harsh ultimatum. Their view was basically the same: one way or the other, this baby had to go. Although I had to wonder if they'd ever really thought of it as a *baby*. Their grandchild, to be exact.

And yet . . . "You're thinking about doing that anyway."

She nodded. "I know. I want what's best for my baby."

"We're always hearing about how many couples are trying to adopt."

"And doing that would solve a bunch of problems, wouldn't it? I could go back to college and basically start my life over. The baby would have good parents with everything to offer her, and I'd be . . . free."

"Maybe that's the solution, then."

"Maybe it is. But I won't take a bribe from my folks just to make life easier for myself," she added almost fiercely.

This was where I backed off. I could see strong arguments on both sides. I couldn't imagine ever giving up Sarah under any circumstances, but I knew how tough life would be for Joella if she kept the baby. Raising a child alone, without family support of any kind, was a daunting prospect. And so many childless couples desperately wanted a baby.

"Did you decide on a name?" I asked tentatively.

She shook her head, but not before I caught a glint of tears in her eyes. "If she has . . . other parents, I figure they'll want to name her themselves."

A tough decision. And a decision, as I'd earlier said to her, she had to make alone.

"No, not alone," Joella had said firmly.

I knew what that meant. God was in all her decisions.

It must be a nice feeling, I thought. A secure feeling, to know help was there, that there was a greater strength to lean on. There'd been times in my life when I felt as alone as a bird lost on a mountaintop. And yet I doubted God was going to be sending her a check to help out every month.

After dinner, I put the dishes in the dishwasher, then said, "Okay, I have to run. See you later."

"What's your hurry?"

"Oh, you know. Things to do."

My evasion didn't work.

"You're going to call that number, aren't you?"

"I can't just ignore it. It might be an important clue."

"It might be a hotline to you. And an hour after the call, the murderer will be knocking on your door!"

"I don't think murderers come politely knocking." I patted

her hand. "But don't worry. I'm going to call from a pay phone. The one up by McDonald's, I think."

"Hey, great idea! I'll come along."

"No reason to do that."

She smiled and slipped her bare feet into sandals. "Maybe nosiness is catching."

We parked in the shopping center where the big yellow arch rose over a stucco building. I couldn't see any danger in this, but I already had a fast exit from the parking lot figured out, just in case some high-tech identification system instantly latched onto me.

I punched in the number. The prefix showed it was located in Vigland. I had an innocent-sounding spiel ready. I was this querulous, confused little old lady wanting to know who I'd reached because this was supposed to be my cousin Phoebe's number.

It rang four times before an answering machine picked up. I held my breath, expecting anything from sultry female tones to the growl of a bookie named Bubba.

I listened a few moments, then hung up the receiver.

Joella pounded my arm. "Who was it? What's wrong? Why did you hang up? Did they sound threatening or dangerous?"

"Not unless you're afraid of chiropractic treatment."

"Chiropractic treatment!"

"It was a chiropractor's office. Their hours are eight thirty to five on weekdays, eight thirty to noon on Saturdays. Although there's another number you can call if you're having a chiropractic emergency."

Joella looked bemused, then giggled, and I maintained my dignity by saying, "It *might* have been an important clue."

Okay, as a sleuth, I was learning things. About Jerry's

gambling. About his stomach problems. About his married state. And that he'd had some unknown condition possibly requiring chiropractic attention.

I was also learning that in real-life sleuthing there were considerably more dead ends than there had been in Ed Montrose's weekly half hour of detective work, where every clue had meaning.

18

On Friday morning I called people in several insurance offices in Vigland, people I knew from a loose network of working together in the past. Some said their offices weren't looking for anyone at the moment, but they'd be happy to keep my résumé on file. I took the résumé I'd typed up (am I the only person in the world still using an old electric typewriter instead of a computer?), ran off copies at a photocopy shop, and dropped them off.

One woman I talked to confided that when another local office had an opening a few days ago, they'd been inundated with ex-F&N employees. "My daughter over in Seattle says the Internet is the only way to go when you're looking for a job these days," she added.

I felt vaguely dinosaurish. "A whole different world from how job hunting used to be."

"Right. But it's how all her friends do it. Though they're looking mostly at big-corporation-type jobs, I think."

"Thanks. I may have to try that." But Vigland didn't have any big corporations, and relocating was far down on my list of life choices. Thinking I might do better in Olympia, I expanded the job search to an employment agency over there that afternoon. The woman nodded approvingly when she saw my résumé.

"Looks good," she said. But she also said finding the right job could take time, especially if I wanted to stay in insurance, because they were getting so many applications from F&N people.

I assured her I wasn't welded to insurance.

"So MONDAY I try the city and county government offices and the schools," I told Joella on Saturday. It was a warm evening, and we were sitting barefoot on my back patio, sipping lemonade. "I was offered a job with the county years ago, but I decided to go with F&N instead."

"I got my job through a newspaper ad. Though it isn't the kind of job you're looking for, of course."

"I'll try that too."

"Are you thinking any more about a limousine service? I still think it's a great idea."

"In case you haven't noticed, there's a problem."

"Okay, no limousine. But you're going to get it back one of these days."

The phone rang in the living room. I set my lemonade glass on the little metal patio table and padded in through the sliding glass doors.

"Hey, sidekick, how're you doing? Got that murder figured out yet?"

Fitz! I was surprised and a little annoyed at how glad I was to hear from him. Glad enough that I let the "sidekick" thing pass without a challenge. "I'm working on it. You're back at the marina?"

"Yeah. We won't be going out again until Tuesday."

I gave him a rundown on my activities, including the possibility of Jerry's father-in-law being involved in the murder and my finding out that Jerry had never actually been divorced. Which gave me the irrelevant thought that perhaps what the world really needed was a detective agency specializing in investigating the jerks who wander into a single woman's life. Call it the CTBO Agency, for Check the Bum Out. I didn't mention to Fitz my phone call to the chiropractor's office, which I felt put my sleuthing talents in a somewhat less-than-complimentary light.

"So how was your trip?"

"Great. Caught a nice lingcod. I was thinking maybe we could get together tomorrow and cook it."

"I already have something planned for tomorrow, but . . . hold on a minute."

I carried the cordless phone out to the patio and covered the mouthpiece with my hand. "Hey, what would you think about Fitz coming along tomorrow?"

"Coming along where?"

"Your birthday celebration, of course. We may be missing the limo, but we're going to do limo-dogs anyway."

"Oh, that's a lot of bother," she protested, but I'd already seen her eyes light up.

"So what about Fitz?"

"Sure. Invite him to come along."

I did, and he agreed, and I said we'd pick him up at the marina about one thirty. Then Joella suggested that since it was her birthday, I really should come to church with her first.

"You'd use your birthday as coercion to get me to church?" I protested indignantly.

Joella just smiled her sweet smile. "Whatever works."

SO I WENT to church with her the following morning, and I ventured one small prayer: *Thanks for bringing Joella into my life, and please help her make the right decision about her baby.*

Okay, that's two. Does God have a quota, especially from an outsider like me? Or maybe I didn't have to be an outsider? An interesting thought, though I wasn't sure I was ready to act on it.

Afterwards we went home to change clothes, then to the grocery store for wieners and onions and buns and everything that went with them. Plus Greek salad from the deli, because Joella was looking at it with such longing, and a big fat dill pickle for her, too, because she said she hadn't had one in a zillion years. I'd baked a cake before going to bed the night before, so I also bought a box of birthday candles.

Fitz, in khaki shorts and forest green T-shirt with the ever-present sailboat logo, was waiting in the parking lot when we arrived at the marina. He had long-handled forks for roasting wieners over a fire, plus chili left over from yesterday's lunch on the boat.

It was a glorious day for a birthday, a picnic, or anything else. The tide was almost out when we reached the park over on the far side of Hornsby Inlet, the long, narrow channel of water that connects Vigland Bay with the main part of Puget Sound. A nice stretch of rocky beach lay exposed below the picnic area.

I'd brought kindling and wood saved from a tree that blew down in my yard a couple winters ago, and Fitz had a fire blazing and crackling in minutes.

"We'll let the fire burn down until we have good coals for roasting the wieners," Fitz said. "That's the best way to do it."

So how long did that good advice last? Just long enough for Joella and me to thread wieners on our long forks and gleefully stick them right into the blaze. Where a few seconds later they were blackened, burned, and splitting. The fat in mine even caught on fire, and I whirled it merrily like a Fourth of July sparkler.

We both piled our garlic-flavored buns high with onions and mustard and pepper-jack cheese, which Joella declared, between chomps of big dill pickle, was "exactly the way limo-dogs should be!"

"Limo-dogs?" Fitz said. He was still waiting for the fire to burn down to those nice coals.

So we had to explain the concept of limo-dogs to him, and then he started singing a song about a long, black limousine. I couldn't tell if he was massacring a real song or making up an incredibly bad one as he went along, but by the time he motioned us to join in on the chorus, which was, "And then I painted my long black limo pearly blue, and we all ate chili beans and Mountain Dew," we were all giggling.

By then he'd given in and had a burned weenie of his own. The chili he'd put in a pot over the fire was hot, and the next round of limo-dogs we smothered in chili. With Greek salad on the side. I stopped there, but Joella and Fitz went on to third and fourth limo-dogs.

Afterwards I brought out my gift for Joella, an inexpensive watch to replace the one that had conked out. Then to my surprise, and Joella's, too, Fitz also had a gift stuck down in the plastic bag in which he'd brought the pot of chili. "I've had this for a while, so maybe today is a good time to give it to you."

It was a little book of stories and songs to read and sing to a baby, and I was as touched as Joella by something so sweet. Although I also guessed this meant Fitz didn't know she was considering giving the baby up for adoption.

Then I stuck twenty-one candles on the cake, with Joella giggling that it looked like a chocolate porcupine, and we sang "Happy Birthday" while she gave a mighty puff and blew them all out.

She gave us both big hugs after we ate cake, Joella claiming an outside piece with the most frosting. "Thank you both so much. This is a twenty-first birthday I'll never forget."

Which turned out to be true in a way none of us anticipated at that moment.

19

We sat around the fire for a while, and then I decided I should work off some of the calories before they homesteaded on my thighs. Fitz said he'd walk on the beach with me, but Joella decided she'd rather take a nap. I spread a blanket from the car on the grass for her.

The tide had gone out even farther while we were eating, exposing all kinds of interesting creatures. Starfish, purple and orange and pink. One a different kind of starfish with seventeen stubby arms. Fitz called it a sunstar. Little blobs of jellyfish. Tiny crabs scuttling around in shallow water. A log occupied by five seagulls, like first-class passengers sightseeing on a cruise, gently floating by.

On this pleasant day I didn't feel like talking about murder and suspects, and Fitz seemed to know that. Here, on the north side of the inlet, the houses weren't as numerous as on the south side opposite. Over there, a man on a riding lawn mower cut geometric swatches on a green lawn sloping to the water. The house I'd once shared with Richard stood on a wooded point to the west, glass soaring from deck to vaulted roof, the azaleas I'd planted long ago now blooming gloriously. But seeing it gave me no pang of loss. Too much of life in that house had been a lie.

The framework for another house was going up to the east, the sound of a hammer hitting a nail reaching us a smidgen after the hammer struck. A girl was throwing a stick into the water, a big black dog enthusiastically retrieving it. A motorboat roared by, its wake sending waves swooshing against the shoreline.

I lifted my face to the sun. A great day to be alive, well fed, healthy, walking in the sunshine, with a nice man telling me about seeing a rare pod of orcas in the inlet a few weeks ago.

Thank You, God.

Now, where did that come from?

Behind us, on our side of the inlet, madrone trees drooped glossy green leaves over the rocky beach, and here and there cliffs eroded by the endless action of the moving water rose above us.

We picked up occasional bits of colorful rock or shell as we walked. A young couple showed us a pretty reddish agate they'd found, as proud as if it were a diamond. They were holding hands, and Fitz gave me a speculative sideways glance. I wondered if he was thinking about holding hands too. Instead he asked about my name.

"Andi. Is that short for something?"

"Andalusia." I said it a bit defensively, maybe even in a wanna-make-something-of-it tone. "I shortened it to Andi when I was a little girl. We moved around so much, and the kids could never pronounce it, much less spell it. Mostly they just made fun of it."

"They should have studied their geography better. It's a region in Spain, isn't it? How'd you get a name like that?"

"My father was there during World War II. He liked the friendly people and the climate and mountains. He wanted to go back after the war was over."

"And did he?"

I shook my head. "The closest he ever got to Andalusia was giving me the name. Never enough money, I suppose. But he was always . . . looking for something, even if he was stuck on this continent. We moved every few months, all over the country. Mom's family disapproved of him, and she pretty much just walked away from them."

"That's too bad. Family is important."

"He always had ideas about starting a business of his own. Big, outlandish ideas, I can see now, although back then I was just impatient for him to *do* it, and then we'd settle down and live in one place forever. I remember once he invented some new kind of beaters for Mom's electric mixer. Except when she used them, it was like an egg hurricane in the kitchen. It took us hours to clean up the walls and woodwork."

I smiled, remembering my father's dismay. And my mother's endless, supportive good humor. "I think it needs a little fine tuning," she'd said diplomatically as she wiped beaten egg off her eyebrows.

I spotted a little crab sitting motionless a dozen feet from the water. I thought he was already lifeless, but when I carried him to the water, he revived and scuttled off. I applauded, and Fitz grinned at me.

"Your folks aren't around here?" he asked.

"When I was about fifteen, they got involved in some back-to-nature, live-off-the-land movement. People came to our house bringing stuff like thistles and lilies and alder bark to eat. Did you know crabgrass is edible? Kind of. The summer I was seventeen, we spent four months camping out on the other side of Mount Rainier."

"Just you and your folks?"

"Other people came and went. Everyone would get up

before sunrise and sit cross-legged in front of their tents with their eyes closed and palms up, waiting for the sun to rise."

"And you?"

I laughed wryly, although I also had a catch in my throat. Looking back, I saw my folks as so young and naive and vulnerable, so much younger than I was now. "I was huddled in my sleeping bag in another tent, wishing I could take a hot shower and have something other than those awful boiled weeds for breakfast."

Fitz picked up a flat rock and skipped it across the smooth surface of the water. The inlet was in that lull between tides now, before the water started rushing back in. I was always astonished by the speed with which the water moved up the inlet toward the bay, like a river running backwards. When Richard and I lived in the big house across the way, Sarah and I'd toss out sticks just to watch them zoom away.

"Did you have a falling-out?"

"Oh, no. Nothing like that. When cold weather froze us out, we moved over to Anacortes. Where I was a month late starting school, of course. Then in early spring my folks got the nature bug again and went out to the mountains to commune with the snow or something. Their pickup got stuck, and they were dead by the time searchers found them several days later."

I could still feel the awful shock of that, the pain, the disbelief and sharp stab of betrayal. Rationally I knew they hadn't chosen to leave me, but deep inside the feeling was there, and I did feel abandoned.

"And you were on your own. Were you resentful and angry?"

Angry? Oh, yes. Angry that they would do such a careless, stupid thing, and then angry at myself for being so angry at them. But a resolve had come out of that anger.

"Mostly I was just determined to marry a man who was totally different from them, and to do it as soon as possible. Someone rooted and rock-solid and dependable. I made the mistake of thinking that someone was Richard McConnell." I glanced over at Fitz and smiled. "So there it is, the story of my life. You'll probably see it on 'Lifestyles of the Muddled and Misguided' any day now."

We turned around, where a creek flowing into the inlet changed the beach from rocks to mud. The fire had burned down to ashes by the time we got back to the picnic area, and at first I thought Joella was still asleep. The blanket was wound around her like a cocoon. Then I realized she was bunched into a fetal position and making small whimpering noises.

I ran to her and yanked back the blanket. Sweat riveleted down her face and plastered her blonde hair to her head. "Jo, what's wrong! What is it?"

"I . . . I think the baby's coming." Her hands were crossed over her abdomen. Her eyes looked not quite focused. "I feel all tight and hard inside. Oh!" A pain hit her, and she balled up even tighter.

But the baby couldn't be coming! Joella was only a little over seven months along. If she had it out here—

"We have to get her to the hospital!"

Fitz didn't ask questions. He shoved everything to the center of the tablecloth on the picnic table, grabbed it all in a bundle, and slammed it into the trunk of the car. I helped Joella to her knees, then to a shaky stand. Together Fitz and I half walked, half carried her to the backseat of the car.

"You get in back with her," Fitz said. "I'll drive. I know where the hospital is."

I got in back with her, but about all I could do was wipe her damp forehead with a tissue. What did I know about childbirth? I'd had one child by caesarean while fully anesthetized in a hospital almost forty years ago.

"Can you tell how often the pains are coming?" I asked anxiously.

"It's all one great big pain."

Fitz drove fast but carefully. Joella groaned. I cursed the minuscule size of the backseat, the seat-belt straps and buckles that kept getting in the way, and the delaying traffic light where the inlet road joined the highway into town. Traffic was heavier on the highway. Some idiot cut around us, making Fitz screech the brakes to keep from hitting him, and I shook my fist at him. I also prayed, recklessly asking for God's help even if I wasn't on some approved list of prayers.

Please, God, this is a child of Yours. Don't desert her now. She and her baby are depending on You!

20

Joella kept groaning and holding her abdomen.

I said the only thing I could think of. "Don't push. Wait till we get to the hospital. Everything will be all right. *Don't push!*"

Joella gritted her teeth. "Easy for you to say. You're not the one . . . trying . . . to hold back a . . . rocket ship about to launch."

"Think soothing thoughts. Ocean waves. Birds singing."

"What does it feel like when your water breaks?"

I had no idea. Sixty years old, I'd be the matriarch in any primitive tribe, the wise old woman. But, product of civilization and caesarean that I am, I knew nothing!

We whipped into the parking area, then under the covering that sheltered the emergency entrance. Fitz ran inside. Thirty seconds later he was back with two guys in white and a gurney. They loaded Joella onto it, and I followed them inside while Fitz went to park the car.

He caught up with me in the emergency room a couple minutes later, as I was giving the woman at the admitting desk information.

She frowned. "You don't have an insurance card or anything for the patient?"

"No." I was pretty sure Joella had no insurance, but I didn't want to reveal that. "We were out at the park on a picnic—"

"Did they take her directly to the delivery room?" Fitz cut in.

"The patient is your daughter?"

"No, but—"

"You are family?"

"Well, in a way."

"What way?"

"Joella lives in my duplex."

"You're roommates?"

"No, I'm the, uh, landlady." Which came off sounding not even third-cousin-once-removed close to being family.

"Please wait over there." The woman motioned in the direction of the chairs arranged around the room, only two of which were occupied. Good. That meant Joella should be getting priority attention.

So we sat. We waited. The chairs had apparently been chosen for longevity rather than comfort. I kept thinking about all that food we'd eaten. Could wieners and onions and chili induce labor?

There was a coffee machine in the corner. Fitz went over and brought back Styrofoam cups of stuff as black as my impounded limousine.

"I guess it's coffee," he muttered, peering at the dense liquid. "Unless it's something they're using to resurface the parking lot. I could run up to one of the espresso stands."

"This is fine," I assured him. I didn't want him to leave. We weren't doing much talking, but his presence was comforting.

"Matt arrived three weeks early," he offered once. "And look how big and strong he is now."

But Joella was almost two months early.

God, Jo says Your timing is always perfect, no matter how it looks to us down here. Please make it perfect this time!

169

After an hour and forty-five minutes, I approached the reception desk. "Can we find out anything about my friend, Joella Picault?"

"I'll check." The woman returned a little later with the information that they were still running tests.

"Is there a problem? Has she had the baby yet?"

All I got was a repetition of the "running tests" information, which is apparently all landladies were entitled to in this day of CIA-level privacy regulations.

After almost three hours, the swinging doors opened, and a woman in a white pantsuit pushed a wheelchair through. Joella stood up, still obviously pregnant.

I rushed over to her. "Jo, what's going on? Why are they letting you go? Are you okay? Are they kicking you out because of money? I can come up with—"

"I'm okay. The baby's okay. I need to go out to the car and get my checkbook. The lady inside said I need to pay something on the bill today and make arrangements about the balance."

"I'll go get it," Fitz offered. He headed out the double glass doors.

"They did something to stop the baby from coming too soon?" I asked anxiously.

"They didn't stop anything. She never was coming. My water didn't break, and I wasn't even dilated." Joella sounded both embarrassed and frustrated.

"But all your pain—"

"I am here in the emergency room, recipient of every test known to pregnant womankind, with a huge, enormous, industrial-strength case of indigestion. A big, bad bellyache."

"Indigestion!"

"With my breath smelling so strongly of onions, I practically asphyxiated the doctor. He asked me what I'd been eating."

I went down the list. "Burned weenies. Garlic-flavored buns. Onions. Pickle. Mustard. Pepper-jack cheese. Greek salad . . . with kalamata olives. Chili. Chocolate cake. Fudge frosting."

"That's what I told him. He said I could have found a healthier menu in a dumpster."

I slammed a palm against my forehead. "It's all my fault. What was I thinking?"

"You were thinking of what would make the day fun for me, and I chose most of that stuff. And it was a glorious picnic." Joella gave me a hug. "The best birthday ever. And if I hadn't been such a pig and eaten about three times as much as I should have, I'd have been fine. But the baby was never in any danger. I just . . . panicked, I guess, when I started feeling a little pain."

"You're sure it's just indigestion? *They're* sure? Doctors make mistakes."

"They did ultrasound, blood, EKG, urine, the works. Indigestion. They gave me some medication. I can't believe it. Telling you the baby was coming when it was just a dumb stomachache." She shook her head in disgust. "What am I going to do when I have real labor pains?"

Laughter came from the other side of the swinging doors.

Joella rolled her eyes. "One guess what they're laughing about back there. They'll be making onion-breath jokes for days."

Fitz returned then and handed Joella her purse, and she dug out a checkbook. I knew today must have run up a mammoth bill.

"I can help out—"

"I'll manage."

She had to take the check to a different desk, and it took quite a while getting the financial arrangements made. I don't suppose they can repossess the baby if you can't pay a bill, but I was pretty sure they could make life miserable. Would "managing" mean she'd have to accept her parents' ultimatum about adoption to get financial help? And though I could and would help her out, I doubted I could do enough to make much of a dent in this bill. *Is this God's way of helping her make a decision?* I wondered with a stab of dismay.

I put a hand over my mouth and breathed into it as we went out to the car. Now I knew why she'd almost asphyxiated the doctor. Why hadn't I noticed this before? Maybe because it was like a skunk-on-skunk situation. If you're a skunk, you probably don't smell the other skunks.

But thank You, God, thank You for indigestion instead of tragedy. Please, please take care of Joella and her baby.

Odd, I thought, how much I was talking to God here lately.

NEXT MORNING I brushed my teeth twice as long as usual, rinsed my mouth with Listerine, and took a breath mint for good measure. I had enough problems without burying innocent bystanders in an onslaught of onion-breath hangover.

Joella had already left for the coffee shop by the time I went out to my car. I'd checked on her earlier, and she was fine, no pains. We were both still apologizing, Joella for her mistake about thinking she was in labor, me for not using better judgment about limo-dog revelry. Fitz was bringing his fish over to cook this evening.

I visited the county personnel offices first, only to find out the hiring situation had changed there. A big sign said all job vacancies were posted on their Web site. A similar situation with the school offices, although I did pick up an application form there. By that time I'd had it with the advances in technology and decided to work on something more productive and perhaps even more important than a job.

Keeping myself out of jail.

21

Only a scattering of cars occupied the big F&N parking lot. They were huddled together as if intimidated by all the empty space. I found the door to the wing where I'd worked locked and had to go around to the main front entrance. A uniformed guard . . . a guard! . . . stood beside it. He checked my ID and called up to Letty's office before he let me pass.

I found my way up the stairs and down the hall to the section of cubicles where I used to work. Everything seemed the same, except that the desks were abnormally uncluttered, the phones silent, and Letty the only occupant.

She stood up and held out her arms. "Andi! It's so good to see you!" She gave me an enthusiastic hug.

We'd never socialized outside the F&N setting—Letty's grandchildren kept her busy—but I'd always considered her a good, dependable friend. She's my age, widowed, plump and energetic, a cheerful mile-a-minute talker. Her skin is enviably unlined, and there's always a flowered barrette in her buttercup yellow hair. Today it was my favorite, daisies.

"Good to see you too. What's with the guard?"

"They hired him after Mr. Findley found some homeless guy washing his feet in the sink in the executives' restroom. He'd just wandered in."

"That's kind of creepy."

"So's sitting here alone day after day. It feels like a deserted island, without the ubiquitous palm tree."

Ubiquitous. I'd forgotten Letty's determined system for improving her vocabulary. Pick a new word or phrase and use it at least once a day for two weeks. It was from Letty that I'd learned such words as *salubrious* and *rubescent*, although I hadn't yet found any particular use for any of them.

"How's everything going here?" I asked.

"I can't believe they expect one person to finish up everything for the entire department." Letty waved both arms as if fighting off work hurtling at her from all directions, like strange creatures in some video game.

"How much longer will it last?"

"I'm not sure. Maybe a month or six weeks. I've been trying to get them to hire someone to help out, but you'd think I was asking for my own private Rent-a-Hunk. But I've made up my mind. Once I'm finished here, I'm *through*. I'd planned to work till I was sixty-five before taking my Social Security. You get more if you wait, you know. But now I'm just going to run. I'm thinking about expanding my herb garden and starting a small business selling herbs and spices."

"Great idea. I'll be an eager customer." I was a little short on basil and thyme right now, since the sheriff's department had custody of mine.

"Oh, but I should have called you. I was so horrified when I heard what happened to Jerry. Murdered! Here, sit down." She pulled a chair from a neighboring empty desk as if the murder must have tired me. "I just made fresh coffee."

She'd moved the shiny metal coffeemaker stand into the aisle closer to her desk. She bustled around, pouring coffee and setting out packets of creamer and sugar. "And how traumatic for you, having it happen right under your nose. Though I've never understood what a limousine was doing there."

I explained about my inheritance, which brought an appreciative "Oooh!" Then a hopeful, "Are you giving rides to old friends?"

"I'd like to, but the sheriff's department impounded the limo. Actually, the reason I'm here has to do with the murder. As you may recall, you were the one who introduced me to Jerry at the company Christmas party—"

"And now I feel so guilty about that! But it wasn't as if I'd planned it. It was, well, you know, *propinquity*. I just happened to be talking to you when he came up. And at the time, I thought it was so wonderful that the two of you right away got started talking about a hiking trail out by some lake and seemed so taken with each other. But now, considering the circumstances . . ."

"The circumstances of his death?"

"Well, that too, of course. But also the circumstances of his life. I guess you know now, he was still married?"

"His brother told me."

"I had no idea when I introduced you."

"You found out later?"

"Not while he was alive! Or I'd have warned you. What happened was, I decided I should come in on the next day after Free Fall Friday to get organized for working alone. I was just walking in from the parking lot when the police arrived. They said they needed information from our personnel files about his next of kin."

"Did they tell you why?"

"No, but I knew it had to be something serious. I tried to call Mr. Findley and then a couple of other executives, but I couldn't reach anyone. I didn't think I could access the personnel files to find out anything for them—I never could before. But San Diego had given me a new computer password a couple days earlier, and it worked. So I got into Jerry's file and gave them the information."

"About his wife being next of kin."

"Right. Which was a shockeroo, I can tell you. And I knew you had no idea he was still married. But it's a very handy little password," she added in a sly way that suggested she'd done some extracurricular browsing of her own.

The thought occurred to me that if the police also figured out I hadn't known Jerry was married, they might consider it another black mark against me. *Unstable woman goes berserk upon learning boyfriend still has a wife.*

"The deputies came back on Monday and questioned both me and Mr. Findley, since he'd been Jerry's boss here. Then they came back again with a search warrant and took a lot of stuff from Jerry's office."

"His computer?"

"Yes, although I don't know why they'd want that."

I did. They were looking for whatever had been on Jerry's home computer that the killer had apparently been desperate to conceal. I doubted they'd found anything. I was sure he wouldn't have put any of his Web site information on the company computer system where someone else might access it.

"How is Mr. Findley taking Jerry's death?"

"After the deputies left, he came in here looking kind of lost and dazed, as if he needed someone to talk to. He seemed pretty broken up. He kept saying how much everyone liked Jerry, and he couldn't understand how anyone could kill him. Jerry was going to be his assistant down in San Diego, I guess you knew."

"Yes, Jerry told me."

Over the months I'd known him, Jerry'd had various unkind things to say about his boss, including a wickedly accurate parody of Mr. Findley's stuffy speeches at company award ceremonies. More importantly, however, he'd also claimed he did more of Mr. Findley's work than Findley did. With the different perspective I now had on Jerry, I couldn't be sure there was any truth in that. But Mr. Findley must have held Jerry in high esteem if he'd wanted Jerry to be his assistant in San Diego.

"Do you think anyone here at F&N was particularly angry or resentful that Jerry was given a transfer and this other person, he or she, *wasn't?*"

"You mean someone who might be angry enough to kill him?" Letty looked shocked when I nodded, but then she leaned back in her chair, her expression thoughtful. Finally she said, "I can't think of anyone who was ticked off at Jerry specifically, but plenty of people were angry and resentful about the whole situation. But isn't it always the quiet, inconspicuous person, the one nobody notices, who suddenly goes off the deep end and does something like committing murder?"

Someone like me was my thought, but what I said was, "If you think of anyone, let me know, okay? Although what I really came for is, I'm wondering if you know about any other girlfriends Jerry had, either while he was dating me or before?"

"Is that important?"

"Possibly. I'm afraid the police think I may have killed him. And I didn't."

"Of course you didn't!" Letty's smooth forehead wrinkled above shocked blue eyes. "How could anyone think that?"

"So now I'm wondering if some other woman could have been angry enough to kill him. Maybe someone he'd dumped, or maybe someone who'd just found out he was also seeing me."

"Oh dear, let me think. You know me. Gossip just goes in one ear and out the other. I don't pay that much attention."

"Yes, I know," I agreed with more tact than truthfulness.

Letty's idea of keeping a secret was to tell only two or three people, not send out a global e-mail. That was the big reason I'd come to her. She always had the latest scoop.

"I don't remember hearing rumors about Jerry and anyone here at F&N." In spite of her claim to being a nongossiper, she sounded apologetic, as if not knowing was a shortcoming on her part.

I was disappointed she didn't have any information, but at the same time relieved. From all I'd learned about Jerry so far, I was beginning to wonder how I could have been so naive and foolish as to be attracted to him, so it was good not to hear any more to add to his sleaze quotient. But there was still the woman Joella had seen him with.

"Have you ever heard of someone named Elena?"

"Elena? No . . . oh, wait. There was an Elena who used to work in the publicity department. But she quit several months ago to do publicity for some pet food company in Olympia. I never heard anything about her and Jerry. She was married anyway." She put her fingertips over her mouth. "Oh dear, you don't suppose—"

Yes, I suddenly did suppose. It was a jolting thought, but ripe with possibilities. If Jerry had been seeing a married woman, and her husband found out . . .

"What did she look like?"

"Very attractive. I heard once she'd been a model down in California before she came up here. Tall and slender. You know, that willowy type?" Letty wrinkled her nose.

Letty is not the willowy type.

"Dark hair, looked like one of those shampoo ads. Do you ever wonder how they get their hair so shiny in those ads? Personally, I think it's all in the lighting. Do you really think she and Jerry could have had something going?"

"Do you remember her last name?"

Letty's forehead scrunched under her buttercup hair, but she finally shook her head. "I'm afraid not. Though I think it was something kind of exotic sounding. The only reason I even remember the Elena name is because I have a cousin named that."

I stood up and dropped my Styrofoam cup in the waste-basket. "Well, I'd better be running along. It's been good seeing you again."

"Sorry I don't know anything helpful. Oh, we've been chattering along and I haven't asked. Have you found another job yet?"

"No, I'm still in free fall. But looking."

"That's what I'm hearing about almost everyone. Hey, if you want to come to the house and use my computer to get on the Internet, you're certainly welcome. You can post your résumé or check job openings on a lot of sites there."

"Thanks. I may just take you up on that. Hey, if they do decide to hire someone to help out here temporarily, keep me in mind, will you?"

"Oh, I will. Definitely. I'm so glad you came by. And keep me in mind when you get the limo back!"

Down on the first-floor hallway, I headed for the exit. Then a thought occurred to me. Would there still be information about the willowy Elena in the personnel files, maybe something Letty could access even with only a first name? I made an abrupt U-turn at the corner. If I could locate a last name, an address, a husband's name—

I rounded the corner in a hurried dash back to Letty's office and thundered headlong into two men rounding the corner from the opposite direction. In a split second, the fact that one was Mr. Findley registered. The other . . . who? Oh, yes,

Mr. Randolph, head of the public relations department. Public relations? Hey, he'd surely known Elena.

Propinquity! I could just casually ask him—

But in the next split second, the momentum of my dash took over, and I shot past identification and right into collision with the man. We belly smashed into each other like a couple of sumo wrestlers. His feet went out from under him, and he *oof*ed to the hallway floor with a fleshy thud. I reeled and steadied myself with a hand on the wall.

I looked down at the considerable bulk of his figure sprawled on the polished floor of the hallway, like a beached whale in a blue suit. "Mr. Randolph, I'm so sorry!"

He shook his head to clear it, and when it did clear, he glared up at me.

"Are you okay?" I fluttered over him, then offered a hand.

"Get away from me," he growled and slapped at my hand as if it were contaminated. His face had now reddened to the color of his tie, and the thought occurred to me that it might even be described as *rubescent.*

Mr. Findley helped him to his feet. By now both men were glaring at me as if they suspected I had designs on the executives' restroom. I wondered if Mr. Findley recognized me. Probably not. Upper-level executives didn't mingle with lower-level people from other departments. Jerry had taken me to a party at the Findleys' posh waterfront home, but I doubted he'd have reason to remember me from that. I'd eaten more than my share of shrimp hors d'oeuvres, but I hadn't crashed into anyone.

"Are you employed here?" Mr. Findley demanded.

"Well, no, not now. I mean, I *did* work here, but today I just came to see a friend." I started to give Letty's name, then realized this might make trouble for her. I also realized, regretfully, that this was probably not a good time to quiz Mr. Randolph about Elena. "I was just leaving," I added hastily.

I started toward the entrance, peering back once. The two men were still watching me. I suspected their topic of conversation was about instituting a tighter screening policy at the door to keep clumsy older females as well as dirty-footed homeless persons out.

22

Back home, I decided it wouldn't be fair to put Letty on the spot by asking her to dig up information about Elena. I studied the Olympia phone book instead.

The phone book listed many stores that handled pet food, of course, but I found only one manufacturer. I was rather impressed. Mountaintop Pet Foods was the company currently running a series of clever TV ads featuring two upscale cats using a sleeping dog as a cushion while discussing their diets. Was that Elena's work?

I prepared a brief spiel before I dialed. I was a former F&N employee looking for work. I'd heard of her through my friend Jerry Norton. If she was involved with him, she'd surely know he'd been murdered, and I hoped her reaction to my mentioning his name would be revealing.

"May I speak to Elena, please?" I asked in an old-friends, we-don't-bother-with-last-names tone when I finally got through to the publicity department.

"Just a moment and I'll connect you."

It had worked. One session with Letty, one phone call, and I'd nailed Elena!

She came on the line: "Elena"—then a word I didn't understand—"speaking."

"I'm sorry, I didn't catch your last name?"

"Loperi." She also spelled it, as if she were accustomed to having to do that. Her voice was cool but not unfriendly. She spoke so clearly and without accent of any kind that I suspected she'd had voice lessons at some time.

But mostly I was into more self-congratulation. Now I had a last name too! I scribbled it on the pad by the phone. I went into my spiel about the downsizing at F&N and my search for a job. "I love those TV ads with the cats," I gushed.

"You have experience in publicity and advertising?"

I froze. Why hadn't I anticipated that question? It was a logical one. But I'd been so focused on my side of this script that I hadn't thought about her rewriting it.

"Well, uh, no. I was thinking more about general office or secretarial work."

"And you acquired my name from—?"

"Jerry Norton at F&N. Friends and Neighbors Insurance. Where you were formerly employed," I added, since my words seemed to be plunging into a bottomless pit.

"I'm sorry. I don't recall anyone at F&N named Jerry Norton. I was there only a few months."

I hadn't expected a straightforward denial of her even knowing Jerry. And the nerves or agitation I'd counted on if she had any connection with him were totally absent. Did that mean she really didn't know Jerry, or that she was a model-cum-actress giving me a snow job?

"He was killed recently. Murdered, actually. Over here in Vigland. Maybe you heard about it?"

I thought I heard a gasp, but maybe it was just a cough.

"When did this happen?"

I gave her a date, then added, "It was sometime in the night, between that Friday evening and the next Saturday morning."

"My husband and I have been on vacation for the last couple of weeks. But I'm sorry to hear about something like that happening to anyone."

A statement as impersonal as a recorded telemarketer spiel, yet with an undertone of something deeper. Something that I might almost think was panic, except that she went on in a normal tone.

"I'd always thought Vigland was a rather nice, safe little town when we lived over there."

"You live in Olympia now?"

That question produced a moment of silence, then a wary-sounding, "What did you say your name was?"

I ignored the question and tossed out my little bombshell. "You say you didn't know Jerry. But someone saw you together over in Olympia."

If I expected nervous, backpedaling explanations, I was mistaken.

"What did you say your name was?" she repeated. This time it was more demand than question, with a sharp turn into hostility.

"That doesn't matter—"

"I think it does. Let's see. . . . I have your number here on my caller ID." She wasn't bluffing. She repeated my phone number to me. "So perhaps you should explain to me what this phone call is *really* about."

Why hadn't I thought of this? I'd been careful with that call to an unknown number, but here I'd blithely plunged right in. She could undoubtedly have my name and address within a few minutes.

After a long, uneasy moment, I finally said, "Well, I, uh,

suppose you'll find out anyway. This is Andi McConnell over in Vigland."

I waited to see if the name brought any sign of recognition, but all she said was, "So?"

"I had a . . . uh . . . relationship with Jerry for several months before he was killed. I think you also had a . . . relationship with him."

"You're basing this on a statement someone made about seeing us together?"

"She heard him call you Elena."

"What did you say this man's name was?"

"Jerry Norton. He was in the Finance Department at F&N."

Another small sound, as if she were tapping the phone with a nervous fingernail. "You know, I think I may know who you're talking about after all. Tall, dark-haired guy, older but athletic and quite nice looking."

She spoke with an I'm-just-remembering dawning in her voice, which sounded a little short on authenticity to me, but mostly I was thinking *generation gap*. She saw him as older; I saw him as younger.

"He was murdered?"

"I'm afraid so."

"How?"

"Gunshot."

"But who would do that? And why?"

"That's what I'm trying to find out."

"And your friend saw us together where?"

"Just outside a restaurant in Olympia."

"I'm sorry, but I don't remember that at all. It's possible we ran into each other in the restaurant, of course, and walked out together, but I don't remember it." Her tone had a that's-my-story-and-I'm-sticking-to-it firmness.

"And you didn't know he'd been killed? It made quite a splash in the news. The limousine and all."

I suspected the limousine aroused her curiosity, but after a small hesitation, all she said was, "I told you, my husband and I just returned from vacation at Cozumel. I didn't see any newspapers while we were away."

Obviously this was going nowhere, and I hadn't the interrogative expertise to turn it around. Lamely I said, "Oh. Well, uh, okay then. Thanks."

"I take it Jerry Norton's murderer hasn't been identified yet?"

"Unfortunately, no."

"Look, it's none of my business, but can I give you a piece of advice?"

"Well, uh, sure." *Uh* seemed to have taken over as the most-used word in my vocabulary.

"You figured I . . . or, let's see, my jealous husband perhaps? . . . killed him. And so you called me."

"I've been considering possibilities."

"Then my advice is this: let the police handle it. Don't go chasing around after a murderer. Or you might find yourself in the same situation as Jerry."

She hung up then, and I was left standing there with phone in hand, thinking two things. Number one was that calling her without a better plan in mind was really dumb, right up there with using a match to test whether you have a gas leak. Number two was wondering if she had just given me an excellent piece of thoughtful advice—or was it a threat?

I WAS RELUCTANT to tell Fitz about the call, because the more I thought about it, the dumber my having done it sounded. But I had to tell him, of course. We were in the kitchen, and he was cooking the lingcod. I'd just watered the nice pot of daisies he'd brought me and was now steaming asparagus. We'd planned to cook out on the patio, but clouds had moved in, along with a cold breeze, so we'd moved inside. We'd also invited Joella over, but she'd headed off for some doings at church.

I started with what I'd learned about Elena from Letty, then segued into the phone call and Elena's "advice."

"I'm thinking now that calling her wasn't a very good idea," I admitted. "Or at least calling her without a better game plan than I had."

Fitz's silver-white eyebrows drew together in a concerned frown, but he didn't chastise me. "Sometimes investigations backfire in unexpected ways."

"No matter what she said, I'm still not convinced she wasn't involved with Jerry."

"And if she was, it's a pretty good motive for murder."

Fitz turned the fish carefully in the frying pan. I checked my asparagus and started making hollandaise sauce from a packet I'd gotten at Safeway. The only time I'd ever tried it from scratch, I'd wound up with curdled glop.

"Do you think she really hadn't known about Jerry being dead before you told her?"

"I thought she sounded shocked. Maybe even scared. But I suppose I'd be shocked, too, hearing someone I'd known, even if I hadn't known him very well, had been murdered. Most people we know don't get murdered."

"So, what are our possibilities here? Her husband found out about the affair and murdered Jerry. Or she tried to dump Jerry and he wouldn't let go, and she murdered him herself to get rid of him. Of course, one basic question remains."

"Which is, why was Jerry here that night?" We kept coming back to that. "What was he doing in my limousine?"

"Along with, why was his computer and everything connected

with it stolen? What reason would this Elena or her jealous husband have for doing that?"

I stirred the sauce mixture in the pan. Fitz put a couple of potatoes in the microwave to nuke.

The doorbell rang, and I stiffened like the handle on my infamous shovel. I wasn't expecting anyone. I'd had what might well be a veiled threat from the willowy Elena. Could she, or the husband—

Then I reminded myself of what I'd told Joella: murderers don't come politely ringing doorbells.

Hopefully this wasn't an exception to that rule.

23

Ryan!"

He smiled, apparently pleased that I was glad to see him. I was glad to see him again, but the enthusiasm was also relief that he wasn't a visiting murderer. His arms were filled with two big paper sacks.

"I don't know why I didn't think of this when you were at the condo, but you might as well have the stuff from Jerry's cupboards and freezer. I'm heading home tomorrow, and I don't like to see good food go to waste. I don't think Cara would object if you have it."

"Cara?"

"She called. She located a will that Jerry had made out back when they were first married. Since he apparently never got around to changing it, it's still in effect. It leaves everything to her, which simplifies the situation considerably."

"Is that . . . okay?"

"Do you mean, am I upset that I won't get anything from Jerry's estate?" He shook his head vigorously. "No way. The will also names her as executor, so she'll have to cope with everything. But she does have her father to help, and he's a very capable person."

"That's good."

"And that stuff I said earlier about his being involved in the murder? Just forget it, okay? Ben's kind of a ruthless old codger, and I think he'd stomp anyone who threatened those grandkids, but Cara says her father and Jerry had reached a deal on a divorce settlement. Odd, isn't it, how the divorce seemed to be more between Jerry and the father-in-law than between Jerry and Cara? Anyway, 'an amicable agreement' between them was how she phrased it. I shouldn't have sounded off about Ben the way I did."

I had the feeling telling me this was the real reason he'd come here, and the groceries were mostly just an excuse.

"Cara's father agreed to give Jerry money?"

"I think that's the only kind of 'agreement' Jerry would go for. I'm thinking now that the cash in the toilet tank may have been the payoff they agreed on. It'd be just like Ben to send it as a big wad of cash."

Fitz had followed me to the door, and I realized his hands were resting lightly on my waist. I also realized Ryan was still standing there holding the heavy bags.

Embarrassed, I moved back from the door. "Where are my manners? Come on in."

Ryan hesitated. "Perhaps I should have called first. Maybe Jerry's leftovers are the last thing you'd ever want."

"Groceries are groceries." And welcome, in my unemployed state. "I appreciate your thinking of me."

"There's an odd assortment of stuff here. Jerry wasn't exactly a Hamburger Helper kind of guy, was he?"

We smiled at each other in rueful conspiracy about his brother's expensive tastes.

I led Ryan into the kitchen, and he deposited the sacks on the counter. I introduced him to Fitz. I could see Ryan was curious about who Fitz was, beyond a name, but I didn't offer details. Especially not the detail that Fitz and I had formed a sleuth-and-sidekick investigative team. Though I was still a little miffed by that sidekick status.

"There's a couple more sacks out in the car. I'll go get them."

The minute Ryan was out the door, Fitz said, "Let's invite him to dinner. There's plenty of food. I'll just throw another potato in the microwave."

"All because you're so good-hearted?"

"Don't you think I'm good-hearted?" Fitz drew himself up in righteous indignation. "The guy's been eating out or cooking for himself all week. He needs a solid, home-cooked meal. Isn't that being good-hearted?"

Okay, I did think Fitz was a good-hearted guy, but—

"I think, at the moment, what you want to do is pick his brain while you feed him."

"Being good-hearted and practical are not mutually exclusive," he pointed out. "Ryan may be backpedaling on the possibility of the not-ex-wife's father's involvement, but I'm not convinced. Are you?"

No. I figured Ryan was sincere in what he said, but quite possibly mistaken. "Just be nice, okay? Ryan's a good guy."

"Not a killer, you mean?"

I was startled. Ryan as murderer had never occurred to me. "He was way off in Denver. And he had no motive."

"No motive that we know about."

"I don't like being suspicious of everybody," I muttered.

"Goes with the territory."

Ryan returned with two more bags, and I suggested his staying for dinner.

"Fitz is cooking a lingcod he caught up around the San

Juan Islands. He's the cook on his son's charter sailboat, and they just came back from there."

"A charter sailboat? Hey, that's neat." Ryan smiled, something I hadn't seen him do often. "Kind of like what I'd like to do when I grow up."

He also accepted the dinner invitation without hesitation. While the men talked sailing and fishing, I put the contents of the sacks away. I felt guilty, but I was really looking forward to those lobsters from Jerry's freezer. Plus steaks and chicken cordon bleu. And there was that can of foie gras, plus a veritable treasure chest of marinated mushrooms, smoked oysters, fancy olives, and crackers, plus a lot of other stuff not on my usual menu.

Fitz's lingcod was boneless and tender, light and delicious. Afterward I dished up raspberry chocolate chunk ice cream for dessert. Well fed and relaxed, and with a little adroit encouragement from Fitz, Ryan started talking about his boyhood days with Jerry back in Colorado. Family camping and fishing trips in the mountains, shooting hoops in the backyard, and cheering for Jerry at high-school football games and track events. He'd definitely hero-worshipped his big brother.

I had the feeling Ryan hadn't thought about those happy times in a long while, and it felt good to him to talk about them. I'd have preferred leaving his relationship with his brother on that upbeat note, but shadowy pictures of Jerry's dead body in the trunk of the limousine kept slithering around in my head. Along with that disturbing possibility Fitz had planted there.

Not Ryan, I assured myself. *Surely not Ryan.* There were any number of reasons Ryan couldn't possibly be the murderer. And yet . . .

I phrased my leading comment carefully. "It's too bad you and Jerry weren't closer in recent years."

"Yeah, it is." Ryan's voice went flat and distant, his gaze unfocused on an empty spot beyond my shoulder. I thought he was going to stop there, but he surprised me by going on. "But Jerry changed. I don't know if it was getting involved with gambling that did it, or if he changed first and the gambling followed. But he turned harder. More ambitious and greedy." He paused. "Less ethical."

He stopped talking, and I refilled his coffee cup. I started to say something small-talkish, but Fitz bumped me with his elbow. I realized what he was getting at. Sometimes silence is like a vacuum that needs filling, more effective than questioning.

"I guess the breaking point between us came when he told me he had a serious medical problem and needed money. I was glad I had it to lend to him. I'd have happily *given* him the money for a medical emergency."

"But there wasn't a medical problem?"

"No. There was a gambling emergency. I never knew the details, but he never paid me back."

He was silent for a moment, and I wondered if he was thinking, as I was, that if Jerry could afford a Rolex, he could surely have repaid this debt. And there was that money in the toilet tank.

"Well, I guess none of that matters now, does it?" Ryan briskly moved on to tell us that he'd been to see the guy who owned the private dock where Jerry kept his boat. "He said it was fine if the boat stayed there until Cara can sell it; then he'd like to buy it. He seemed like a really nice guy, as puzzled as the rest of us about Jerry's death."

"It won't be easy for Cara to take care of all these details from back in Georgia," Fitz said.

"She'll probably make a trip out here. She said her father might be interested in keeping the condo as a vacation place.

He's never seen it, but he liked the Puget Sound area when he visited here before Cara and Jerry broke up."

"Will he come along?" Fitz asked. "Maybe he'd be interested in a charter sailboat trip while he's here."

My first thought was that Fitz was just trying to drum up business, but then I realized he had something else in mind.

"Didn't I hear something about his being in the timber business in Georgia? Southern pine, I imagine it would be. Most people don't think of the South as a timber area, but a good percentage of the country's timber is produced there now."

Leave it to Fitz to know an irrelevant fact like that and toss it out to muddle what he was really doing, which was digging for information. He apparently thought, as I did, that Ryan would be reluctant to tell us anything about Cara's father if he thought we were still suspicious of him.

"What's his company's name?" Fitz added, as if it were an afterthought.

"Something about timber. Well, that figures, doesn't it? Southern Gold Timber, I think."

"He didn't give the company a family name, then, like the big timber barons often did around here. Vigland Timber Products and the town of Vigland itself, in fact, are named after one of the early timber men here."

More camouflaging facts.

"No, Cara's father is Benton Sutherland, although everyone calls him Ben. Jerry always grumbled that what he really wanted to be called was Big Daddy, like that character from *Cat on a Hot Tin Roof*. Remember him? But Ben's really a pretty good guy. He's sent several nieces and nephews through college."

"Maybe he'd be interested in a tour through the mill while he's here," Fitz said. "I took one a while back, and it was interesting."

"If I talk to Cara again, I'll mention it."

So there we were, smoothly in and out of the subject of Ben Sutherland. Yet what could we do with the information? Calling him up and asking if he could recommend a good hit man probably wouldn't be a productive start.

At the door we shared good-bye handshakes with Ryan. "Thanks again for all the groceries," I said. "I'll make good use of them."

"It's been great meeting both of you. And thanks, Andi, for helping me there at the condo."

We watched from the door as he gave us a final wave from the rental Honda.

"What do you think now?" Fitz asked.

"I don't think Ryan had anything to do with Jerry's murder."

Fitz nodded agreement.

"I also think Big Daddy Sutherland could have decided hiring a hit man was cheaper and more satisfactory than paying Jerry off. I have no idea where that ten thousand dollars in the toilet tank came from, but I doubt Jerry'd have settled for that amount. I think he'd have played for bigger stakes."

"Maybe he did," Fitz said somberly.

Right. Maybe he'd gambled and lost.

Fitz's serious demeanor changed, and he grabbed my hand. "C'mon, we're going up to the CyberClam Café."

"But we just ate—"

"You don't eat at the CyberClam. Not if you value the inner workings of your anatomy."

24

A few minutes later I found out what you *do* do at the CyberClam. Several rows of computers stood off to the left side of the room. About half were occupied, the others showing screen savers of hurtling stars or toothy-fished predators. Hey, maybe I could come here to do some job hunting on the Internet.

Only one guy sat at the counter, eating.

We picked up soft drinks, and Fitz got us set up at a computer back in the corner. A few clicks, and a search engine was eagerly awaiting input. He typed *Southern Gold Timber* into the blank space.

"You've done this before?"

"I spent a lot of time in here looking up information about identity theft. That's what I had to see the lawyer about."

Identity theft! At last, an answer for my curiosity. I was also relieved. I know identity theft can be a big problem, but I was thankful it wasn't something such as marriage entanglements Fitz hadn't told me about, or lawsuits filed by jealous husbands. Maybe revelations about Jerry's secrets had given me a jaundiced outlook on males in general.

I kept my unwarranted suspicions to myself. "I've never

known anyone personally who had an identity stolen, but I keep hearing about what a mess it can be."

"A huge mess. Somebody got hold of everything. My Social Security number, date of birth, credit card account number, checking account number, address. Maybe my shoe size, for all I know. They drained bank accounts, opened credit accounts, borrowed money, and bought enough stuff to stock an electronics store. I don't tend to use credit much, but I don't like having a credit rating number that looks like the IQ of a ham sandwich."

"It's scary to think someone could really do that. You don't know how they acquired the information?"

"No idea at all. I never had my wallet lost or stolen. Never used a credit card on the Internet. Never gave out personal information over the phone. Never, so far as I know, anyway, had mail stolen."

"How long has it been going on?"

"It started a couple months before I left California. I've straightened out most of it, but I needed legal help with a couple of things. One of the strangest problems was my house down in LA. Somebody actually tried to sell it using my identity. I was telling a woman who writes for the local newspaper about all the problems I've had, and she's using me in an article she's doing on identity theft."

He made a couple of clicks with the mouse. "Look, here's a bunch of Web sites about Southern Gold Timber."

Southern Gold had a Web site of its own, but it was mostly hype about what an outstanding company it was. There was no personal information about Ben Sutherland, although there was a photo of him as CEO. It showed him standing beside an acre or so of desks in a dark-paneled office: a beefy-shouldered, big-bellied guy with bushy eyebrows and jutting shocks of white hair that looked like a haystack hit by a tornado. Family photos stood prominently on the desk, but a stuffed boar's head and a bearskin, complete with head and claws, dominated the wall behind him. Horns of some other unidentifiable creature poked into a corner of the photo.

"He might consider spending less money on preserving dead animals and invest in a decent haircut," I suggested.

"The man definitely doesn't need Rogaine," Fitz agreed. "I'd say he probably has a collection of guns big enough to arm a small country. And knows how to use them."

A do-it-yourselfer rather than a hire-a-hit-man guy?

"Hey, here's something interesting," Fitz said as he opened a new window. "Southern Gold has a recently acquired subsidiary called Shoreline Timber Products right here in Washington, headquarters up in Bremerton. I wonder if the big boss ever comes out here to visit his subsidiary."

I also wondered if Ryan knew about this company. Ben Sutherland in Georgia had seemed a safe distance away. Ben Sutherland with a company right here in the state felt dangerously close. Had he, in fact, been right out in my driveway, sneaking up on Jerry . . . and hitting me over the head?

Fitz frowned. "But we're back to the same old problem. What was Jerry doing in your limousine that night? I keep thinking if we knew the answer to that, we'd have a better handle on why he was killed and who might have done it."

"And what could possibly have been on Jerry's computer that would worry Sutherland?"

We spent the better part of an hour on the Internet, but most of the remainder of what we found had to do with lawsuits filed against Southern Gold Timber by various environmental groups concerned with the company's overlogging and destruction of wetlands. Paying Jerry off to get rid of him would surely have been small change compared to what Sutherland was spending on lawyers. But maybe it was the principle of the thing more than the size of the payoff that mattered.

We were back at the house by nine thirty, had a cup of green tea, and then Fitz was off, saying he'd call me from somewhere on the *Miss Nora* in a day or two.

I yawned and flicked the remote to see what was on TV, but the phone rang. I answered eagerly, thinking it might be a late call from Sarah, but after my hello, a nondaughterly voice said, "Is this Andi McConnell?"

"Yes."

"This is Elena Loperi."

"Oh." I couldn't think of anything to add. *How nice to hear from you* would be a hard line to say with sincerity.

"I don't suppose you were expecting to hear from me."

"Well, uh, no. Are you calling for some, uh, particular reason?"

Elena seemed to bring out the *uh* in me.

"I'd like to talk to you."

"We're talking now," I said warily.

"No, in person."

Talking to Elena was not on my schedule of Fun Things to Do. She hadn't directly threatened me during our earlier conversation, but neither had she been telling me to have a nice day. I wished Fitz were still here. "What did you want to talk about?"

"I think you know." Her cultured tone was meaningful.

I did know, of course, but I had the odd feeling she was reluctant to say Jerry's name. Why was that? I hesitated, tapping the arm of the sofa nervously. Okay, this was good, I decided. Elena was right up there with Big Daddy Sutherland on my list of suspects. I'd set up a meeting in some public place for after Fitz got back, and he could use some Ed Montrose interrogation skills to get more information out of her.

"How about Friday evening? We can meet over there in Olympia. A restaurant or parking lot, whatever you'd prefer."

"I've been parked at the end of your street for almost an hour waiting for you to get home and then for your friend to leave. I was beginning to think he was going to stay all night." She sounded a bit snappish. "I'll be there in two minutes."

She hung up before I had a chance to protest.

25

I peered out the window. Headlights pulled to the curb in front of the house. I couldn't identify the model of car, but it didn't look sleek and expensive, which rather surprised me. Although someone who looked as I expected Elena Loperi to look slid out and headed up my walkway. When she rang the bell, I opened the door, but left the chain on and one-eyed her through the narrow crack.

Letty's description fit. Long legged and slender, dark hair loose and shiny under the entry light. Her clothing . . . jeans, nondescript dark sweatshirt, and black sneakers . . . was what I might wear on a dark night when I wanted to be as little visible as possible. But where I'd look like a potential bag lady in the outfit, she managed to look svelte and stunning, ready to waltz down a fashion runway heralding this year's do-your-own-thing look.

But I also noted a worry crease between the perfect line of her eyebrows. "Why couldn't we talk on the phone?"

"I was afraid it might be bugged or tapped or however it is someone can listen in on your calls."

"Can that be done with a cell phone?"

"If it can be, I'm sure my husband knows how to do it." She

glanced down the street as if afraid someone might be lurking in the shadows.

"You think he might be following you?"

"He's down in Portland now." Small hesitation. "At least that's where he's supposed to be." She jumped when Moose started barking from behind his fence, then turned back to me. "I didn't kill Jerry, if that's what you're thinking."

I wasn't convinced of her innocence, although her nerves were a point in her favor.

"And I'm not carrying a gun, knife, or any more creative murder device to do you in." She lifted her arms to show me she wasn't concealing anything, but what I mostly saw was a to-die-for figure.

I eyed the black leather purse hanging from a shoulder strap. "That purse looks big enough to be lethal."

"Any woman who carries some itsy-bitsy purse with only a credit card and eye shadow in it isn't to be trusted."

I could go along with that. Real women need big purses. We carry everything from pocketknife to the small pharmacy of aspirin, Tylenol, and Tums that is in mine to the screwdriver I saw daughter Sarah pull out of her purse last winter.

"But if you'd like, I can dump the contents on the sidewalk and you can take inventory," she offered.

It was a facetious statement, and yet I figured she'd do it if I insisted. "That won't be necessary."

I unloosened the chain and let her in. I dispensed with a polite offer of refreshments. I flicked the TV off, then motioned her to the sofa and took a chair across the coffee table from her. Since I hit forty, I tend to acquire muddy freckles and blotches under the sun, but Elena's vacation tan glowed gloriously golden. It didn't, however, change the way her dark eyes kept darting nervously to the door.

"Okay, you're here. Somehow I don't think it's to call a meeting of the Jerry Norton Fan Club. So what's this all about?"

"I'm afraid you aren't going to pay attention to what I said on the phone. Afraid you're just going to blunder ahead—"

"Blunder!" I repeated indignantly.

"Blunder," she confirmed. "Which could put you on a collision course with my husband. With consequences that might be . . . dire."

"Out of the goodness of your heart, you're here to tell me to back off?"

"My ethics and good judgment on some matters may be up for debate, but I'm not without a conscience. And I don't want your dead body in there cluttering it up."

"Goody for you," I muttered. "One gold star, coming up. You want it on your forehead or your butt?"

Elena looked startled, but then she gave me a wry smile. "I can see why Jerry liked you. He liked . . . sass."

Warily I said, "You really didn't know he was dead until I told you?"

"No, I had no idea. As I told you, we'd been away on vacation."

"It happened right here, in my driveway. Jerry's body was stuffed in the trunk of my limousine."

"You'd been out somewhere . . . in a limousine?"

So then I had to go through the whole uncle-and-limouzeen story, which actually brought a hint of smile to the tense line of her lips. Until I got to the part about the body and getting knocked in the head myself.

"You didn't see who hit you?"

"No."

"So you don't know if it was Jerry or the killer."

I blinked. The thought that Jerry could have hit me had never entered my head. People were always coming up with these points that hadn't occurred to me, which did not bode well, I suspected, for my success as a sleuth/sidekick. Was there a *Sleuthing for Dummies* book I should be studying?

Jerry knocking me unconscious seemed implausible. *Jerry wouldn't do that, would he?* Yet, on second thought, it wasn't beyond possibility. If he hadn't wanted me to catch him in the limousine, maybe he had clobbered me. And then someone had done even worse to him. A deadly food chain.

Elena ran her hand through that long mane of hair. "This is all so . . . incredible."

"I suppose it is a shock, if you were having an affair with Jerry and didn't even know he was dead until I announced it to you," I agreed bluntly. "Didn't you wonder why you didn't hear from him after your vacation?"

"I wasn't having an affair with him!" The denial burst out like an explosion of fireworks, but then she hesitated and seemed to crumple as she added, "It had been over for three months."

Three months. Interesting timing in regard to my *four*-months relationship with Jerry. Two-timing both of us there for a while. Jerry's sleaze quotient rose again.

"What ended it?"

She lifted her head and gave me a ghost of smile. "I'd like to say I came to my senses and dumped him. But that wasn't what happened. Jerry dumped me."

Dumped her because he'd started seeing me? Yeah, right. About as likely as his choosing leftover meat loaf when he could have those lobsters in his freezer. There must have been some more compelling reason. I picked one and asked, "Did your husband find out about the affair and threaten him?"

"I don't know. It's possible. I . . . I was thinking about leaving Donny for him."

"I wouldn't take getting dumped by Jerry too personally," I advised. "According to his brother, Jerry dumped women the way some men toss beer cans out car windows."

"He was married once," she said. It sounded like a protest of my harsh view of Jerry, but then she reconsidered and said, "A mistake he probably didn't intend to make again."

"He was still married. He and Cara were never divorced."

"Still married? He lied to me!"

True, although that seemed a moot point to get indignant about, considering that she was also married.

"He broke up with me, too, just before he was killed. He already had the next lucky winner picked out."

Speculation glimmered in her eyes.

I shook my head. "I didn't kill him either. Though I'm not sure the police believe that. They seem a little suspicious, since I'd taken after him with a shovel just a couple days earlier."

"A shovel?" Her eyebrows rose, but then, without asking questions, she muttered, "Good for you."

"But somebody else got him with a gun, not me. Do you own a gun?"

"No . . ."

"But?"

"But my husband has several."

"Okay, I think it's time you told me a little more about this husband. Whose name is—?"

"Donny. Donaldo, actually. Our marriage has been on the rocks for quite a while." Elena twisted her shimmery-nailed hands together, then tucked them between her knees as if she had to do something to keep them from flying off into space. A wedding ring encircled her finger, plain gold band, no other jewelry except gold hoops in her ears. "That isn't any excuse for my relationship with Jerry, of course, but maybe it helps explain why it happened."

"But your marriage is mended now?"

"No. We're getting a divorce."

"But you just got back from vacation together!"

"It was one of those last-ditch efforts. You know, fly off to some exotic setting, get to know each other again, recapture the romance. Moonlight and champagne. Yada, yada, yada."

She made a snorty noise that didn't go with her elegant looks but made me feel a little warmer toward her.

"We might as well have gone to Motel 6 and Burger King and saved ourselves a bundle."

"Your husband found out about your relationship with Jerry, so now he wants a divorce?"

"I don't know if he knows about Jerry or not. I know I just can't take his moods and his paranoid suspicions and the way he just blows up about every little thing." Now she was twisting the wedding band as if she were trying to light a fire with it. "He got in an argument with some guy right on the dance floor down in Cozumel. The guy looked like he'd come straight out of a Mafia-R-Us photo. I was terrified."

"So the two of you have decided a divorce is the only answer?"

"The two of us haven't decided anything. Donny doesn't know yet that I'm seeing a lawyer next week. He isn't going to be a happy camper when he finds out."

"Are you afraid of him?"

"I don't think he'd hurt me, but . . ." Her voice trailed off. Then in a defensive tone she added, "The problems in our marriage started long before I met Jerry. Before we ever came up here."

"Came here from where?"

"Southern California. Donny was a cop down there. He was a cop before we married, so it wasn't as if I didn't know what I was getting into. But I had no idea about the strange hours or how often I'd be home alone, scared that something terrible had happened to him, or how he'd get all uptight and moody. Though I can't blame him for that, I suppose. Cops are exposed to . . . awful things."

"So he quit being a cop because you didn't like it?"

She shook her head. "No. I couldn't take that away from him. He loved being a cop even when it upset him. But there was a lot of . . . politics, I'd guess you'd call it, in the department. Donny didn't get a promotion he was entitled to. A buddy of the police chief got it. And then a witness was killed after the police questioned him. It wasn't Donny's fault, but someone had to be blamed, and it wound up being him."

"So he got fired?"

"No, not that either. I think they figured he'd sue them if he got fired over that. But it made a big black mark on his record, and he was furious about that as well as not getting the promotion. Then he got assigned an old police car instead of one of the new ones the department bought. He saw it all as a big conspiracy. He made a noisy stink, got the police chief in trouble with the city council, and quit."

"So you moved up here so he could be a cop here?"

"That was the idea, but all he's been able to find so far is a rent-a-cop job as a night security guard. He hates it. And he figures the reason he can't get on with a police force here is because the department down in California is sabotaging him. Another conspiracy."

"But his night hours as a security guard made your relationship with Jerry easier to carry off. A little conspiracy of your own."

She nodded unhappily.

"And how did you feel about the move up here? Is that part of the problem? I heard you'd been a model down in California."

"I was fairly successful. Not as big-time as New York, but I kept busy with catalog work and private showings for some stores. I was hoping I could still get some modeling work up here, but I was willing to give it all up if Donny could just make a new start."

"And you did give it up. You went to work for F&N."

"We were short on money. I needed a job quick. And I do have a degree in communications, with an emphasis on advertising and public relations. Being in advertising probably has a longer shelf life than being a model anyway."

I agreed, but switched back to the basics here and put the situation in crisp outline form. "So you went to work at F&N and started an affair with Jerry. Your husband found out about it and killed Jerry with one of those several guns you say he has. Now you're here warning me about him, that maybe he's going to kill me too."

"No!" She sounded rattled, as if she didn't know which part of my scenario to protest first. "I mean, I don't know that Donny ever found out about the affair—"

"Oh, c'mon. He was a cop. Don't you think he was observant enough to know something was going on? And if he got suspicious, had the experience and skills to check up on you without your knowing it?"

Another unhappy nod.

"Is he capable of killing someone?"

"Donny . . . killed a man once. But it was self-defense. A drug dealer who came after him with a knife. So I guess he's capable of it. But I don't think he's a cold-blooded killer who'd just . . . murder someone."

"But you're not sure. Or you just don't want to think it?"

She made a dismissive move with her shoulders. Shapely shoulders.

"So do you think he really could have killed Jerry or not? The circumstances are suspicious, to say the least."

The wedding ring went round and round again. "If he found out about the affair, yes, I think he could have done it."

"But why would he wait until now, if the affair had been over for three months?"

"Sometimes things . . . work on Donny. He might seem not too upset about something at the time. Like when a neighbor ran over a nice dog we had down in California. But then he thinks about it, like he did with the neighbor and the dog, and it just grows on him. Until he explodes."

"What happened with the neighbor?"

"Several months later he sent the guy to the hospital with a broken collarbone."

Not a guy you wanted teed off at you. "Okay, you may be suspicious of Donny, apparently with good reason. But he has an alibi. You and he were out of the country. You were away on vacation since before Jerry was killed."

"Not exactly."

26

We stared at each other across the coffee table.

"But you told me you'd been on vacation for two weeks!"

"Do you believe everything anyone tells you?" she snapped. "You'd just told me Jerry was murdered. I was horrified and scared and imagining all kinds of things."

"So you real quick thought it would be a good idea to cover your back. Or Donny's back."

"I . . . I'm not covering anyone's back now. Our flight left for Cozumel around eleven Saturday morning. Which, from what you tell me, was after Jerry was killed."

"But if Donny had been at home with you all night—"

"He wasn't. He worked the previous night. I thought it was a bad idea, working right up until we were practically ready to take off, but he said we needed the money."

"*Was* he working?"

"I don't know. This particular job was at a warehouse. He could have left for several hours, and if the place wasn't broken into during that time, no one would know. He could have gone to Jerry's condo, followed him to your place, killed him, and gone back to the warehouse."

"You've done some thinking about this."

"Oh, yes."

I gave all this some thought too, then pointed out a different twist on the murder. "So if Donny was at the warehouse, you were home alone. Which means you could have gone to the condo, followed Jerry to the limo, killed him, and got home in time to meet your husband with a smile and a suitcase full of bikinis and suntan lotion."

"I didn't kill him! What reason would I have to kill him?"

"A woman scorned, etc."

She frowned but repeated her statement, this time with an emphatic shake of head. "I didn't do it."

"There's something else, something you don't know," I said. "All Jerry's computer equipment was stolen out of his condo the same night he was murdered. And the murderer took his cell phone and that flash drive thing he always carried in his pocket. His Rolex watch too. The police have kept it quiet, but the computer theft had to be connected to the killing. But your Donny didn't have any reason to—" I broke off at the stricken look on Elena's face. "Or did he?"

She got up and paced back and forth between the sofa and the window, swinging hair and swift turns graceful as a prowling cat.

"I didn't tell you how Jerry and I met."

"You were both working at F&N."

"Donny changed after what happened with his job down in California. He thought everybody was out to get him."

This sounded like an off-subject tangent, but I knew there must be a connection.

"We had an income tax problem. He saw that as a government conspiracy. The rich can get away with anything, and the IRS was after *him*. Our car got totaled in an accident, which is why I'm driving the clunker out there. But to Donny, it was another conspiracy between the other driver and the insurance company."

"A little paranoid, as you said."

"A *lot* paranoid. He started spending time on the Internet while I was at work. Through that he got tangled up with some strange, quasi-military group called the Twenty-first Minutemen and even started going to their meetings. He brought some of their literature home. It was all this awful hate stuff. How the government was on the verge of collapse and was conspiring against innocent citizens. How it was every man for himself, and we all needed to be armed and ready. And beware of anyone not like *us*. It scared me. I looked up the Web site. And down at the bottom I saw this little notice: Site Design and Maintenance by Jerry Norton Web Design."

Jerry had told me about that particular Web site, although I hadn't known the name before. He said most of the guys were "weekend commando" types playing war games and seeing conspiracies everywhere, but a couple of them might really be dangerous. Was Donny Loperi one of the dangerous ones?

"I knew there was a Jerry Norton at F&N. I didn't think it could be him doing the Web site, but one time I made kind of a joke out of it and asked him."

"And it was."

"Right. So we talked . . . and laughed. He was older and mature, like you, but still so much fun."

I almost choked at that, but I doubted she even realized how it sounded to me. At least she wasn't making malicious cracks about my being too old for Jerry. So all I said was, "Yeah, Jerry could be fun."

"Donny took the group seriously, but Jerry thought they were just a bunch of kooks and crackpots and laughed at them.

He was that proverbial breath of fresh air after all Donny's anger and paranoia."

"And the talking and laughing escalated into an affair."

Another nod.

"You must have been very discreet. I don't think anyone at F&N knew about it. At least it never got onto the gossip express."

"We were careful. Looking back, I think Jerry enjoyed the cloak-and-dagger part of our relationship. Made it more exciting."

Until Elena started making waves about a different kind of relationship, something wifey and permanent, and then he ducked out.

"Did Jerry and Donny ever meet?"

"Jerry went to a few of the group's meetings. He met Donny then, although that was before Jerry and I . . . got together."

"I remember Jerry telling me that he closed the Web site down because they didn't pay their bill."

"Donny mentioned that." She smiled without humor. "To him that meant Jerry was part of some vicious conspiracy to destroy the group and keep them from getting the truth out."

"Would Donny feel strongly enough about that to kill Jerry?"

She paused and tapped her fingertips together nervously. "Maybe, if he got paranoid enough. But I'd think it more likely that if Donny killed Jerry, it was about me."

"But what could possibly have been on Jerry's computer that would make Donny steal everything to keep it hidden, especially if the Web site had already been shut down?"

"I don't know." Elena returned to the sofa, her slim body graceful in spite of the dispirited slump as she dropped to the cushion and clutched a pillow to her chest. "Jerry liked to dig into stuff, you know. He thought hacking into places he wasn't supposed to be was fun. He said once he'd gotten into the computers of some rival insurance company and could have sabotaged every one of their accounts if he'd wanted to."

"I didn't know that." Although I remembered he'd laughed once about how he'd hacked into a dating site and teamed up several of the most incompatible couples he could find.

"So maybe he had some kind of confidential information about Donny. Or maybe it was just more of Donny's paranoia, thinking Jerry *might* have something on the computer that would tie him to the murder if the police saw it."

Donny Loperi was more and more looking like a major suspect. Although one of my hot theories had to be wrong. Elena's husband and Big Daddy Sutherland couldn't both have killed Jerry.

"Why is Donny down in Portland now?"

"He heard about an opening on some suburban police force there. He sent in a résumé and got called for an interview. I'm hoping he gets the job. I feel bad divorcing him when he's so . . . down-and-out."

"But you're afraid of him."

"Wouldn't you be, if you were me?"

"And you're telling me I should be afraid of him too."

"I don't think he's going to deliberately come after you. But if you keep trying to find out who killed Jerry, and you get close enough to Donny that he starts to feel cornered, I think he'll do something to . . . protect himself."

"Protect himself by getting me out of the way."

"Stay out of it. Let the police handle it. It's their job, not yours. If he did it, they'll catch up with him sooner or later."

"Sometimes killers never get caught."

We sat there in silence until finally she picked a word out of something I'd said earlier. "You said Jerry had a Rolex?"

"He got it a month or so after I met him. You sound surprised."

"I am. Jerry had expensive tastes—I'm sure you know that—but he didn't have that kind of money."

"His brother said he used to be heavily into gambling. Maybe he still was, though if he was, I didn't know anything about it. But maybe he won a bundle. Was he gambling when you knew him?"

"Not that I knew. But he could have been, I suppose. We never went out anywhere together where someone we knew might see us." She shook her head. "I don't know what ever made me think that kind of relationship could go anywhere."

"Maybe you should work a little more on your relationship with Donny. It sounds as if he needs some help."

"Counselor? Psychiatrist? Good whack alongside the head?"

"Maybe it's God he needs." I almost looked around to see who'd said that. *Me?* Okay, I'd gone that far, so I added, "Maybe you need God too."

She looked thoughtful, but what she said was, "When you called me, you said you were looking for a job. Is that true, or was it just some ploy to talk to me?"

"Both," I admitted. "I don't know if you've heard, since you've been away, but F&N merged with another company. They're closing down here and moving everything to San Diego. Jerry was supposed to transfer there, as an assistant to his boss."

"Really? I'm surprised he wanted to keep working with Findley. He thought the guy was a real jerk and was always making fun of him. I hope you find another job," she added.

"Thank you." I looked at her hopefully, but no offer was forthcoming.

She stood up. "Well, I should be getting home. Donny might try to call."

I looked at my watch. "At this hour? It's past midnight."

"An hour Donny thinks is the perfect time to call and check on me."

Oh, Donny had known about Jerry, all right. I had no doubt about that. We walked to the door, and I opened it for her.

"Thanks for taking time to talk to me," she said.

"Thanks for taking time to come all the way over here. I appreciate your concern."

She put a slim hand on my arm. "And please, please listen to what I've said."

A new thought suddenly hit me. "Maybe you're trying to protect Donny. Maybe all this stuff about divorce and being afraid of him is just a big smoke screen. Maybe you just want to stop any investigation that might lead to him and give him time to get out of the country!"

"You do have a suspicious mind." She didn't sound critical, merely observant.

I offered Fitz's comment. "Goes with the territory."

"Believe what you want, but I really was thinking of the danger to you. As I said before, I don't want another dead body on my conscience."

"Jerry is on your conscience?"

"I can't help thinking that if I hadn't had a relationship with him, he'd still be alive."

"You could be a responsible citizen and go to the police and tell them everything you've told me."

"Yeah, I could, couldn't I? But Donny would know who'd

tipped them off, and I'm afraid my desire for self-preservation exceeds my desire for exemplary citizenship. But *you* could go to them."

Right. I could tell them all about how I thought Jerry's ex-girlfriend's husband may have done him in, or maybe it was his not-quite-ex-father-in-law.

Anyone else you're suspicious of? I could hear Detective Sergeant Molino saying politely. *Maybe his cleaning lady's cousin's ex-husband? Or his condo neighbor's former brother-in-law?*

No, I needed something more solid than what I had here to take to the authorities. Although I'd rather that *something solid* wasn't my dead body.

"You know, there's one puzzling point about Jerry's murder that I keep coming back to, and nothing you've said explains it. What was he doing here at my place that night?"

She looked thoughtful. "Maybe he wanted to make up with you."

"It was the middle of the night. And he didn't come to the house, just to the limousine."

"I don't know. That is odd, isn't it? For a while, I thought Jerry and I were soul mates. But, looking back, I think maybe I saw in him . . . what I wanted to see. And I think now that there was a lot I *didn't* see. So I have no idea what he may have been up to."

Me too. Multifaceted Jerry, showing a different face to each of us. Which was the real Jerry? Or did he show that face to anyone?

Elena looked both ways down the street before heading out to her car.

"I really do like those TV ads with the two cats and the dog," I called after her. ◦

"Thanks. Watch for the next one. The cats are at a ritzy pet spa, having their nails and hair done."

I watched until Elena's car was safely around the corner, then closed the door. I didn't see myself and Elena ever being big buddies, and I certainly couldn't condone her relationship with Jerry no matter how bad her marriage was. But I liked more than disliked her. Whether or not her husband had killed Jerry, I suspected she had good reason to be afraid of him.

And maybe I did too. I shivered.

27

It had been a long day, with unsettling surprises along the way, and I didn't think I'd sleep. But I did, and it was after nine when I woke the next morning. I might not have wakened even then, but for the persistent jangling of the phone. I picked it up and grunted into it.

"Mom, are you okay? The phone must have rung seventeen times. I'm standing here worrying that you're lying there murdered in your bed!"

"I'm fine," I muttered. "Except for this persistent ringing in my ears."

I sat up in bed, and we brought each other up to date on what was going on with murder, limo, college plans, and Rachel's graduation this coming Friday night. Which reminded me I hadn't sent her a present yet. Which reminded me I needed to send flowers to Lancaster for Jerry's funeral, too. There was also a job to look for. Sarah again reminded me that I could come stay for a while or live with them permanently. I said I'd think about it.

I got the flowers taken care of by phone and credit card. I considered spending hours looking for some just-right graduation present for Rachel, but finally decided to send her what she liked best. Money. I already had a card, so I added a check and a stamp, and that was done.

Which left the more difficult problem of a job. But before I went to the Internet, I decided I'd try another route. I dressed and drove down to the Sweet Breeze, which was busy this morning. I asked Joella for a mocha latte rather than my usual French roast. I have this theory that changing your usual routine, even in so minor a matter as coffee, may break some cosmic rut and shoot your life off in a whole new direction.

I sat off in a corner with my latte—nonfat milk cancels out whipped cream on top, right?—and perused the help-wanted ads in the Olympia newspaper. I rationalized the cost of the latte as well by telling myself I'd have had to buy the newspaper if I weren't reading it here for free.

And what a dazzling array of jobs was available! Car salesman, backhoe operator, bartender, exotic dancer, fence builder, hairstylist, lifeguard, pharmacist, rigging slinger. None of which I was even remotely qualified to do.

In a spare moment, Joella plopped down at my little table with a sigh of relief. "Finding anything?"

"Not unless the fact that I once slung a plate at my ex-husband qualifies me to be a rigging slinger, which I doubt. How are you doing? No more indigestion, I hope?"

"I'm fine. I'm thinking that after I'm not pregnant, maybe I'll wear a little pillow." She patted her tummy. "There's something about pregnancy that brings out the generosity in people." She opened her pocket and showed me a nice collection of bills and change.

"You're too honest to do that," I said, and she gave a sigh that said that was true. "But you could bring the baby here with you. A cute baby would surely encourage fantastic tips."

I was just making idle small talk, but Joella gave me an odd, cheerless look. "A lady came in the other day and said she knows a couple who are desperate to adopt a baby." She poked at a tiny dent in the table, as if she were trying to excavate it with a fingernail. "Wonderful people, she says, and they'd take care of all the medical bills, including the ones I've already run up."

I knew that pocketful of tips wouldn't much more than pay postage on the heavyweight bill she'd be receiving from the hospital for her visit to the emergency room.

"She wants me to meet this couple."

"Are you going to do it?"

"I'm thinking about it. It wouldn't be like just dumping the baby out there for someone else to decide who gets her."

I couldn't tell if that's what she really thought or if she was trying to convince herself. But it was quite possible Joella would never even know her baby for more than a few precious minutes. That struck me as so sad. But adoption would solve so many problems for her and maybe the baby too. And adoption was a good thing, not something ugly or evil.

Joella briskly changed the subject. "I didn't have a chance to tell you before, but Detective Sergeant Molino was in again yesterday."

"To update you on his cat's skin condition?"

"He wanted to know about your 'activities' since the murder. If anyone different had been coming to the house, or if you'd been acting any differently than usual. He really got down to the nitty-gritty about your relationship with Jerry too. I think he's been talking to Jerry's neighbors at the condo."

She didn't mention my late visitor last night, so apparently she hadn't heard Elena arrive or leave. I couldn't say for certain why, but I'd just as soon dear Detective Sergeant Molino . . . DDS Molino, I was thinking of him now . . . didn't know about that.

"Hey," she said as I got up to leave, "someone was telling me there's an old-fashioned band concert in the park Thursday night. Want to go?"

"Sure. Let's do it."

I'd circled the jobs that said to send a résumé to their business address. I ran off more copies of my résumé and did that. Several ads said to apply in person, so I drove over to Olympia to do that. I'd thought "apply in person" might mean an interview, but it meant only that they wanted you to show up in person to fill out an application; then they'd call if they were interested. I'd already registered with an employment agency over there, but I came back and registered with another one in Vigland.

I tried to feel as if I was making progress with all this activity, but mostly I felt as if I were trapped on some slow-moving treadmill.

THE FOLLOWING MORNING, however, I had a pleasant surprise. The Vigland agency called. An assisted-living facility on the north side of town needed someone knowledgeable about insurance. Could I go right out there? Yes, indeedy.

The interview went okay, but I saw the applicants before and after me. Both were at least twenty years younger, and I was fairly certain both were also former F&N employees. I hoped age wouldn't matter here. This was, after all, a home for older people, and the manager wasn't much below sixty herself.

On the way home I picked up a copy of the weekly *Vigland Tides*, thinking I'd check the ads. And there, right on the front page, was a photo of Fitz sitting at a computer at the CyberClam Café!

It was an excellent article, well written and informative. In addition to detailing Fitz's problems, it included information about a local woman who'd been "phished" on the Internet, which meant she'd received an e-mail that looked like a legitimate communication from her bank. She'd gone to the site they'd instructed for bringing her personal information up to date, and only later learned the site was a scam and her information had been stolen. Another older man had given personal information over the phone because the caller made him think she was from his credit-card company.

The article also pointed out that none of the usual methods of identity theft applied to Fitz, however, so it could happen to almost anyone. From there the article went on with what steps to take if you did find yourself a victim. I cut the article out to save for Fitz and studied the photo a minute longer.

A very attractive man, Keegan "Fitz" Fitzpatrick. I suspected senior ladies all over town were trying to figure some way to meet him. And they didn't even know he could cook.

I optimistically waited for the assisted-living facility to call. I did some housecleaning, noticing for the first time that I still had that photo of Jerry in the bedroom. I started to toss it, then felt a little guilty—he was, after all, dead—and stuffed it into a drawer instead.

The call came from the assisted-living facility on Thursday morning. They were sorry, but they had decided on another applicant. I suspected age had something to do with the decision, but I had no proof of that, of course.

Disappointing, but not the end of the world. I went back to the help-wanted ads in the Vigland newspaper. The only job possibility was at a burger place. Not my ideal choice, but if I had to sling burgers, so be it.

The job wasn't filled yet when I arrived, and the nineteen-year-old manager let me fill out an application, but I could tell I made him nervous. In looking over the workers on duty, I could see why. The males were near clones of the manager himself, the females young and cute and curvy.

"Do you ever hire older workers?" I asked.

"Well, uh . . ." His gaze followed mine to the fresh-cheeked girl handing over a tray of burgers. "We, uh, haven't so far, but we, uh, *might.*"

Right. They also *might* hire a robot in a clown suit. But not likely. Age discrimination, I was reasonably certain, was alive and well no matter what the law said.

I drowned my sorrows in a cheeseburger deluxe with curly fries and a chocolate milk shake. If it weren't for DDS Molino having my limo in his clutches, I might soon be desperate enough to consider starting a limousine service.

THE BAND CONCERT was scheduled for eight o'clock. There were chairs set up, but Joella and I spread a blanket on the grass. We heard rousing Sousa marches, patriotic songs, and some surprisingly swingy numbers too.

On the way out of the park, we ran into Letty Bishop and a couple of her grandkids. "Hey, are you still interested in a temporary job?" she asked.

"At the moment I'm interested in any kind of job."

"I think they're going to let me hire someone. I should know in a day or two. I'll give you a call."

"Great!"

Afterward we went to KeKo's Ice Cream Parlor for strawberry sundaes. The small size. No more pigging out, followed by expensive trips to the emergency room. We got home about ten thirty. I'd left the lights on in the living room. After what had happened in my driveway, I'd gotten uneasy about coming home to a dark house. I unlocked the door . . . and walked into a disaster area.

28

Sofa overturned, cushions scattered. Pictures ripped off walls. Videotapes and DVDs tumbling out of the cabinet and across the carpet. Cans of chili mingled with boxes of cake mix and cornflakes spilled on the kitchen counters. Refrigerator and freezer wide open, contents strewn on the floor.

Lobster! I dashed around frantically gathering up my precious lobster tails and steaks and cheesecake and stuffing them back into the freezer.

Then I stopped short, frozen chicken cordon bleu in hand. The burglar might still be in the house, and I was worrying about lobster tails?

I stood as frozen as the chicken cordon bleu for a moment. Was that a noise from the bedroom? Or footsteps behind the house?

I ran for the garage to go over to Joella's, then turned and dashed for the front door instead. What I did not need was to find myself face-to-face with a burglar lurking in the dark garage. Joella, in her wispy little nightgown, let me in when I pounded on the door.

"Andi, what's wrong? What happened?"

"Someone broke in. The place is a wreck! I need to call 911—"

"Are you okay?"

I touched my hand to my rampaging heart. Sure, fine. If I didn't have a heart attack or stroke in the next two minutes.

Joella pulled me inside. "Detective Sergeant Molino gave me a card. I'll call him. He should know about this."

I started to protest. I wasn't eager to see DDS Molino again. But she was right. He was the person to call. This had to be connected with the murder.

She locked the door behind me, got his business card from her purse and, very calm and collected, punched numbers into the phone. She listened a moment, then started on new numbers.

"That was his home phone. It's an answering machine. I'm trying his cell phone now."

I plopped on the sofa, feeling a combination of panicky and drained, my thoughts jumpy as hyped-up grasshoppers. Had the murderer come back? Why? To frighten me? Or to search for something he hadn't found in the limo or Jerry's condo?

Joella sat down beside me after she hung up the phone. "He'd gone to give his sister's car a jump-start. The battery was dead 'cause she left the lights on while she and a friend went to a movie. He'll be here in a few minutes. He says don't go back over there."

We sat at the window and watched. The detective arrived with admirable speed. He was not in an official car, nor was he in uniform. I had difficulty picturing DDS Molino as a helpful brother . . . with a cat . . . but obviously even hard-edged detectives had a life beyond chasing murderers and snatching limousines.

Joella had dressed and was right behind me. I momentarily wondered if we'd have gotten such quick off-duty service if I, rather than cute Joella, had called. DDS Molino did, in fact, look at her and say, "You okay?"

"My place wasn't broken into, just Andi's."

"I'm sorry about interrupting your evening," I said. "But I think the break-in must be connected with the murder."

"I'll check it out. You both wait here while I see what's going on."

He was, I noted, carrying a gun in a holster strapped to his belt, even though he was in jeans. He had the gun out as he approached the door. He turned before entering, emphatically waving us back inside.

He was inside the house for some ten minutes. Then he came to Joella's door and asked me to come back to the house with him.

"I know it's difficult to tell at this point, but do you see anything missing?" he asked when we were inside.

My house hadn't been neat after the police search, but now my bedroom looked like the last day of a three-day yard sale, when everything has been pawed through and rejected. Clothes scattered, blankets torn off the bed, mattress shoved aside. Nightstand and dresser drawers emptied on the floor. Contents of my jewelry box dumped on the bed. I poked through the items with a stiff finger, feeling squeamish knowing someone else had also just done so.

"I don't see my diamond-stud earrings." I said it reluctantly, because I was sorry to lose them, but also because I was afraid how this would look to DDS Molino.

He didn't have a notebook, so he appropriated the scratch pad by the phone. "Could you describe them, please."

I did. Plain old diamond studs. A quarter-carat each, in a plain gold setting. A long-ago present from Richard. Actually, I'd been surprised he hadn't grabbed them when he left. He'd taken most everything else of value, including an expensive bottle of Dom Pérignon champagne I'd naively been saving for our anniversary.

"Anything else?"

"An old watch that belonged to my mother, a Hamilton. It won't run anymore, but it might look valuable to someone." I described that too.

In the bathroom, the medicine cabinet had been emptied, contents flung across the counter and into the sink. Towels and sheets yanked from the linen closet.

"Anything missing here? Prescriptions or drugs of any kind?"

"Maybe some old Vicodin painkillers I had left over from when I hurt my elbow a couple years ago." I hesitated, trying to remember. "Although I may have thrown them out," I hedged, again not wanting to encourage any this-is-just-an-ordinary-burglary thoughts. "How did they get in?"

He led me to the sliding glass doors that opened onto the patio out back. They were still open.

"Nothing high-tech about the entry. They just pried the door open. Looks as if the frame is bent. The glass is cracked too." He frowned disapprovingly. "You should at least use a stick or rod along the bottom to hold the door in place. That would have made prying it open more difficult. Is Joella's door like this too?"

"Yes."

"Then get something to brace her door too. What time did you leave the house?"

"About seven thirty. Joella and I went to the band concert in the park. It was a little past ten thirty when we got home. I'd left the lights on while we were gone."

Which had undoubtedly been convenient for the burglar, I thought unhappily. Maybe I should have left cookies out for him, too, so he'd have felt extra welcome.

The detective took a flashlight and searched for tracks in the grass, both front and back, but found nothing. That didn't surprise me. Even if the burglar hadn't stayed on the narrow sidewalk leading around the house, the grass was clipped short and the ground dry, not conducive to revealing footprints of anything smaller than the Northwest's mythical Bigfoot.

The detective started to shove the door back into place. I stopped him, appalled at what he was doing.

"Shouldn't the door be dusted for fingerprints before it's touched?"

"I know it probably seems unreasonable to the general public, but the department doesn't have the money to do that kind of investigation on every minor burglary."

"That's all you think this is?" I asked in dismay. "A minor burglary?"

"Unless you discover something more, only the earrings and watch are missing. It's basically just a big cleanup job. And I'd strongly guess whoever did this wore gloves anyway."

"But if it's connected to the murder—"

"You think it is?"

"Of course I do. Isn't a murder and then a break-in on the same property too much of a coincidence? And if they were just ordinary burglars, wouldn't they have taken more than the few little things that are missing?"

DDS Molino looked around. He didn't say anything, but I could see what he was thinking: *And that something more would be . . . ?*

Okay, I could see his point. No burglar was likely to bother with my toaster or my old VHS tape of *Grease*.

"So why do you think the killer would be in your house?"

"To search for something connected to the murder. Or to frighten or intimidate me by vandalizing my home."

"To intimidate you into doing something? Or *not* doing something?"

Put that way, frightening or intimidating me seemed less of a possibility. Yes, I was frightened. But what did that accomplish? It wasn't as if I was in a position to finger anyone for the crime of murder, and this would silence me.

"Okay, they were searching for something, then."

"Such as?"

"Something the killer didn't find in the limo or in Jerry's condo. Maybe that flash drive Jerry always carried! Or his cell phone. They weren't on his body."

"Is there any chance they could be in here?"

"Well, no, I don't think so," I admitted reluctantly. Jerry had never spent nights here. "But the killer doesn't know that."

"And why would this flash drive be important?"

I hesitated, suddenly wary of these questions. DDS Molino was not a stupid or unobservant man. So what was the point in acting so dense? Because I was still a suspect, and he was trying to catch me in some incriminating remark? I barged ahead anyway.

"Because he was undoubtedly using it as a backup for whatever was on his computer. The killer knows the flash drive exists and is afraid if he doesn't find it first, that you'll find it. And there's something on it that incriminates him!"

"We'd already searched the house. It wasn't here."

"But the killer doesn't necessarily know that either. Have you ever heard of something called the Twenty-first Minutemen?"

"No. What is it? Some rock group?" He sounded more impatient than interested.

"They're the group I first mentioned when you questioned me about Jerry. I don't know if it's located in Vigland or elsewhere in the area, but it's kind of a semimilitary group. Minutemen of the twenty-first century, or something like that. Big on conspiracy theories and do-it-yourself survival."

"So why would they be after Jerry Norton?"

"He did a Web site for them, then shut it down. He thought at least a few of the members might be dangerous."

I started to mention Donny Loperi's name in connection with the group, then hesitated. Elena had said if the police came after him, he'd know who'd put them on his trail. He'd surely blame Elena if they sought him out for questioning now. And if he did blame her . . . I shivered. I didn't want her dead body on *my* conscience.

"I'll send someone over in the morning to dust for fingerprints. I don't think anything will show up, but just in case."

He sounded as if he was making a big concession on the fingerprint issue, which rather annoyed me, but all I said was, "I'd appreciate that."

"Don't touch anything more until then. And I think it would be better if you don't stay here tonight."

I didn't need any encouragement in that direction. "I can sleep on Joella's sofa."

"Good. And brace that sliding glass door at her place."

I locked the front door, which seemed a bit superfluous, considering that the sliding glass door in back couldn't be closed because of the bent frame. He walked me over to Joella's door.

"I wonder how the burglar happened to choose tonight? I'm usually home in the evenings. Odd that they'd strike on the rare night I wasn't."

"If it's an ordinary burglary, probably just an opportunistic thing. They saw a place that looked like no one was home and broke in. If it's something else, although I consider that unlikely, maybe someone has been watching your place."

I didn't find that possibility unlikely. I shivered again at the thought of someone sneaking around, peering in windows without my knowing it.

"Well, thanks for coming," I said at Joella's door. I realized I should have picked up some pajamas before I left the house, but I wasn't about to ask DDS Molino to go back with me while I pawed through my scattered lingerie.

He was headed toward his car when Joella locked the door, but a minute later the doorbell rang.

"It's me again," the detective said through the door. "I forgot to tell you something."

I opened the door with a feeling of dread. Now what?

"I intended to call you in the morning, but I may as well tell you now. You can come to the station and pick up your limousine whenever you want."

My limousine was a minor detail he'd forgotten? Then my big rush of joy overshadowed my indignation. My limousine. I was getting it back!

"I'm surprised the techs have released it this soon, but they have." He sounded disapproving, as if he'd have liked to keep it squirreled away from my eager hands much longer. "You can stop by my office and pick up the keys."

"Thank you!" Then, thinking about what they may have done looking for evidence, I asked anxiously, "Is it okay?"

"Mostly."

And with that laconic comment, DDS Molino left me to spend the night sleeping in one of Joella's wispy nightgowns and worrying about exactly what that cryptic "mostly" might mean.

29

Before going to bed, we made a brace for Joella's sliding glass door by whacking off an old broom handle. I wouldn't put it past DDS Molino to come back and check to see if one was in place. In spite of the sags in Joella's secondhand sofa, I drifted off to sleep with surprising speed. Only to wake with a phone jangling somewhere near my toes and a disoriented *Where-am-I?* feeling as I shot upright.

I scrambled for the phone before it could waken Joella, then hesitated a moment before picking it up. The red numbers on Joella's clock radio showed 2:10. Phone calls at 2:10 AM are not generally joyous occasions.

"Yes?" I said warily.

"Andi?" The voice sounded surprised.

"Fitz? What are you doing calling me at this hour?"

"I was calling Joella—"

"Joella does not need to be scared out of her wits by a strange phone call in the middle of the night!"

"You're right. But I was worried. I tried to call *you* several times this evening, and you were never home. I tried again a few minutes ago, and when you didn't answer at 2 AM, I started thinking of all kinds of terrible possibilities. So I decided to see if Joella knew anything."

I flicked on the lamp. His concern was nice, but at the same time I felt a bit miffed that his imagination was so one-dimensional. "Didn't it occur to you that maybe I was, oh, out with someone, dancing on tabletops or swinging from chandeliers?"

"No, that didn't occur to me." He paused as if trying to picture that.

Okay, it was a stretch. About as likely as Rachel's old Barbie Doll acing a Mensa test.

"But if that's what you do on dates, I'll need to practice up."

"Oh, never mind."

"So why are you at Joella's? She isn't sick, is she?"

"No. She's fine. Detective Sergeant Molino advised my staying here."

"Molino? Why?"

"The sliding glass door wouldn't close because the frame was bent—"

"Bent? How'd that happen?"

"That's where the burglars broke in."

"Burglars!" Then he gave a resigned sigh. "Okay, we're obviously going at this backwards. Start at the beginning."

So I did. Band concert. Break-in. Night on Joella's sofa.

"You think this is connected with Jerry's murder?"

"Detective Sergeant Molino doesn't seem to, but I do. My diamond earrings and a watch were taken, so he seems to think it's just a generic burglary. But I think the burglar was looking for something connected to the murder and just grabbed those items as a bonus."

I wiggled my mouth and stretched my jaw trying to get everything into shape. I read a list of differences between men and women not long ago. One was that men get up in the morning as good-looking as when they go to bed. Women deteriorate overnight.

"But let's talk about it later, okay? My head doesn't work right at this hour. Why were you calling me to begin with?"

"Can't I just want to talk to you? Hear your lilting voice?"

"I'm fresh out of lilt."

"And also to tell you that I called Ben Sutherland's Shoreline Timber Products office in Bremerton before we left. I have some interesting information. We should be back at the marina by midafternoon—why don't you come over, and I'll fix dinner? Bring Joella too. She's never seen the boat."

"Joella has enough problems to worry about without hearing about murder suspects."

"We'll slip off alone for a few minutes."

Hmmm. That sounded interesting. But then I remembered his son's less-than-enthusiastic reception the other time I was at the boat. "What about Matt?"

"He can find his own sidekick to slip off with," Fitz said airily. "Actually, he has to run over to Tacoma on business and probably won't be there anyway. Seven thirty?"

"Sounds good."

IN THE MORNING I left a note on the door telling the fingerprint technician to go around back to get in. I was in too much of a hurry to retrieve my limo to wait around for him. Joella dropped me off at the sheriff's station on her way to work.

And there it sat in the parking lot, a long, black jewel gleaming in the sun, radiating power and luxury. *My* jewel! Calling to me the way those tempting nymphs that lived on rocks in the sea called to lost sailors. Of course, giving in to that pull tended to result in a watery grave for the sailors, so I dropped the comparison there.

But what I really felt like doing was proclaiming my owner-
ship and doing a happy dance of joy around the car. Running my
fingers over every glorious inch. Patting hubcaps and hugging
fenders and sniffing leather upholstery. My limouzeen!

That first rush of glee abruptly floundered, torpedoed by
the sobering memory of the open trunk with Jerry's body
stuffed inside. I felt subdued when I walked inside the station
and asked for Detective Sergeant Molino.

The officer on duty said he'd already gone out on a call,
but when I stated my purpose, she pulled keys out of a drawer.
She, unlike DDS Molino, apparently had no regrets about
returning the vehicle to me. After I provided identification she
dropped the keys in my hand with a cheerful, "It's a real beaut,
isn't it? Have fun."

My arrival home brought Tom, the vulture in plaid, to his
front deck to take a good look. Even from a distance he radi-
ated disapproval. I smiled and waved.

The crime-scene van was parked at the curb, the fingerprint person apparently inside. I didn't disturb his work.

Instead, with feelings carefully set on numb neutrality, I
inspected the interior of the limo from end to end. I was
braced to find that the technicians had done anything from
tear seats loose to rip out carpeting in their search for evidence. I did find that the tarp mural had been removed from
the ceiling and folded into a neat square on a seat, apparently
so the technicians could search under it. That was a big plus.
Saved me the trouble.

Finally all that remained was the trunk. I steeled myself as
I lifted the lid, prepared for anything from bloody stains to a
chalk outline.

Nothing like that, but now I saw what DDS Molino had
meant. The trunk was not okay. It had been stripped to bare

metal. What had once been a lushly carpeted compartment was now a stark metal cave, like something abandoned in a junkyard.

I had expected to feel panic or even revulsion when I looked into this space that had held Jerry's body. And I did feel a great rush of horror at the memory. *Murder.*

Yet, oddly, what peering into this empty hole also did was fill me with a fresh surge of anger and determination. The killer wasn't going to get away with this, not if I could help it.

I had just shut the lid on the trunk . . . gently, a slam would have felt disrespectful . . . when JoAnne Metzger came running down the street, waving wildly.

"Andi, you got it back! Oh, and just in time. My niece's wedding is tomorrow afternoon. Can you pick her up and take her to the church, and then to Sea-Tac afterward?"

"Hasn't she already made other arrangements?"

"She'll scrap 'em for a chance to do it in a limousine!"

"But won't you . . . or *she* . . . mind, you know, about the murder?"

"Andi, it was an awful thing, but I don't see that it contaminates the limo. And it would just *make* Tanya's day to have a limousine for her wedding."

I hesitated, but then with a certain recklessness thought, *Why not?* It would be good to have the limo used for some joyful occasion to counteract the grisliness of what had happened in it.

On a practical basis, there was also the fact that I'd probably have to get the trunk repaired before I could sell it. Might as well let the limo itself earn the money to do that.

We settled on a price, something more affordable for JoAnne than the price the limo service outfits had said they'd charge her. She said she'd call me later with addresses and details. I unexpectedly realized I was looking forward to this.

I met the fingerprint technician coming out of the house. We exchanged a few words, but I didn't even try to get any information out of her. I knew she wouldn't tell. After she left, I called a retired guy who did repair work in the neighborhood.

What I unhappily learned when he arrived was that I needed a whole new sliding glass door. He managed to straighten the frame enough that, with sufficient application of muscle, this one could be opened and closed. It still couldn't be locked, but he fixed a rod to brace it. We agreed he'd pick up a new door and install it on Monday.

After he left, I just stood there for a moment, overwhelmed by both the unexpected expense and the cleanup job facing me here in the house. Then I sternly told myself to look on the bright side: the place needed a good going-over anyway. Think how I'd feel if I'd just *done* a big housecleaning, and then this happened.

30

By seven I wasn't done cleaning and putting away, but I quit to shower, change to clean white capris, and add a spritz of the almost-empty bottle of Eternity I hoarded for special occasions. Joella had agreed to come, so I called her when I was ready, and she met me outside. On the way I cut a big bouquet of daisies to take along.

"You've been working so hard. I can drive," she offered.

"Oh, that's okay. We can take my car—" I broke off, and we looked at the elegant black jewel sitting in the driveway, then at each other.

Oh, yes!

I drove out of Secret View Lane airily confident of my ability to handle the limo, only to realize a few minutes later that the gas gauge was sitting on empty. And then to realize that I had no idea where the gas cap was located. I pulled into the first gas station we came to—unfortunately the busiest one in town—and Joella jumped out to look. And discovered I'd pulled in on the wrong side of the gas pumps, of course.

So then I had to back up, with the back end of the limo sticking out there like a long, black target in the midst of a demolition derby. Joella guided me, arms waving wildly, and I jacked the wheel around, feeling as if I were trying to fit a baseball bat into a keyhole.

Sweat ran down my back, and a muscle cramped in my leg. I barely squeaked by a gas pump, missed a fender on a Lincoln by an eyelash, and kissed a trash can into a wild rock 'n' roll. But finally I was lined up properly, though I was hogging two spaces at the tanks to do it. I got out, head ducked in embarrassment, only to be greeted with a round of applause from spectators.

I looked up in astonishment. I'd expected hisses and boos, but people were clapping and whistling as if we'd just put on a command performance. Joella laughed and acknowledged the applause with a sweeping bow . . . at least as sweeping a bow as one can make when thoroughly pregnant.

A young guy gave me a thumbs-up gesture—I was relieved it wasn't a gesture of a different type—and I returned it with giddy relief. Then I thought, *Why not?* and bowed grandly too.

I filled the tank and watched incredulously as the meter rolled up into the stratosphere while gas gurgled into Uncle Ned's oversized tank. He must have wanted to be able to waltz across Texas and back without stopping to refuel.

Fortunately, it was clear sailing out of the gas station, and we drove on to the marina without incident. Although I suspected the effect of my Eternity had been considerably diluted by the deluge of nervous sweat.

Fitz happened to be looking up from the boat when I pulled up to the front edge of the parking lot, and he dashed up to meet us. Behind him, though with considerably less enthusiasm, came son Matt.

"Matt didn't have to go to Tacoma after all," Fitz said. "So he'll be here for dinner."

Matt was looking at the limo as if his opinion of limousines in the neighborhood matched Tom's. "This is the limo your friend was killed in?" he asked.

Of course it was this limo, I muttered to myself. *What did you think, that it was my* other *limo?* But all I said was, "Yes. The sheriff's department let me have it back this morning."

Fitz hadn't seen the limo before, and he walked around it admiringly, giving the tires the ol' testosterone kick. "Wow. Impressive. Want to look at the engine, Matt?"

"No."

Fitz ignored his son's negative response. "Open it up, would you, Andi?"

I slipped back into the driver's seat and poked at various controls until I found a lever that released the hood. Fitz shoved his hands in the pockets of his khaki shorts as he inspected the engine, and I remembered what Matt had said about his father's mechanical expertise.

Standing alongside him I said, "There's the battery."

"Sure is," Fitz agreed with enthusiasm. We exchanged congratulatory glances.

Matt, however, reached into the engine and pulled out what I surprised myself by recognizing as a dipstick to check the oil. "Oil's clean."

"And it's a very safe vehicle," Joella said. "It even has bulletproof windows."

Matt frowned. "And why is that?"

I explained about Uncle Ned's eccentricity and paranoia, adding Cousin Larry's comment that I'd be safe if I ever decided to take up bank robbing.

Matt was not amused. "There's no such thing as actual bulletproof glass," he said. "The correct term is bullet *resistant.* Bullets may not go through it, but they aren't going to bounce off like Ping-Pong balls. Isn't that right, Dad?"

"That's right," Fitz agreed, although he didn't sound happy about having to back up his son's grumpy opinion.

Matt closed the hood. "Nice vehicle. Looks to be in good shape. Too bad the murder puts kind of a stigma on it."

"There's no—no stigma!" I argued testily. "A neighbor has already asked me to use it for her niece's wedding tomorrow."

"Hey, great," Fitz said. "You're in business!" To Matt he added, "Andi is thinking about starting her own limousine service."

Matt just folded his arms and scowled as if I'd announced I was going into business taking local terrorists on scouting jaunts. "I hope you're prepared for a mountain of red tape and regulations and permits. And you'd better be loaded with insurance. People like to sue, you know," he added gloomily.

"Andi is very competent at that sort of thing," Fitz said. "She knows all about insurance."

I appreciated the vote of confidence, but I had to admit I'd never thought about such complications as permits. And it occurred to me now that my liability policy might *not* extend to cover a new vehicle being used to transport paying customers. F&N handled property and life insurance, not vehicle insurance, so I had no experience in that area.

We went on board then, where Fitz had a barbecue grill set up in the cockpit area. I gave him the article I'd cut out of the newspaper, along with the bouquet of daisies.

"Hey, Shastas, aren't they?" He sounded delighted. "Thanks."

"It's a really good photo of you in the newspaper," I added.

"What can I say? I'm photogenic. Aging like fine wine."

Matt unexpectedly laughed, reminding me that I probably shouldn't take his grumpiness too seriously. "What you are is a senior citizen full of hot air."

Joella asked if she could see inside the boat, and Matt looked pleased and motioned her through the cabin door. Fitz went inside for a vase and then set it and daisies on a little table near the grill.

By the time Matt and Joella returned, a fragrant scent of barbecuing chicken drifted from the grill, and Fitz and I were enthusiastically discussing daisies.

"I've had really good luck with those Cape Town Blues in the window box in the galley," he said. "They don't get as much sun there as daisies need, but I set the box outside when I can."

"He babies those daisies as if they were—"

"The grandchildren you've never gotten around to providing me?" Fitz asked tartly.

To head off what looked like trouble brewing, I jumped in. "I've never tried Cape Town Blues, but I had good luck growing the dwarf Snowcap variety in indoor pots."

Matt looked at Joella. "How do you feel about daisies?"

"I guess I can take 'em or leave 'em," Joella admitted, and he awarded her an approving smile.

A few minutes later we were sitting on the padded bench seats surrounding the cockpit, with plates on our laps. The marina lay in the shadow of the hills around the bay now. Fitz's chicken was golden on the outside, tender and tasty inside. Crisp salad, heavy on the alfalfa sprouts. Garlic French bread toasted on the barbecue.

As Fitz and I had agreed, we didn't talk about the murder, but after we'd eaten, he said, "Andi and I are going to take a stroll around the marina and look at the other boats, okay?"

Joella said, "Sure," and Matt, though he gave the two of us a suspicious glance, asked if she'd like to go inside and see what was on TV.

Fitz and I walked out on one of the side docks that branched off the main dock and, with a circling of seagulls squawking in hope of a handout, sat on a bench at the end. I told him about my late-night visit from Elena and her warning about husband Donny.

"So I think he's a pretty strong candidate. He had motive and opportunity, plus a gun and the expertise to use it."

"Don't count Big Daddy Sutherland out yet," Fitz said. He went on to tell me that when he called Shoreline Timber, he'd asked about Benton Sutherland's availability for an interview for an article he was working on.

"What article?" I cut in.

"I might write an article; who knows?" He gave an airy wave. "I've done a few. Anyway, they said they doubted he'd be in this area in the near future, because—get this—he'd recently spent several days here."

"Did you pin them down on a date?"

"He arrived three days before Jerry's murder and left the day after it. Although the woman I talked to didn't phrase it that way, of course."

Interesting. Also interesting that no one back in Georgia had clued Ryan in on this trip. "What was he doing here?"

"Holding meetings with management, touring the facilities, talking with workers, etc. But not so busy, I'm thinking, that he couldn't have made a quick jaunt down to Vigland to get rid of a bothersome son-in-law. Which I suspect may have been the real reason for his trip."

"But what about the break-in at my place last night? He couldn't have done that."

Fitz's eyebrows scrunched thoughtfully. "That seems to point more toward the Donny guy, all right."

"Unless Big Daddy made a return trip."

"I'll make another phone call to Sutherland's office in Georgia and try to find out if he's been out here again."

"And I'll see if Elena can tell me anything about Donny's whereabouts during the break-in time."

When we got back to the boat, Fitz dished up strawberry shortcake with whipped cream for dessert.

Then Matt, obviously knowing his father and I hadn't gone off to look at boats, said, "I suppose you two have now worked up some wild James Bond scheme for capturing the murderer?"

"What we really need is a Batmobile," Fitz said. "It's hard to be a real crime buster without a Batmobile." He frowned and spoke as seriously as if he'd been searching the classifieds for a used model.

"Dad, you've got to be serious about this," Matt said. "You're both getting in way over your heads. Murder isn't for amateurs. It's not a TV show."

Fitz sighed. "It isn't as if we're trying to corner the killer in a dark alley."

"Doesn't it occur to you that if the killer didn't find whatever he was looking for when he broke into Andi's house, he may decide to try some other tactic? Like coming after Andi herself?"

It wasn't a thought that had occurred to me, and I felt something cold and slimy slither up my spine. "Why would he do that?"

"He may think this guy who was killed—what was his name?"

"Jerry," Fitz supplied.

"He may think this Jerry confided in Andi before he was killed, and Andi may know where whatever it is he's after is located."

"But Jerry didn't confide in me—"

"The killer doesn't know that. He may even think the two

of you were involved together in whatever it was that got Jerry killed. You go stomping around in this like the Keystone Kops, and he may decide to eliminate *you* like he did Jerry."

Much like what Elena had said regarding her husband. Only somehow it sounded even more menacing in Matt's angry tones. Even Fitz looked worried, and Joella gave a little gasp.

"You're in danger, both of you, don't you realize that? You're daisy detectives"—Matt flicked his fingers disdainfully at the flowers in the vase—"meddling in a shark-eat-shark world."

I thought Fitz might be getting angry too. Matt was really laying it on about our level of amateurism and incompetence.

But after a long moment, Fitz leaned back, a thoughtful look on his face. "The Daisy Detectives," he mused. Then he smiled. "I like it! There we have it, Andi, a ready-made name for our private investigative business when we add it to your limousine service."

Matt made no further comment, just made a noise that sounded something like *aarrghh*, threw up his hands in disgust, and stalked off into the cabin.

I looked at Fitz. "A detective business *and* a limousine service? Not for me, thank you. All I want is to find Jerry's murderer, and then I'm out of the murder business."

Fitz smiled. "I just like to rattle his cage now and then. Matt can be a fussbudget at times." He hesitated. "Although he made a pretty good point there about the killer thinking you may know more than you do."

Right.

Now my cage felt a little rattled too.

31

With the sliding door not yet fixed, and with both Fitz and Joella nagging at me about safety, I spent another night on Joella's sofa. Next day, JoAnne's niece's wedding went off without a hitch. I wore my snappy uniform, picked Tanya up at her parents' home, and afterwards ferried the newlyweds to Sea-Tac. JoAnne had invited me into the reception, where I glommed onto some spectacular crab hors d'oeuvres and a hunk of wedding cake, picked up a nice check for a few hours' enjoyable work . . . and landed another limo job!

An elegantly coiffed and dressed older woman named Trudy Vandervort, someone JoAnne knew from a library fund-raising thing, said she'd like to hire the limo for a trip up to the Port Townsend area the following Tuesday. It was a considerable distance up to the north end of the Olympic Peninsula, so I quoted her a fairly hefty price, to which she responded, "Fine," and wrote out a check for half the amount on the spot. She gave me her home address, and I agreed to be there at two thirty on Tuesday.

Hey, maybe I *was* in the limousine business!

I INTENDED TO go into the DMV on Monday morning to get the title on the limo transferred and check on that ominous permit business Matt had mentioned, but Letty Bishop called before I got out of the house. She said the higher-ups in San Diego had just approved her request for an assistant. Could I come in right away, this morning, in fact? There wouldn't be any benefits with the job, but the hourly rate sounded good.

Oh, yes! With no steady job in sight, I needed this.

A complication, however. I was already scheduled for the limo trip up to Port Townsend Tuesday afternoon. I called the woman, explained my problem, and asked if starting the trip later in the day, about five thirty, would be okay.

"That's fine. Just so you get there before dark. The Captain doesn't like to travel at night."

"There'll be two of you for the trip, then?"

"No, dear, just the Captain. He'll be staying with my niece while I go on a cruise."

That settled, I rushed to the F&N offices. Letty immediately put me to work on some client computer files that had been corrupted and on which information had to be resurrected from their original insurance applications.

On my lunch hour I tried to call Elena, but someone in the publicity department at the pet food company said she was out for a few days. I didn't have a home phone number for her, so that temporarily ended that.

Fitz had better luck. He called that evening from near Port Orchard, where the *Miss Nora* was anchored for the night, to say he'd talked with Ben Sutherland's offices in Georgia. A woman there had told him Mr. Sutherland was "out of the office for a few days," but she wouldn't give any further information.

"So," Fitz said, "he could be off trying to add some other unfortunate creature to the trophies on his wall—"

"Or he could have been here in Vigland when my house was broken into!"

"He could still be here, trying to decide how big a danger you pose to him," Fitz warned. "Is the door fixed yet?"

"No. The repairman called and said he had the new door, but his back went out, and he has to see a chiropractor before he can do anything."

"Andi, I don't like you being there alone with the door broken."

"The repairman fixed a metal rod to brace it, but I'll stay with Joella again, okay?"

He hesitated, as if doubtful about our joint competence to hold off a burglar. Finally he said, "Just don't take any chances, okay? Call 911 if you hear *anything*."

I DECIDED TO drive the limo to work the following morning. That would enable me to go directly to Trudy Vandervort's house after work. When Letty found out the limo was right there in the parking lot, she got excited and begged for a ride on our lunch hour. I'd have taken her anyway, but when she offered lunch at The Log House, one of Vigland's nicer establishments, as an inducement, I gave her my best bow and sweep of hand. "Your chariot awaits, madam."

When we went out at noon, she was chattering gaily about the only other time she'd ever ridden in a limousine. When she saw the car, she slapped her palms to her plump cheeks. "Oh, Andi, it's so elegant! How can you even think of selling it?"

I was just ushering her into the rear door when Mr. Findley and Mr. Randolph started across the parking lot. I'd angled the limo behind a tree, because it was too long for the parking spaces, so they didn't see it until they were almost behind it. Mr. Findley stopped short. His gaze went from limo to me and back to limo.

"What's this doing here?" he demanded as if I'd appropriated his private parking space, though I'd been careful not to do that.

"This is Andi McConnell," Letty interposed. "She used to work here, and now she's come back to help out temporarily. We were just going to lunch."

"Andi McConnell . . ." Mr. Findley frowned as he studied me, as if he thought he should know me but couldn't quite place either the name or face.

Mr. Randolph just looked at his watch. I was grateful he didn't appear to be connecting me with the belly-buster attack in the hallway.

Then Mr. Findley apparently made a connection, because a lightbulb look came on in his eyes. "Is this the limousine in which Jerry Norton—"

"I'm afraid so."

More connections apparently snapped into place. "You were a friend of his, weren't you?"

Unfortunately, connections snapped in Mr. Randolph's mind too. "You're the idiot who crashed into me a few days ago!"

Mr. Findley, bless his heart, ignored that. "A terrible thing, Jerry's death. An *incredible* thing. Could I speak to you privately after lunch, Mrs. McConnell?"

"Yes, of course."

Lunch at The Log House was fantastic, shrimp scampi and grilled salmon, although I'd have enjoyed it more if I hadn't been nervous about meeting with Mr. Findley. Did he object to my temporary employment at F&N? Had he power to veto it? Could he think I had something to do with Jerry's death?

A few minutes after we were back at work, Mr. Findley called down and asked me to come up to his office. Once I was there, he motioned me to a sofa rather than the chair by his desk and perched on the arm of the couch himself.

"I hope you don't mind my asking to speak to you."

Flimsy white lie. "Not at all."

"I've been so upset ever since Jerry's . . . demise. *Baffled* by it, in fact. We were quite close, as you may know. Not as close as the two of you were, of course, but he was supposed to transfer to San Diego as my top assistant."

"He'd told me about the transfer. I think he was quite excited about it."

"I just can't imagine anyone doing such a terrible thing to Jerry. He was very well liked, you know. Competent, knowledgeable, a real go-getter. And then to have all his computer equipment at the condo stolen too. Very strange."

I was surprised Mr. Findley knew about the burglary. "The sheriff's department has been rather closemouthed about what happened at the condo. Not many people know about it."

"I heard about it from a detective. They were asking if any company information could have been on the computer, but I told them I doubted it. Jerry was very conscientious about company confidentiality. A man with the kind of character we could all admire."

I might quibble about some details of Jerry's fine character, but I just said, "My own thought is that the theft may have had something to do with his computer Web site business."

"I was never familiar with details of the business, although I understood it was quite successful. And something Jerry enjoyed doing."

"I've mentioned it to Detective Sergeant Molino."

"Do you think the murder may also have been connected with that business?"

"I think it's possible. Or perhaps something to do with a . . . former relationship." I tossed that out hoping Mr. Findley might jump in with something about Elena, but he just looked puzzled.

"Have *you* any ideas about who could have murdered him?" I asked.

"No, not really." He stood up and paced back and forth in front of his desk as if frustrated. "I've wondered if someone resented his getting the transfer when so many others here at F&N were let go. Although that hardly seems sufficient motive for murder. And then I've wondered . . ."

"Yes?"

"I don't know quite how to put this, but I had the impression Jerry may have gotten himself involved in something . . . troublesome. I have no idea what, but on that very Friday he was murdered, he'd asked to talk privately with me the following Monday. I had the feeling he was about to confide something of a very serious nature to me. But then, come Monday, he was . . . dead."

Mr. Findley didn't tear up, but I had the impression he was about to, and I felt uncomfortable. Especially remembering that Jerry'd had a lot less nice things to say about Mr. Findley than Mr. Findley was saying about him.

"Yes, it was a terrible shock."

"You found the body, didn't you? I remember reading that in the newspaper. Jerry was at your house that night, and then his body was found in the limousine."

I swallowed. His saying it brought back all too clearly the appalling vision of Jerry's body lying there in the trunk. I hadn't been totally successful at blocking it before this, but I had managed to stuff it back where it wasn't sticking out in my mind like the tail of the limo in traffic. Now it was right upfront in vivid color again.

Mr. Findley unexpectedly seemed aware of my distress. He reached over and gave me an awkward pat on the shoulder. "I keep thinking about what losing Jerry means to me, and I know that's selfish. It must be much worse for you, losing someone you loved."

"A friend and I have been asking around, trying to come up with any information that might help the police locate the murderer."

"If I can do anything, will you let me know? The detectives asked me a lot of questions, but I don't think I was much help. But if there's anything I can do . . ."

"Thank you. I'll remember that."

Mr. Findley stroked his chin, and then, as if he were making a deliberate effort to pull himself together, his shoulders straightened and his tone went brisk. "Well, Mrs. McConnell, we're glad to have you back with us here at F&N, even though it will be for only a short time. I'm wondering . . . this is off the subject, but is the limousine available for hire?"

"I'm taking a passenger up to Port Townsend after work today, but I understand that if I'm going to start a real limousine service, there are permits involved."

Mr. Findley grimaced. "Red tape. It's a nightmare, isn't it? We added onto the house last year, and you wouldn't believe what we had to go through. But what I'm thinking is, if you could manage it, I have a meeting to attend with some of the executives of Friends & Neighbors Worldwide. That's the name of the new, merged company, you know."

"You'll be going down to San Diego?" I asked, wondering what this had to do with me and my limo.

"No, Mr. Delgrade has a vacation home on a lake—a private lake—northwest of town. The meeting will be held there." He frowned. "Making a tax deduction out of what is basically a vacation trip." The frown reversed to a guilty smile. "Though you don't need to tell anyone I said that."

A bit of friction between the F&N transferees from

Vigland and the executives already established in the other company?

"I'm not sure of the exact date yet. Sometime within the next couple weeks, I think. I guess I should just come right out and admit that what I'd like to do is impress these guys. Mr. Delgrade calls his place his 'hard-times cabin' and acts as if it's just some shack in the woods, but I'll bet anything it's really a showplace fancy lodge. You know the kind." He grimaced. "Fireplace big enough to roast a bull. Kitchen fit for a five-star restaurant. Ten bathrooms."

"I'm not really familiar with expensive lodges."

"They're looking on us up here as a bunch of unsophisticated country hicks, and arriving in a limousine might give me a bit of an advantage. If Jerry were alive, he'd be coming with me, of course. I really depended on him." He moved his shoulders as if they were stiff. "Well, I shouldn't be laying all that on you. My problem, not yours."

"I'll be glad to do it for you, Mr. Findley," I said quickly. I found a vulnerable Mr. Findley a much more sympathetic figure than the stuffy jerk I'd always thought he was. "We hicks have to stick together."

As soon as I said that, I thought maybe it was a mistake and he'd take offense, but he smiled.

"Right. No wonder Jerry was . . ." He hesitated as if uncertain how to put it. "Attracted to you. And remember, if there's anything I can do to help in bringing his killer to justice, just let me know."

32

I changed to my uniform in the ladies' room at F&N and arrived at the Vandervort place only five minutes late. The house topped a forested hill south of town, with spectacular views of the south end of Puget Sound and Olympic Mountains to the north. Trudy Vandervort herself, in pink shorts, diamond tennis bracelet, and dangling earrings with some pink gem I couldn't name, answered my ring of the doorbell.

"Oh, there you are! And don't you look spiffy! I'll write you a check for the balance, and then I'll get the Captain."

I peered around. The house wasn't quite a mansion, but probably as close as I'd ever get to one. The foyer was bigger than my living room, a graceful staircase winding to the second floor; off to the left was a living room with an enormous fireplace and impressive oil paintings of what I assumed were rich ancestors.

A moment later she returned with the check in one hand and a huge brass cage in the other. In the cage I was astonished to see an enormous, brightly colored parrot.

"You're taking your parrot along?"

"Captain, this is Andi McConnell. She'll be your chauffer today." She made a little kissy moue at the bird.

"You're not going?"

"No, of course not. I told you, I'm going on a cruise." She clapped her fingertips over her mouth as she peered at the bird. "Oh, I didn't mean to say that in front of the Captain." In a surreptitious aside she whispered, "I let him think I was doing this just as a vacation for him."

I blinked. "You want . . . I mean, you've hired me to drive a *parrot* up to Port Townsend?" *A parrot you find it necessary to fib to?*

Her eyes went a little flinty. "Is there a problem?"

I'd been picturing the Captain as a snowy-haired old salt, her father probably, maybe a retired naval officer. But on second thought, with substantial check in hand, what did I care if my passenger sported feathers instead of hair?

I shook my head hastily. "No, certainly not. No problem. Does he need any, uh, special care?"

"He likes company. Perhaps you could leave the partition open and talk to him occasionally."

Lightbulb going on. "I could ask my assistant to come along. She can ride in back with him. It won't cost anything extra."

She beamed. "That's very nice of you. I'd appreciate that."

"Does he talk?" I asked as we trundled out to the limo.

"If he wants to."

We set the cage on the floor of the limo, along with a box of food and toys, which included a Rubik's Cube. I decided he probably couldn't actually work it. But I wouldn't try to match wits with him, just in case. I drove off with Trudy standing there waving, tissue to her nose, as if she might be having second thoughts about all this.

"Okay, Captain, you want to talk?" I inquired as we headed back toward town, speaking loudly enough to be heard through the open partition. "What's your opinion on Einstein's theory of relativity?"

I didn't want to insult him with *Captain want a cracker?* For all I knew, maybe he could work that Rubik's Cube.

Silence. He probably figured I wouldn't know what he was talking about even if he explained it with equations. I tried another tack. "Can you say your name? Captain?"

More silence, but I had the feeling he was muttering to himself, *I know my name, dummy. And I could say it if I wanted to. I just don't want to.*

I made a detour by the Sweet Breeze and ran in to ask Joella if she'd like to come along. She was just getting off work, and I was surprised when she hesitated. Joella was usually so eager for any out-of-routine activity, but she did look a bit frazzled today. She stretched her shoulders and rubbed her lower back.

"Come on out and meet my passenger," I suggested, thinking the drive might do her good. "I understand he likes company."

Joella gave me a puzzled look, but when she saw the Captain, she clapped her hands delightedly. "My grandmother used to have a parrot. He liked to ride around on my head and yell, 'Comin' through, comin' through.'"

For his part, the Captain looked at Joella in her long, fluttery sundress, one of her Goodwill picks, and declared, "Bodacious babe!"

She laughed. "It isn't often I get a compliment like that. I have to come now, don't I?"

She checked out with Neil in the bakery, climbed into the limo with the Captain, and off we went. We'd pick up her car when we got back.

"Bodacious babe," the Captain repeated as he strutted in his cage.

It was cute the first few times, but after about the twenty-ninth repetition, the cute had definitely paled. Then he abruptly switched to TV commercials, first a ditty from some local real-estate company, then one about a detergent.

Joella and I both laughed when he did a lusty version of the Oscar Mayer wiener song. Maybe we shouldn't have, because he did it again. And again. All the way to Port Townsend, over and over, that cheerful, and eventually nerve-scraping, "Oh, I wish I were an Oscar Mayer wiener."

I was ready to stuff him in a hot-dog bun by the time niece Elaine took him off our hands, although he was back in silent mode when I handed her the cage.

"It's so hard to get him to say anything, isn't it?" she complained.

Count your blessings, was my silent advice

"You want to sit up here with me?" I asked Joella.

"No, I think I'll lie down in back, if that's okay with you. I didn't sleep very well last night."

The frazzled look hadn't gone away, I noticed. "Sure. Take a nap. Want to get a bite to eat first?"

"I'm not hungry right now. I had a big corned beef sandwich for lunch. But maybe later."

I turned the radio to soothing music and enjoyed the peaceful drive back toward Vigland. Beautiful views of broad Hood Canal, which was actually a natural cut running from the sea deep into the Olympic Peninsula, water like ruffled pewter. The dense forests lining the road, with green underbrush thick as a tangled tapestry. All the interesting names. Quilcene. Dabob Bay. Duckabush. Hamma Hamma.

The curvy road required full attention, but traffic was light. Dusk had settled in now, and I had the headlights on and was remembering that there was a place to get really good oyster soup along here somewhere.

Then came Joella's voice, a small, thin voice, through the open partition. "Andi, I don't feel so good."

I looked up and in the rearview mirror saw her face, pale and ghostly in the dim light. "Maybe you're hungry. It's getting late."

"I'm not hungry. I probably shouldn't have eaten that corned-beef sandwich at lunch. My stomach doesn't feel so great."

"I have Tums in my purse. Do you want a couple?"

"Okay."

I dug one-handed in my purse and handed her the plastic carton. "How long have you been feeling like this?"

"I wasn't feeling great even before we left Vigland. My back's been hurting all day. I'd probably have gone home early, except there was no one to take my place."

"Why didn't you say something earlier?"

Actually, I could guess why. She was still embarrassed about that rush to the hospital with indigestion. But I felt a jolt of alarm now. Backache. Abdominal pain. Another false alarm? Or could this be the real thing?

"It can't be labor," she added. "I'm not due for at least another month. I really shouldn't have eaten that sandwich."

"Does it feel like last time?"

"Well, kind of. Except now I get all tight and crampy . . . and then it kind of lets go. It didn't do that last time."

That had the scary sound of contractions to me. I pressed down on the gas pedal. Surely there was plenty of time, but it wouldn't hurt to hurry along. "Are the pains coming regularly, so you can time how far apart they are?"

"About five minutes, I think."

Five minutes! Wasn't that awfully close? I tried not to panic. But first babies take a long time to arrive, right? Sarah had been in labor almost eighteen hours when Rachel was born. I just hoped this one knew the proper schedule. Even more, I hoped this *was* just another bout of indigestion. Maybe the Tums would take care of it. But I wasn't going to take a chance.

"I think I'll swing by the hospital when we get to Vigland. We're only about thirty miles away. You lie down, okay?"

"Okay."

My eyes kept flicking from the odometer to the clock to the partition into the back. After five miles I said softly, hoping the pains had let up and Joella had drifted off to sleep, "Joella? You okay?"

"I . . . I'm all . . . wet. Maybe we should stop and see if I'm bleeding. I really . . . hurt."

I spotted a pull-out area on the canal side of the road up ahead. I parked the limo and raced around back. A dim light, along with other pinpoints of light under the wine racks, came on when I opened the door. Just what we needed right now. A romantic ambiance.

Joella was lying on her side on the long, sofalike seat that ran along the side of the limo, sweat beading her forehead even though it was comfortably cool here. I couldn't see any blood, but I scrunched the gauzy fabric of her dress. Wet.

Did that mean her water had broken? I had no idea how much wetness would signify that it had. A gallon? A tablespoon? "We've got to get you to the hospital right now, before—"

"I'm not sure there's time."

"Babies don't come this fast. It's not like going through the express lane at Wal-Mart!"

She gave a small cry, fists clenched and face twisted with pain. "Wanna bet?"

33

The he pain retreated. I grabbed the hem of her long, gauzy skirt and wiped her forehead.

"Can you look at me, Andi?" she asked.

I peered at her in the dim light. How come ol' Ned didn't have something in the 300-watt range in here so he could see to count his millions? "You look a little sweaty. And pale, but—"

"Not my face, Andi. I don't need to know how my face looks."

"Oh!" I gulped as it got through to me what she meant. "I can't do that! I'm no doctor. I wouldn't know what to look for—"

"You look to see if there's a *baby*, okay?" she asked, her tone going uncharacteristically tart at my reluctance. Another pain brought a louder cry this time. "Help me . . . get undressed."

I helped her off with her underthings and warily lifted the flowered sundress. In my own lone pregnancy, I was under anesthesia for the caesarean, with the doctor picking the date, and none of what was happening to Joella ever happened to me.

"Tell me what you see," she gasped as another contraction clamped down on her.

"I . . . I think I see something . . ."

"What, Andi? Daisies? Or *what*?"

Not a daisy, that was for sure. "I . . . I think it may be the top of the baby's head."

But that couldn't be! It was way before Joella's due date. We weren't in a hospital. And she hadn't been in labor all that long. Unless maybe you counted her back pain this afternoon, and the time *before* she told me about the contractions . . . But, no, this couldn't be the baby coming. I was surely mistaken about what I was seeing.

"Maybe you'd better call 911."

Which is when I finally realized that you can't argue a baby out of coming. I wiggled my upper body through the open partition and grabbed my purse from the seat up front. I dialed 911, afraid we were in a dead zone and nothing would go through. But, no, there was a person, a real, live person.

"I'm in a limousine out here on the highway to Port Townsend, and my friend is pregnant, and I think I can see the top of the baby's head—"

"Hey, hey, slow down," the woman soothed. "You're where, and what is happening?"

I tried again. "We're parked alongside the road—"

"In a limousine?"

"*Yes* . . ."

She let the peculiarity of the limousine go and led me through the more important points of what was happening with Joella and our exact location. "Okay, I'm sending an ambulance."

"Do you need a description of the limousine? It's long and black—"

"Somehow I doubt there'll be so many limousines parked alongside the road that we need to identify this particular one."

"Oh. Yeah."

"I'm going to connect with a doctor in the emergency room at the hospital. You won't be able to talk to him directly, but you can talk through me, okay?"

"Okay." I wiped my damp palm on the pant leg of the uniform.

A little silence, and then she was back. "Okay, he's on the line now. He wants you to look again and tell him what you see now."

I looked, cell phone scrunched awkwardly between shoulder and cheek. "I don't see anything! What do I *do?*"

A moment as she passed that information along. "He says don't do anything. Everything sounds normal. You can see the top of the baby's head when the mother pushes; then it goes out of view between pushes."

"But it isn't time for pushes," I argued. "She isn't due for at least a month. She hasn't been in labor long enough!"

"Should I push?" Joella cut in. "I don't think I can keep from pushing! Oh!" Another gasp.

"Yes, there, I see it again!" I yelled into the phone.

"He wants to know how long it is between contractions."

"I think it's down to maybe two or three minutes. Or less."

"Has the mother's water already broken, or is the bag still around the baby's head?"

"I think maybe it broke earlier. Everything's all wet. I don't see anything around the head. When I can see it."

"Good."

Doctor and 911 woman walked me through it, like leading a blind person through a landscape littered with booby traps and sinkholes. Through contractions that got ever closer together. Through Joella's screams and panting gasps. Through her abdomen feeling like a drum about to burst when I fearfully touched it. Through my panic. Through half-dollar-sized glimpses of fine, dark baby hair. Through a check on Joella's pulse, me with hand clenched around her wrist while trying to look at the second hand on my watch and keep from losing my shoulder-to-cheek grip on the cell phone.

I found myself in nonstop prayer. *God, take care of her, please. Take care of the baby. Don't let anything go wrong. Keep me from doing anything wrong or dumb!*

Where is that ambulance? Why isn't it here yet? I didn't realize I'd yelled the words until the woman's voice assured me the ambulance was on its way.

"Be patient. It's coming. You're quite a ways out there. What's your friend's name?"

"Joella . . . but she shouldn't be having the baby yet! It's not time. Doesn't it take hours and hours for a first baby?"

"I don't think babies pay much attention to statistics."

Right. This one apparently hadn't a clue.

"The baby's head is coming farther out now . . . but it's facedown!"

Nothing wrong there. Facedown was good, the doctor via the 911 woman assured me. Was the umbilical cord wrapped around the baby's neck? No. That was good too. Now I should wipe out the baby's mouth. I stood up and frantically felt in the pockets of the chauffeur's uniform. Paper napkin from Tanya's wedding reception! It had silver wedding bells on one side, but it was clean and unused.

No, baby, you weren't born with a silver spoon in your mouth, but you did have silver bells! The head was out now. I knelt again and followed their instructions about wiping.

"I can see a shoulder . . . but it isn't moving! Does that mean it's stuck?"

"Don't pull," the woman said, almost yelling now. "Just let things happen naturally! Don't pull."

Pull? Like I was trying to yank an oversized carrot out of the ground? You've got to be kidding, lady. No way. The last thing I had in mind was pulling.

"Doctor says just try to catch the baby, support it as it comes out. And be careful! Babies are slippery."

Slippery. Yes, oh yes, indeed. Very slippery. Shoulders, arms, tiny hands! Long, agonizing pause in the action, while I kept up my one-sided dialogue with God. *Help her, help her, help her! She's in Your hands. The baby's in Your hands. I'm in Your hands!* Body, legs—

Another mind-bending push from Joella, and I stared in astonishment, my throat choked up. Head, body, arms, legs, itsy-bitsy feet. It was all there. "I-I have a baby in my hands!"

God, thank You! A baby! A miracle right here in my hands!

"Is the baby breathing?"

"I don't know. . . . No, I don't think so!" Plunge from awe back to panic mode.

"Hold it upside down—"

"*Upside down?*"

"Upside down. By the ankles. But hold on tight. Tap the bottom of its feet—"

I did, and a lusty yowl followed that so startled me I almost dropped the yowler.

"She's breathing!"

"Good. Hold her normally now. But don't pull on the cord."

I snuggled the baby up close between Joella and me, kneeling with the baby in my arms. She was still howling, as if, now that she'd found out how to do it, she didn't intend to quit. She was definitely breathing, and so was Joella, and that was reassuring, but—

"Now what?" I asked frantically. "Doesn't something have to be done with the cord? Cut or something?" I eyed the lifeline that still tied baby and mother together. Inspiration! "I . . . I always carry a pocketknife in my purse."

"The doctor says just leave it alone." The woman sounded alarmed. "The cord doesn't have to be cut immediately. Don't try to do anything. The paramedics will take care of everything when the ambulance arrives. *Don't do anything.*"

I got the gist of that frantic message. Leave it alone, lady! Don't start sawing away like you're trying to hack the rope on a boat anchor in two. Not that I wanted to cut anything anyway.

But I'd have done it if they'd said it had to be done, I realized. *You'd have helped, wouldn't You, God?*

"Everything okay?" the woman asked.

"Joella, are you okay?"

She tried to lift her head to see down to where I was still on my knees. "Is my baby okay?"

"She's fine. She's wonderful. She's a baby!"

Voice from the cell phone. "The doctor says now you should just wrap the baby in something and lay it on the mother's abdomen."

New panic. "Wrap it in *what*?" We weren't exactly rolling in receiving blankets here.

"My skirt," Joella said. "Your jacket. Anything!"

I tore off the jacket of my chauffeur's uniform, glad it was nicely lined with silky stuff, and got it wrapped around the baby. I laid her on Joella's abdomen.

Somebody gave a relaxed sigh. Joella? The baby? Me? Maybe all three of us.

Then I just looked at what we had here. A baby. Where before there was one, now there were two!

"I'm a mother," Joella said, in the wondering way of some astronaut announcing, *Hey, here I am, on the far side of the moon.*

And I suddenly felt God right there, just as if He were

standing beside me, looking over my shoulder with satisfaction at this new life. God and His miracle of creation that had happened right before my eyes. I'd been present when Sarah was born, obviously. I'd been awed when I came out from under the anesthesia and she was there. But this—! To see it all happen, to hold this new creation in my hands the very moment it happened! Could anyone experience this and *not* believe in God?

"Hey, are you still there?" Tiny voice coming from the cell phone that I'd dropped in my struggle with the jacket. I picked it up.

"I'm here." In the distance I could hear a faint wail. "I think I hear the ambulance."

"Good. How's the mother doing?"

"There's a lot of blood . . ."

"The doctor says having babies is a messy business. Don't panic."

Joella gave a muffled groan as she shifted on the limo seat. "Next time, I am going to camp out at the hospital. No more of this do-it-yourself stuff."

"The mother is grumpy but doing fine," I said to the 911 woman.

"The doctor says congratulations. To both of you."

The ambulance wailed to a stop beside the limo. The 911 woman and I ended our conversation, and I thanked God for her too.

The guys in white got Joella and the baby on a stretcher. She touched my hand as I followed the stretcher to the ambulance.

"Thanks, Andi," she whispered. She sounded weaker now than she had in the midst of the birth. "I think I made a mess of your nice limousine."

"Limousine, shmimozine. Who cares? Think what a story

you'll have to tell your baby when she's older! How many people can say they were born in a limousine?"

And then I realized maybe Joella might not know this baby when it was older, never have a chance to tell her the story of a zero-to-sixty-in-thirty-seconds-type birth in a limousine alongside the road.

This was no time to talk, and yet I asked anyway. "Can you do it, Jo? Can you really give her up?"

But the paramedics were already scooting her into the ambulance, and there was no answer. I wasn't sure she'd heard me anyway.

Perhaps just as well. If she'd already made up her mind . . . The ambulance pulled away, siren wailing again. I leaned against the limousine for a few minutes, catching my breath, my legs feeling prickly as they returned to normal after kneeling so long. The rocky beach at the edge of Hood Canal was only a few feet below the road, and I scrambled down to wash my hands.

Then I just stood there looking at the forested hills on the far side, the glimmer of stars above gently reflected in the deep water.

Thank You, God. And then that didn't seem enough, so even though I figured God knew my thoughts, I said it aloud. "Thank You, God. Thank You for bringing Joella's baby safely into the world."

No reply, and yet I had the funny feeling that somewhere out there, God was smiling. Probably He didn't care what I thought, but I couldn't help saying it anyway. "Good work, God."

What came now with Joella and the baby? *It's in Your hands, God.*

Yet even as I felt so very sure not only of God's existence but His very presence in those moments, as if He had reached out and touched me, I also felt very small, very ignorant.

So much I didn't know.

There'd been another baby, far back in time. Jesus. The Son of God. The Jesus Joella spoke of as if He were a friend and confidant.

Who was this Jesus, beyond a baby in a manger, celebrated at Christmas? How did He fit into my newfound awareness of God? Was tonight the shove Joella said I might get?

34

I was walking into the ER before I realized I was covered with blood and probably should have gone home to change. Then I decided not to worry about it. Blood was a hospital's stock in trade.

I asked about Joella, but she'd arrived only twenty minutes or so before I did, and they didn't have anything to report yet. I headed off the "Are you family?" question by announcing I was Joella's sister. A stretch of truth, but fortunately the woman was too busy to question it. And after what we'd been through together in the limo, I felt as if I really was kind of an older sister. I was also only now realizing how tired I was.

A couple of hours later, when they could tell me something, it was only that she was sleeping now. So I went on home, showered, and fell into bed, too tired even to check on the sliding glass door.

In the morning, I called the bakery to tell Neil what had happened. The F&N office wasn't open yet, so I called Letty at home to let her know I'd be late getting in, then drove up to the hospital. Vigland General had a generous policy on visitors, and I was allowed to go right up to Joella's room.

She was sitting up, eating breakfast with what looked like a logger's appetite.

"Congratulations." I said it a little awkwardly, because I didn't know how things stood here. I'd heard new babies usually stayed in the same room as the mothers these days, but there was no baby here. Maybe Joella had decided making the break from the very beginning would be best. "Are you okay?"

"Not ready to run a marathon, but pretty good. How about you?"

"I just thought I'd stop in for a minute before I go to work. How long will you be here?"

"They shove new mothers out pretty quick. Tomorrow, I think. But the baby will be here longer. She was early—"

"Don't I know!" A month and a good thirty miles early.

"They want to monitor her for a few days."

Another moment of awkwardness. "I'll get your car brought back to the house and come see you again this evening."

"Don't you want to know what I named her?"

I felt a little catch in my throat. "You named her?"

"Tricia A. Picault."

"That's very nice. What's the *A* for?"

"What do you think it's for? Andalusia!"

"You can't do that to a helpless little baby!"

"She'll be proud of it when I tell her why she has the name."

"Tell her?" I got this big, funny feeling inside, as if I'd swallowed a balloon that was about to burst. "Does that mean—?"

"I'm going to keep her, Andi. I know it's going to be tough, and I have a lot of things to work out, but I could never let her go. I'm amazed now that I ever even considered it. God sent her to me—"

"He did, didn't He?"

"By limousine express!"

I gave her a hug. "Can I see her?"

"Not until later. She's in a special place for preemies, and they have her hooked up to some monitors."

"Is something wrong?" I suddenly felt very proprietary toward this little one. After all, mine had been the first hands in this world to hold her.

"No. She's barely five pounds, so they're just being careful. But I've already nursed her once."

My mind was spinning. A baby in the house! "We're going to need all kinds of things. Diapers, clothes . . . a crib!"

"I've got a stash of stuff that I've picked up now and then," Joella admitted, and I knew then that even though her conscious mind may have been considering letting the baby go, her subconscious had another agenda. "And I was looking at a crib at Goodwill just a couple days ago."

"If it isn't already gone, I'll grab it!"

I started to leave then, but Joella called me back.

"Hey, Andi?"

"Yeah?"

"Thanks. Thanks for being there. Thanks for . . . well, everything."

"The 911 lady also deserves some credit. And God was right in there too, you know."

"I know. I was talking to Him all the time. And now I'm thanking Him, big-time."

"I was praying every minute too."

"You were?"

"I had quite a little conversation with God. I've decided I should . . . you know, go a little deeper into this. I feel as if . . ." I paused, trying to figure out what I really felt. "As if a door has just opened up on a whole new world for me."

"More than a world," she said. "An eternity."

She gave me big smile and a snappy thumbs-up signal, and after a moment, I returned it.

I WAS EVEN later getting to work, because I went by Goodwill and bought the crib. Then to Wal-Mart for a new mattress and blankets. And then the sweetest little pink sleepers that I just couldn't resist. Okay, they were a little big, but Tricia A. would grow into them.

I finally got to the office about ten thirty. Letty was astonished to hear all that had happened since I'd left work yesterday. She said Mr. Findley had stopped by to see me, and I hadn't been at my desk more than fifteen minutes when he showed up again. I started to explain my lateness, but he brushed the explanation aside.

"You remember my telling you about the meeting with the new execs at the 'cabin' out in the woods? You said you could take me there in the limousine?"

"Yes."

"It's set for tomorrow night. Seven thirty. I've never been there, but I have directions. It's supposed to be about a half-hour drive, but I think we'd better allow forty-five minutes in case we have trouble finding it. Can you do it? I'll pay whatever the going rate is."

"You want me to drop you off and leave you there?"

"No, you'll have to wait. But I'll pay for that time too, of course."

He was obviously nervous about the meeting. I might have thought it served him right, because he'd made enough people at F&N nervous when they got an ominous summons to his office. But mostly I felt sorry for him. He apparently wasn't going to be nearly as big a VIP in the newly merged company as he'd been in the old. And maybe, without Jerry to lean on, he realized he could be in for big problems.

THE PHONE WAS ringing when I got home from work. The *Miss Nora* had just gotten into the marina. Fitz didn't know I was back at F&N, so that was a surprise to him, but I skipped over details of the temporary job to tell him the more exciting news about Joella and Tricia A. Picault. He picked me up later, and we drove to the hospital together. He, too, was jubilant that Joella had decided to keep her baby.

This time we did get to see the baby for a minute. Tiny, inside a kind of glass-enclosed container, with wires and tubes hooked here and there and a monitor above with ragged green lines of information. But possessor of a crown of wild, dark hair, a pink face, and wiggly toes.

Joella was positively radiant as we looked through the glass at the baby together. She was supposed to be released as a patient about midmorning the next day, but she would be staying on in a sleeping room so she could be near the baby. Afterward we drove over to the bakery and took Joella's car home.

We were just sitting down to coffee and cookies when the phone rang again. I mouthed the name to Fitz when I found out who it was. *Elena.*

To Elena I asked, "Is everything okay?"

"I've been off work for a couple days. I wasn't feeling too good. And now something's . . . come up."

"Did your husband get that job down in Portland?"

"He's under consideration for it, but he doesn't know for sure yet. Right now he's still working the security guard job. Andi, I need to talk to you. Not on the phone."

"Talk about what?" I asked warily.

"I . . . found something. Something I think may be important."

"About the murder?"

I heard a little gasp at my mention of the *M* word. Was she still afraid Donny might somehow be recording or listening to her phone calls? I scribbled on a scratch pad and shoved it at Fitz. *Elena wants to meet. Says she's found something.*

"Tell her she should go to the police," Fitz whispered.

I repeated that to Elena.

"I need to talk to you and see what you think first."

That intrigued me, I had to admit. "What did you have in mind?"

"I can come to your house tomorrow evening." Regretfully I told her I already had something scheduled. I wished now that I hadn't agreed to help Mr. Findley out. Whatever Elena had found or knew could be the break we needed. I didn't like asking her to postpone a meeting; it gave her too much time to change her mind. But I'd promised Mr. Findley, and I didn't want to back out now, when I knew how jittery he already was about the meeting.

"How about the next evening?" I suggested. I was just about to set a time when Fitz started waving his hands frantically in front of my face.

"Could you hold on a minute?" I asked Elena. I covered the phone.

"She wants to come here to talk to you?"

"Yes—"

"Think about it," he said, his tone low but urgent. "She's told you she's suspicious of her husband. I'm not counting Big Daddy Sutherland out yet, but from everything this Elena has said, husband Donny sounds as if he could be our guy."

"Right. She's scared of him. She's filing for divorce."

"But women in love do strange things. Maybe she's changed her mind. Maybe she's sorry now for telling you anything. Maybe she and her husband have gotten together and decided you know too much. Maybe this meeting she's so eager to set up is to set *you* up."

"Are you still there?" Elena asked.

A new thought rocketed into my head. Was she alone? Or was husband Donny there, orchestrating this call?

Yet if that wasn't true, and she really did have something important to tell me . . .

"How about somewhere other than here?" I suggested to Elena. "Maybe a restaurant over there in Olympia. There's that good Chinese buffet." That busy, crowded, you-couldn't-possibly-murder-anyone-in-here Chinese buffet.

"No. I can't expose myself like that." She paused. "Look, let's just forget the whole thing. Maybe it's nothing anyway."

"Wait! Don't hang up." I hesitated too. This could be like one of those frantic-salesmen pitches: *You have to act now! This offer is only good for the next fifteen minutes!* Blatant attempt at manipulation. Yet there was that edge of panic in her voice. . .

"Okay. Here. Eight o'clock Friday."

Elena hesitated, but finally she said, "That's too early. Make it nine."

"Okay. Nine o'clock on Friday."

She clicked off without saying good-bye.

"I don't think this is a good idea," Fitz muttered. "It feels too much like seeing a black widow, and instead of stomping it, you're saying, 'Here spider, spider. Come right in, little spider.'"

Could be. I juggled possibilities and grabbed the only one that sounded workable. "You have a gun, don't you?"

"A couple of them. Some women's group gave me a little

.22 as an award because they liked the Ed Montrose show. The other one was my dad's."

Not exactly the modern, high-powered weaponry I'd hoped for, but a bullet's a bullet. "Can you shoot them?"

"I'm, uh, sure I can."

That gave me an uneasy clue. "*Have* you shot them?"

"Well, no. Though I certainly know how to aim a gun and pull the trigger. I shot a lot of blanks on the show."

Also not the level of expertise I'd hoped for, but just a gun in hand as threat should do it.

"Okay, here's my plan. You'll hide right behind that door from the kitchen out to the garage, with the door half open. If Elena shows up alone, I let her in. You listen, and if anything goes wrong, you and your gun come through the door like gangbusters. I remember you doing that, back in your Ed Montrose days."

"Maybe Elena will have her own gun. Ed Montrose didn't have to contend with the possibility of a real gun blazing back at him." He rubbed a finger across his chin. "Though it might work. But what if she isn't alone? What if the husband is with her?"

"Then we can figure they're up to something not conducive to my good health, and we could . . . not open the door to them."

My thinking stalled there. Hiding and pretending not to be home when they rang the bell didn't really sound like a high-concept defense.

"Okay, Plan B." Fitz said. "We wait out in the limo, curtains pulled except for a crack to see through. If Elena and her husband both show up, we let them get up to the door—" He broke off as if his thinking also stalled. "But what we need is to get them inside."

"I could leave a note. 'Come on in. I'll be back in a minute.' Then we can trap them inside!"

"Well, uh, actually, I was thinking that when they're inside, we simply drive off."

"Drive off?" I considered the scenario with dismay. "It's not a particularly *heroic*-sounding plan."

"You know the old saying. He who sleuths and runs away, lives to sleuth another day. You want to be a dead hero or a live sleuth?"

"Would Ed Montrose just sneak off?"

"Ed Montrose had very good script writers to save him. We're just muddling around on our own."

True. "Then what? We just drive around until they go away?"

"No. We drive direct to the sheriff's station and tell them our suspicions, even if we don't have ironclad proof. They'll rush back out here and grab Donny with a loaded gun."

I wasn't convinced it was a foolproof plan, and I doubted Fitz was either, but it appeared to be all we had to work with at the moment. Hopefully, Donny *wouldn't* be with Elena, and she'd have some meaningful information. Then I realized Fitz had something else on his mind.

"What's this deal about your being busy tomorrow night?" he asked. "Some big dancing-on-tabletops, swinging-from-chandeliers date?"

Nice of him to think so, but I had to admit the truth. "No, it's business. Mr. Findley at F&N has asked me to take him in the limo to a meeting with some executives at a place out in the woods northwest of town."

"Seems like an odd place for meeting."

"One of them has a vacation house out there. He calls it a cabin, but Findley figures it's some big, ritzy sort of place. He wants to impress them by arriving in the limo."

Fitz's face brightened. "Hey, you aren't even actually *in*

business yet, and already business is booming! Doesn't that tell you something?"

"And you're all eager to help me get going?"

"Of course."

I went to the cleaning closet next to the door leading out to the garage and started digging out supplies. Scrub brush, carpet and upholstery cleaners, bucket, detergent, Lysol spray.

"What's all this?"

I handed him a bucket. "Just a little cleanup job in the limo, detective dear. Come along."

35

We spent a couple of hours on the cleanup job, and I left all the limo doors open to let the upholstery and carpet air out. I junked both the chauffeur's uniform and the T-shirt I'd worn under it, but I still had the second uniform to wear for Mr. Findley's trip.

The next morning, he called me at the office to make sure I'd be there on time with the limo.

"What will you do while Mr. Findley's in the meeting?" Letty asked.

"I'll take a book. The dome light's enough to read by. Or maybe I'll get out and walk around the lake."

Actually, I was looking forward to this . . . good money, much of it for just sitting-around time. Except the more I reflected on Elena's call, the more I thought she'd be coming alone and was onto something important. Maybe, if Mr. Findley's meeting didn't run too late, I'd call Elena when I got home and ask if she could come over then. No, wouldn't work, I realized in frustration. I still didn't have her number.

I grabbed a sandwich for supper, showered, and changed into the chauffeur's uniform. I was just pinning the waist to take up the slack when I heard a commotion outside. I peered out the window.

Moose! Moose on the loose and ripping into my daisy flower bed like a black-and-white digging machine. What was it with that dog and my daisies?

I dashed outside, yelling as I went. "Moose! Moose, you get out of there!"

Dirt flew. Flowers flew. Moose's spotted hind end stuck up in the air, his tail flashing back and forth like a white whip. Something hit me on the knee. I thought it was a rock and started to throw it back at Moose's rump. Then I stopped short. Not a rock. A small, black oblong, with a key chain attached.

Jerry's flash drive! I stared at it in astonishment. He must have lost it when I was chasing him with the shovel and he stumbled and fell in the flower bed. It had been hidden down in there all this time.

"Moose, you stop that! Bad dog!" Lola Sheerson came running down the street, yelling at the top of her lungs, her two kids following. She grabbed Moose's collar and yanked him out of the flower bed.

"Andi, I'm sorry. I don't know how he got out. We fix one place, and he finds or digs another."

"Dad says we should've named him Howdy Ini," the little boy said.

"Houdini?" I guessed.

"Yeah."

Lola apologized again, then added, "You'll probably be glad to hear we're moving. Ol' Tom there will be so glad, he might even break down and smile."

"Oh, Lola, I'll miss you. And Moose too."

Tom Bolton was on his deck, scribbling in a notebook, no doubt making a log of Moose's infractions for the next time he called Animal Control.

"It won't be for a while yet. We'll try to keep Houdini here under control until we go. If the kids weren't so crazy about him . . ." She rolled her eyes suggestively.

I brushed dirt off the flash drive as I went inside. The piece of the puzzle about why Jerry had been in my limo that night had fallen into place. He'd discovered the flash drive was missing, and mistakenly thought he lost it in the limo when he and Joella were riding back there and I bumped them around. He'd come back to look for it and, not wanting to encounter me when he searched, parked some distance away so I wouldn't hear his car. And someone had followed him.

I still didn't know who that someone was, or why Jerry was killed, but I was certain whatever was on the flash drive would point an *aha!* finger at the guilty person.

And whoever had killed Jerry and stolen the computer equipment also knew the flash drive existed and was still looking for it. That was why my house had been broken into and searched. My earrings and my mother's old watch were just opportunistic thefts. *So, DDS Molino, I was right about that!*

Now that flash drive with its incriminating information was right here in my hands. Another thought jolted me. Were Elena and Donny after this? Was that what the meeting tomorrow night was really about? And how far would they go to get it?

What to do with it? Get rid of it! I dashed inside. I'd put DDS Molino's card in my purse after that interview at the station. I found it and dialed his home number. Answering machine. I looked at my watch. No time to take the flash drive to the station and explain everything to someone else. I'd call Molino again when I got home. I hastily stuffed the flash drive under a sofa cushion.

In spite of the excitement, I arrived at Mr. Findley's house right on time. I was feeling rushed and frazzled, but I had my cap set at a jaunty angle and I'd decided on black heels, which I thought added a touch of sophistication to the uniform. Although I wouldn't be doing any hiking around the lake in them, of course.

Mr. Findley came out of the house as soon as I pulled into the circular driveway. Under different circumstances I'd have felt odd stepping out to open the door for a man, but the uniform put me in chauffeur mode. I gave it the full treatment.

"Your chariot awaits, sir." I opened the door with a flourish.

"I really appreciate this, you know." Mr. Findley paused with one foot inside the limo. He seemed a bit out of breath. "I just did a last-minute change of clothes. Amanda is complaining that I'm acting like a teenager on a first date, but I just don't know what to expect from this bunch."

Mr. Findley was now wearing a dark gray suit, pale blue shirt, and burgundy tie.

"You look very nice."

Although he'd overdone the cologne or aftershave lotion, and he was going to be out of place if everyone else was roughing it in jeans and boots.

"Okay, let's get this show on the road." He settled in the rear seat and consulted a scrap of paper. "There's a two-lane highway going west out of Vigland to a little place called Bogg's Junction, but we don't have to go that far. About twenty miles out of town, watch for a gravel road to the right. There should be a sign that says Ryland Road."

Those directions were easy enough to follow, and traffic on the country road was light. I drove along feeling very chauffeurish, though I wished I could open the window. I wondered if the thickness of bulletproof glass prevented the windows from opening, or if that had been some special requirement of paranoid Uncle Ned.

The temperature wasn't high, but a faint scent of the cleansers lingered. Along with Mr. Findley's industrial-strength cologne.

Ryland Road was rough and potholed, with washboard sections that made Secret View Lane look cushiony. The countryside was rough and hilly, some of it logged over but much still heavily forested. Mr. Findley's face appeared in the space where the partition between us was open.

"When we're about seven or eight miles out here, it says to watch for a three-way fork in the road. It won't have a sign, but there's a big madrone tree with a peculiar gnarled trunk. Take the middle fork. Then it's several miles up that road."

I'd showed him how to use the intercom system to talk to me, but apparently he preferred the yell-in-your-ear system.

The road after the forks got worse. In fact, it looked as if the main road had ended at the fork, and these were just seldom-used branches angling off it. The road was dirt, rutted and uneven, barely wide enough for a single vehicle. I thought maybe Mr. Delgrade had been telling the truth: maybe his vacation place *was* just a shack out here in the boondocks. Slanting evening sunshine hit only the tops of the trees, and below them, everything was in shadows. I didn't like the way branches and drooping vines brushed and scraped the sides and top of the limo.

"Are you sure this is the right road?" I asked after a couple of miles. It was beginning to look like not much more than an old logging road. In spite of the deep ruts, none of the tracks appeared recent. The ground was hilly, the dirt road rough bedrock in places but marshy and squishy in others.

"This is what the directions say."

"Are you okay, Mr. Findley?" I asked after we slogged through a deep mudhole.

"I'm beginning to think I should have worn something other than this suit."

We're on a road that could double as a mud-wrestling tank, and Mr. Findley is worried about the correctness of his attire. I should have doubled the hourly price I'd quoted him. How much did a limo wash job cost?

Apparently he was now having doubts of his own, because he finally said, "If we don't find the cabin in another mile or so, we'll turn around and go back."

Maybe we would and maybe we wouldn't. The limo is not your turn-on-a-dime vehicle, and I hadn't seen any place yet where I could scrunch it around.

Then I spotted something in the road up ahead. The light was so dim I couldn't make it out clearly. I braked and switched on the headlights. Two somethings, actually, I realized as they moved closer. Bear? Bigfoot?

No, two human figures. But not human faces . . .

Ski masks, I realized with a jolt. Black ski masks, making the figures look like earless, two-legged snakes.

Not good. Nice, friendly country folk do not go around wearing ski masks. And carrying guns.

"Mr. Findley, l-look!"

His face appeared in the partition. "Oh, no! Who are they? Hunters?"

"I don't think hunters hunt with handguns or cover their faces with ski masks. I think we'd better get out of here." I shoved the gear lever into reverse and jammed my foot on the gas, but we were right in the middle of another mudhole, and all my effort did was make the tires spin and spit clods of mud like ol' Moose digging at warp speed.

"Something's wrong here," Mr. Findley said, which struck me as a big understatement—like *I smell smoke* when your hair is on fire. "I'm calling 911. Stay calm."

I figured we were in a dead zone for cell phones for sure,

but a minute later I heard him talking. He leaned through the opening again.

"They're sending someone. But it's probably going to take a while to get anyone way out here. We'll have to play it by ear until then."

With two guys with guns approaching, I'd have liked to have something more potent than an ear to rely on. One man was short and stocky, the other taller and scarecrow bony. Along with the ski masks, both were wearing scruffy jeans, dark T-shirts, and gloves.

"Get out!" the short one yelled. He emphasized the command with a wave of the gun at me through the windshield.

I was inclined to stay put. I could lock all the doors from the driver's seat and we could just sit tight, or maybe I could even prod the limo into action. But before I could find the lock button, Mr. Findley was stepping out. That meant the guys could get in through the back way no matter what I did. Reluctantly I opened my door too. Mr. Findley had his hands up.

"You too," Short Guy said to me with another jab of the gun.

I slid out of the limo, my high heels squishing into water and mud to my ankles. I put my hands in the air. Not a time to worry about such niceties as drooping trousers, but I had to wonder how securely I'd fastened that pin.

"Gimme your wallet," Scarecrow Man said to Mr. Findley.

Mr. Findley pulled the wallet out of his pocket and handed it over. I could see a stash of green bills protruding.

Good! With a haul like that, maybe they'd fade into the woods now. This seemed an unlikely place to wait for a rich victim to show up, but here we were, so maybe they knew what they were doing.

"I'll . . . uh . . . get my purse," I said. I made a move toward the open door, but Short Guy targeted me dead center with his gun.

"You don't do nuthin' until I tell you to."

I had a brilliant idea, something to speed up their exit. "You can take the limo too! It'll take us hours to walk out of here. You can sell it to"—I searched my mind for the right word, something I'd read somewhere—"to one of those chop shops!" An ugly demise for the limo, but better than what could happen here.

Both men stopped what they were doing to look at the vehicle as if they were considering the idea.

"Great condition," I said. "Low mileage."

"Don't be an idiot," Mr. Findley snapped.

His dismissal of my desperate ploy seemed a little harsh, given our circumstances.

Scarecrow Man looked back at the wallet in his hand and started flipping through it. But he was having a hard time keeping his gun targeted on Mr. Findley and managing the wallet too. He dropped the wallet. Right in the muddy rut.

Mr. Findley exploded. "You stupid idiot!" He fished the wallet out of the dirty water and shook it under Scarecrow Man's nose. "Can't you do anything right?"

My jaw dropped. "Wh-what's going on?" I was shaking in my snappy uniform, but Mr. Findley was just flicking a speck of mud off the gray suit.

"Okay, let's get this over with," he said. "I don't know how soon the cops may get here."

"Get w-what over with?"

"I'm sorry this turned out to be necessary, Mrs. McConnell, but that's the way it is. I figure you were just biding your time before you hit me up like Jerry did."

"I-I have no idea what you're talking about." I said. Short Guy waved his gun at me again, and I noticed a watch on his wrist. A Rolex.

Connections here, obviously. But it was like trying to

thread a needle in a dark room. I just couldn't see what went where.

"There isn't any meeting, is there?" I said to him. "You staged all this."

"Of course there's a meeting. It just isn't here." He smiled and touched a finger to his jaw. "Oh, dear. I must have misunderstood the directions, and we wound up way out here in the middle of nowhere. And then a couple of ruffians attacked us and demanded money. They shot you when you resisted giving up your purse." He gave me a how's-that-for-a-story lift of eyebrows.

Me, I was hung up on two words back there: *shot you*. I tried to swallow, but my throat felt frozen. "But, Mr. Findley, there really isn't any need to, uh, *dispose* of me. Honestly, Jerry never told me anything. I figured he was killed because of something to do with that weird Twenty-first Minutemen group he set up a Web site for. Or maybe an old girlfriend."

Mr. Findley looked at me, double lines crunched between his eyebrows. "Well, that may be, in which case this unpleasant episode may have been unnecessary. But unfortunately, you do know something now, don't you?"

Yeah, I did. I still didn't know *why* Jerry was killed, but I knew Mr. Findley was behind it.

"Maybe we ought to, you know, give you a little flesh wound or something," Short-Guy-with-Rolex suggested to Mr. Findley. He fingered the gun like a kid eager to start playing a video game. "Make the whole thing look authentic when the cops get here. Like you tried to protect her or something."

"Her body and the fact that I was robbed will be sufficient to show that we were attacked by ruthless killers who stole my wallet. Don't start trying to improve on the plan," Mr. Findley snapped. "And if you use any of the credit cards in that wallet, you're dead too."

I wasn't worried about Mr. Findley's credit cards or the life expectancy of these two guys. I was stuck again, this time on *her body*. Which was *my* body. Sometimes, like bear traps, words just snap and grab you.

"We're wasting time here," Mr. Findley said impatiently. He handed his wallet back to Scarecrow Man. "You've got to be long gone when the cops get here. Do it."

Short Guy gave me a sideways glance. "We killed the guy at the limo for you."

Surprisingly, in spite of that admission and his eagerness to give Mr. Findley a flesh wound, 1 sensed Short Guy was a little squeamish about shooting me.

"And a sloppy job you did of it. If you'd done her"—Mr. Findley jerked his head at me—"we wouldn't be having this complication now."

I felt a peculiar moment of relief. Jerry had turned out to be a sleazy guy, but at least he hadn't clobbered me. These guys had done it.

"You're so good at all this, you do this one," Scarecrow Man challenged. He held the gun out to Mr. Findley. "Or come up with a whole lot bigger payoff."

Okay, maybe squeamishness gave him too much credit. What he really wanted was a pay hike. Killers probably didn't get retirement benefits. If the money was good enough, I was dead meat.

"You're the ones who broke into my house, aren't you?" I said, trying to buy some time. "You stole my diamond earrings. And my mother's watch."

"Not one of our more upscale jobs," Scarecrow Man muttered. "I've seen better stuff at a yard sale. How about it, Emeril?" he added. "You gonna up the ante?"

Mr. Findley didn't appear pleased at what he apparently considered overfamiliarity. He looked as if he were about to stomp the guy's bones into the mud, but finally he said, "Okay, give me the gloves and the gun. I'll do it. No, the gloves *first*, stupid."

While they were fumbling with gloves and gun, I saw a narrow window of opportunity. I jumped into the limo, slammed the door, and punched the lock button as if I were running for my life. Which I was. I turned the key, shoved the gearshift into drive, and rammed the gas pedal to the floor. The tires spun uselessly again. No, no, no! Down, down we went . . . another minute and the limo'd be buried to the hubcaps.

You watching this, God? Help!

The spinning tires suddenly grabbed hold, and the limo shot forward. We roared up the steep hill on the other side of the mudhole, around a bend, down the other side and through more muddy ruts. Branches whapped the windshield like the arms of a green octopus. I automatically ducked.

Where was I going? What did it matter? Anywhere was better than where I'd been. The road must come out somewhere. Maybe the forks joined back in here, or maybe the road went on through to Bogg's Junction.

An opening in the trees up ahead. I careened into it and braked. An old log landing, where logs had once been gathered for loading onto trucks, now a gathering spot for drinkers and shooters. Blackened chunks of wood, remains of an old campfire, jumbled within a circle of rocks. Beer cans and bottles, scattered and broken. A weathered target punctured with bullet holes. Several piles of dumped yard rubbish and old boards.

I scanned the forested edge of the rough circle of clearing, then frantically scanned it again. My heart plummeted like an anchor plunging to the bottom of Vigland Bay. Only one road led into the clearing, the one I was on. No other road led out of it.

Trapped.

For a moment I speculated hopefully on how the two men had arrived. On foot, from what I'd seen, but they must have a vehicle stashed close by, and a planned escape route. Was there another road nearby? Could I crash the limo through to it?

Not likely, since I had no idea where the road might be.

I could get out and make a run for it on foot. Maybe hide out in the woods until the cops arrived.

If Mr. Findley had even called the cops . . .

Yes, I decided, he'd called them. They were a crucial element of his plan. They were supposed to arrive to find me dead, Mr. Findley robbed and terrified. With no reason for any of it ever to be connected to Jerry's murder.

Of course, there was the flash drive hidden back in my sofa. Maybe it would eventually be found and the information retrieved. I still didn't know what could be on it to incriminate Mr. Findley, but justice might catch up with these guys someday.

Long after I was dead.

Mr. Findley and his goons would probably be here in another minute. Now what? Cower inside the limo? They could shoot the door locks open.

Only one way out, I realized. *Back the way I'd come.* I swallowed and eased the limo into a turn while dodging the piles of trash. This was no time to get stuck or puncture a tire. I had a straight shot at the old road now.

Cousin Larry said the limo's windows were bulletproof.

Were they?

36

Old logging debris crunched under the tires. A beer bottle popped. A deep rut threw the limo sideways and almost yanked the steering wheel out of my sweaty hands. I let go of the wheel one hand at a time and swiped each palm across the uniform so I could get a better grip.

Here we go, God. You with me?

I locked my hands on the wheel and roared full blast into the green tunnel of the narrow road. An octopus branch whammed the windshield. Caught vines dangled down a side window. I spotted shadowy figures in the road ahead. Guns pointing at me. No turning back now. I stomped down on the gas pedal as if I were trying to annihilate an oversized cockroach.

The first bullet didn't hit the limo. I saw it take off a tree limb alongside the road. Good! Maybe they were all really lousy shots, the kind of guys who never could win teddy bears for their girlfriends at carnivals.

But the next one was a bull's-eye. *Wham!* It smashed dead-on into the windshield in front of my face. I automatically ducked behind the steering wheel. Matt was right. Bullets didn't bounce off like Ping-Pong balls. The driver's side of the windshield blossomed into a crisscrossed tangle that looked like splintered ice. But the maze of cracks held. No bullet blasted through!

The hit slowed me down. I couldn't see the road through the web of cracks. My next thought was, *Okay, so I hit something while I'm careening along blindly. Maybe it'll be one of those goons.* But even if it were a solid tree trunk I wouldn't be in a much worse situation than I was now.

I leaned over to the right, peered around the central spider-web of cracks, and hit the gas pedal again. More shots, a gauntlet of them. Something thudded on the roof. Falling branch? The windshield in front of me took another direct hit. The web of cracks expanded. Could enough shots in one place break through?

I saw Short Guy's face through a side window as I hurtled past him, so close I could have reached out and ripped off his ski mask. But he didn't have a gun now; he'd passed it along to Mr. Findley, and all he could do was slam a fist into the side window. Which, I was pleased to see when I glanced back in the rearview mirror, left him holding his arm and howling in pain. Fistproof as well as bulletproof!

But a few feet farther on, Scarecrow Guy was on the far side, and he did have one of their two-gun arsenal. I saw a flash as he fired. The passenger's side window took the hit and turned into a kaleidoscope of ragged cracks . . . but again no bullet burst through.

Thank You, God! Thank You for Uncle Ned and his paranoia!

Pudgy Mr. Findley hadn't been able to keep up with his goons and was a hundred feet behind them. I ducked down to peer under the labyrinth of cracks in the windshield and spotted him standing dead center in the beam of the headlights.

He had a gun.

I had a limo.

I'd never played a game of chicken in my life. I didn't want to play one now. But it looked as if I hadn't much choice.

The gun blazed. He wasn't deadly accurate, but the right side of the windshield formed a new jigsaw puzzle of cracks. I shot back with what I had, a blast of the horn, and kept going.

Mr. Findley stood his ground in the middle of the road. More shots. I couldn't tell if he was hitting anything, although the headlight beams looked lopsided now, and I could feel an odd lurch in the limo.

But the limo's powerful engine gobbled up the space between us, and at the last minute Mr. Findley threw up his hands and jumped aside. The last I saw of him was a gray blob tangled in blackberry bushes alongside the road. I guessed that meant I was the winner, although I didn't feel too victorious. Something pinged into the limo from behind, but I didn't stop to check.

Thank You, God. Thank You for bringing me through that.

I roared on down the road, rocketing over stones, barreling through mudholes, hoping for the best with my limited vision. Without the seat belt fastened, I was a loose cannon in the seat, bouncing up, down, and sideways. Past the forks, on down the gravel road. The limo felt strange, sluggish, and hard to steer, but I didn't slow down. I had no idea where the goons had stashed a vehicle. They could be coming right behind me.

At the highway I almost collided with a sheriff's car turning onto the gravel road. Oh, happy day! I wanted to jump out and embrace them. But the two deputies didn't appear to be looking for grateful hugs.

They slammed to a stop in front of me, blocking the road, and, headlights still blazing, jumped out with guns drawn. I couldn't get the window down, of course, so I opened the door.

"Freeze!" one cop yelled.

How about that? I thought irrelevantly. *They really do say, "Freeze!" Just like on TV.*

I stayed right where I was and raised my hands. "You've got the wrong person!" I yelled. "The killers are back there!"

They looked at the shot-up windshield, then back at me. Puzzled. Wary. Suspicious.

"Are you hurt?" one officer asked as he approached, gun still drawn.

How come *I'm* suddenly the target *du jour?*

"I'm okay. It's bulletproof—bullet-resistant—glass. You got here quicker than I expected."

"We happened to be near Bogg's Junction when the call came in. But I understood the call was from a male."

"That was Mr. Findley. It's a long story. He told me he wanted me to drive him to a meeting—"

"Step outside, please," he interrupted.

"But—"

"Keep your hands up."

I fumed at the delay, but I followed orders. One of the officers yanked the rear door open and peered inside. "No one else in here."

"There are two guys, well, three, actually, back there in the woods who were shooting at me." I started to gesture toward the wooded hills, realized that might not be wise, and jerked my head instead.

"The call came from a man who said he and a woman were under attack by two gunmen. Where's he?"

"That was Mr. Findley. He's an executive at F&N, but he turned out to be one of the gunmen." I pointed to the spiderweb on the passenger's side of the windshield. "He did that."

"We need to see your vehicle registration and driver's license."

I groaned. Protocol. If criminals weren't in hot pursuit, protocol came first. Which was a complication, because I didn't have anything to show I owned the limo, and it still had Uncle Ned's Texas plates. But I dragged out my driver's license and gave them a high-speed rundown on Uncle Ned and Mr. Findley and the goons and what I was doing out here in the limo.

Both deputies looked more suspicious—and maybe confused—than impressed by my story. I suppose it's not every day a wild woman in a shot-up limo comes barreling out of the woods. Mud to my ankles probably didn't upscale my image.

Sudden inspiration.

"I know Detective Sergeant Molino. You can ask him about me!"

On second thought, maybe that wasn't such a good idea. DDS Molino might just tell them to slap on the handcuffs and haul me in.

But I'd started this, so I plunged ahead. "Tell him I know who killed Jerry."

"Jerry?" one officer repeated.

"Detective Sergeant Molino is investigating the murder of a friend that happened right here in the limo back in Vigland, Jerry Norton."

"The limousine murder? What's that got to do with all this?"

Everything! I felt momentarily overwhelmed. So much to tell and so little time to tell it. "Mr. Findley—he was Jerry's boss at F&N—hired the two guys who are back there in the woods right now to kill Jerry. And then he arranged all this today to have me killed, too, but so it would look like a robbery . . . but they may all be escaping right now! Because they must have another car—"

I wasn't sure they believed me, but one officer snapped a command. "I think we'd better call for backup."

The other officer ran back to their car, and I heard the crackle of the radio.

To me the first officer said, "I realize it may look to you as if we're wasting time, but we need a few more facts here."

So I expanded on what I'd already told them. The officer nodded a couple of times, and I was no longer looking down the muzzle of his gun. But it didn't go back in the holster until two more cars arrived. Big conference then, more squawks from the radio, and then two cars with four officers inside headed into the woods the way I had come. It was almost dark now, and their headlight beams shot strange patterns of light into the trees as they bounced over the rough road. The third car and two officers stayed with me. Although I didn't know if their intention was to protect me or keep me from taking off.

Not that I could. On a squishy-footed tour around the limo I discovered more casualties. Two bullet holes in the trunk, one headlight shot out, and one front tire flat. More than flat. Shredded. One of the bullets must have struck it, and I'd driven all that way with it flat.

The adrenaline rush that had gotten me this far fizzled, and I leaned against the fender. I felt as shredded as the tire.

"May I make a cell phone call?" I asked the closest officer. "I'm going to need some help here." I motioned to my un-drivable vehicle.

"It looks as if there are a couple of slugs embedded in the windshield. We'll probably need to have it towed in so the technicians can go over it."

That figured. So far, police technicians had spent more time with my limo than I had.

"I'd still like to call someone if it's okay."

I didn't stop to examine my feelings or make some big decision about whom to call. I just knew that right then I needed Fitz.

THE OFFICER HIMSELF made the call. Apparently, even though they were courteous and sympathetic, they didn't totally trust my wild story about an important executive at F&N shooting at me. But whatever Fitz said to them seemed to meet their approval, and they reported that he would be here as soon as possible.

Then we waited. Full darkness descended. The stars came out. My mind felt as if it had gone numb, overloaded by all that had happened. Mr. Findley, murderer. Maybe he hadn't pulled the trigger, but he was the one behind Jerry's death. The kingpin. But of what?

Stray thoughts on disconnected subjects shot around in my mind. Big Daddy Sutherland wasn't involved. Neither was Elena's husband. So what had her so worked up that she needed to talk to me?

My best black heels . . . my only black heels . . . were ruined. Squishy mud gritted between my toes. Who knew what potent little organisms lived in stagnant mud?

How was I going to get the limo repaired? Maybe the damage was even worse than showed on the surface.

How was Joella going to manage financially now? She had a strong belief that God would meet the needs of those who trusted in Him. Once, when I'd said how much I admired her strength in the face of adversity, she'd said, "I don't have any strength of my own. I just lean on Jesus." Okay, leaning was fine, but what could God do now? Change her parents' unforgiving attitude?

I had a mosquito bite on my left elbow.

Hurry, Fitz, please hurry.

Fitz didn't arrive, but headlights arced out of the woods. The lone car pulled up next to the car of the deputies that had been waiting with me, headlights blazing, overhead red and blue lights circling. One officer got out. I couldn't see inside the car. Did they have Mr. Findley and his goons back there? Where was the other police car? Would anyone tell me what was going on?

I got out of the limo.

The passenger's door of the deputy's car flew open. "Mrs. McConnell, I'm so glad to see you're okay!"

Mr. Findley headed toward me as if we were long-lost buddies. I backed off.

"What's going on?" I yelled at the officers. "Why isn't he handcuffed or something?"

Mr. Findley stopped short. "Handcuffed? Why would I be handcuffed? Look what they did to me!"

In the beam of the headlights he stretched his pants leg away from his leg and stuck his finger through a bullet hole.

"Look! A couple of inches to the side and they'd have smashed my leg!"

I felt dizzy with the spin he was putting on everything, too flabbergasted to be furious. "What happened to the two guys with the guns?" I asked.

"They took off through the woods. The other deputies are still out searching for them." He turned to the officers. "Look, I need to make a phone call. I was supposed to be at a meeting with some company executives this evening, but Mrs. McConnell and I got off on this wrong road somehow, and these two ruffians attacked us."

"He's lying! He told me where to go. He had these guys waiting out there to kill me!"

Mr. Findley drew back his head and looked at me in astonishment. "Mrs. McConnell, what in the world are you talking about? I know you're resentful because we had to let you go at F&N, but—"

"You used to work at F&N?" an officer asked, as if the scales on some unseen balance had just shifted.

"That has nothing to do with this!"

But I could see Mr. Findley was having an effect on them. The bullet hole in his pants leg struck me as a weak substitute for the flesh wound he'd rejected, but it seemed to be working with the deputies. And he sounded so reasonable! Then I thought of something.

"Check his hands! He shot at me." I pointed to the right side of the windshield. "There'll be . . . whatever it is that gets on your hands when you shoot a gun! I've seen it on TV."

"Gunshot residue."

The officers, now clustered around us like gawking sightseers, gave Mr. Findley speculative looks.

"Yes, gunshot residue! If he's telling the truth, there won't be any. But if it's there—"

"It takes a lab test to identify gunshot residue," one of the officers said. "Though I suppose we could swab for it."

No one made any move to do that, however, and Mr. Findley lifted his hands and looked at them in the glare of the police car headlights.

"Well, yes, I suppose there is gunshot residue on them. I did have hold of the gun when it went off—"

"You see? He admits it."

"—after you ran off and abandoned me out there—"

It was like a bad tennis match, and now the deputies' attention swiveled from Mr. Findley back to me. I could almost hear their thoughts.

You abandoned this guy out there? Ran off and left him helpless with two guys with guns?

"After she ran off and left, I tried to wrestle a gun away from one of the men. It went off while I was holding it. Then the second guy rushed in and kicked me in the groin."

He made a protective male gesture and got a collective groan of sympathy from the male officers. *The testosterone fraternity*, I thought in frustration.

"And they got the gun back. That's when one of them tried to shoot me. And almost did." He stretched out the bullet-holed pants leg again.

"So why didn't they just go ahead and finish the job?" I demanded.

"Because I yelled, 'The cops are coming!' And they ran off."

I just stood there, flabbergasted. It sounded so plausible. If I hadn't known it was all a made-up story, I'd have believed him myself.

"But that isn't what happened," I protested.

I appealed to the two officers to whom I'd given the most complete story of Jerry's murder and what had happened tonight.

"I told you what really happened. They even talked about giving Mr. Findley a flesh wound to make the attack look authentic!"

Mr. Findley shook his head as if baffled by my accusations. "Mrs. McConnell, I know you're under a lot of stress here, but this is ridiculous."

Big silence, the only sound a lone car passing on the highway and the call of some night bird back in the woods. The lights on the deputies' car went round and round, disorienting and yet oddly hypnotic. Finally one of the officers spoke.

"We seem to have some . . . ah . . . rather large discrepancies here."

37

There aren't any discrepancies," I yelled. "He's lying! It was all a setup to have me killed!"

Mr. Findley looked distressed. Oh, he was good. Give the man an Emmy for Most Convincing Crook of the Year.

"Mrs. McConnell, please—"

Then I finally remembered my trump card. "I have the flash drive, Mr. Findley. Jerry's flash drive, remember? He lost it in my flower bed a couple days before you had him killed and his computer equipment stolen. And I found it tonight!"

I saw the look of mixed dismay and fury cross Mr. Findley's usually bland face. But he was facing me, not the officers, so only I had that privilege. Then, as smoothly as if he were adjusting a mask, his expression shifted back to good-ol'-boy bewilderment before he turned to face them, and he played his bluff like a high-stakes poker expert.

He shrugged as if he had no idea what I was talking about. "May I make my phone call now, please?"

"Give us the number, and we'll make it."

Mr. Findley fumbled in a pocket and brought out a small, leather bound day planner. He opened a page and handed it to the officer.

"See what else he has in his pockets!" I said. "He had directions that took us right out there in the woods where those guys were waiting to ambush us!"

The deputies obviously had their doubts about my version of events, but they weren't playing favorites here.

"Would you empty your pockets please, Mr. Findley?" one asked.

He did. No incriminating scrap of paper.

"Maybe he chewed it up and swallowed it," I muttered, which earned me lady-you've-been-reading-too-many-spy-novels looks from everyone present.

An officer dialed the number from his own cell phone. He briefly interrogated whoever answered, then handed the phone to Mr. Findley. Then we all heard Mr. Findley give his apologetic "lost" story. Very convincing.

"You did that very well," I said when he was done. "But I still have the flash drive."

"I don't know what Mrs. McConnell is trying to pull here, and I have no idea what this flash drive is that she keeps talking about."

Mr. Findley heaved a big sigh, as if he were bone weary. Or maybe he really was tired. He'd jitterbugged some tricky mental footwork coming up with instant and convincing rebuttals to my accusations.

"But I'd really like to go home now. Unless I'm under arrest?"

"No, you're not under arrest, Mr. Findley. But we'd like you to come into the station tomorrow morning so we can take a formal statement."

"Of course. Glad to help any way I can. Now, if someone could give me a ride home?"

I felt a big *whoosh* of doubt. Was the flash drive really

irrelevant? Mr. Findley's glance at me was more pitying than frightened. *Poor deluded woman*, it plainly said. Was it possible the flash drive didn't hold any incriminating information, that it was just copies of Web site work Jerry'd done and had nothing to do with his murder?

More radio squawks, and then the police car, with Mr. Findley inside, pulled onto the paved road. No arrest, no handcuffs, nothing. The second car that had been back in the woods arrived just as the one with Mr. Findley inside was leaving. The three officers got out.

"We can't do any more tonight," one of them reported. "Too dark and way too much underbrush out there. We'll have to bring in the K-9 unit in the morning and try to track them."

I couldn't tell them what the gunmen's faces looked like, but I gave as much description as I could about height, weight, and clothing. A discussion with someone by radio confirmed that they wanted the limo towed in, and I was also told to come to the station for a formal statement in the morning.

Fitz arrived just as I walked back to sit in the limo. Wobbled back, more accurately, considering the state of my black heels. One officer checked out Fitz's ID before letting him come over to me.

Fitz gave the ruined windshield and shredded tire a surprised but fleeting glance and wrapped his arms around me. I was grateful for his warmth and strength.

"You okay?" he asked.

I was grateful that his first question was about me, not the *why* of the battered limousine.

"The glass really is bulletproof." I didn't care what Matt called it. It had gone beyond resisting the bullets; it had stopped them. Bulletproof. Blessedly. Because I knew *I* was not. More now than when the bullets were flying, I realized my vulnerability, how life could have ended in an instant.

"Thank God," Fitz said.

I knew Fitz meant that in a figurative way, but in the last couple of days I'd acquired a new perspective on God's activities.

"Yes," I said fervently. "That's what I'm doing. Thanking God."

"Can you leave?"

"I think I should wait until the tow truck for the limo gets here. Did the officer tell you anything on the phone?"

"Only that you were out here and your vehicle was 'incapacitated.' I'd say that's something of an understatement."

I leaned back in his arms. "I've been shot at umpteen times. My limo is a mess. And I've ruined my shoes."

I held one out to the side to show him and, ridiculously, a tear trickled down my cheek. All that had happened, and I was crying over shoes. "I thought you told me sixty was prime time."

"There can be days like this at any age." Fitz paused, and we looked at each other, and unexpectedly I felt a smile breaking through the tears. "Well, okay, not exactly like *this*. You know what I mean. Bad-hair-type days."

"After this I will be grateful if they're only bad hair days."

"Okay, let's get you home."

"Fitz, I know who killed Jerry. We were wrong about Elena's husband and Big Daddy Sutherland. Mr. Findley did it. At least he hired the goons who pulled the trigger."

"Mr. Findley?" Fitz repeated.

It took almost forty-five minutes for the tow truck to arrive, and I used the time to tell Fitz all that had happened, from Moose's disinterment of the flash drive to Mr. Findley's plan, with my poor limousine the innocent victim in tonight's shoot-out.

Then, once more, away went my limousine. Before we

left in Fitz's car, one of the officers said, "I talked with Detective Sergeant Molino. He's going to meet you at your house and pick up that flash drive. He thinks it may be important."

"Okay, thanks."

Just before we reached Secret View Lane, Fitz said, "I don't think you should stay at the house tonight. With Joella staying at the hospital with the baby, you'd be alone. After the detective comes, we'll go to the boat. You can have one of the guest cabins."

I was too tired to protest. I didn't want to protest anyway.

DDS MOLINO HADN'T yet arrived when we reached the house. I was just putting the key into the front door lock when Fitz put a restraining hand on my arm.

"Did you leave a light on when you left?" he whispered.

I looked where he was pointing, at a peculiar flicker of faint light showing around the drapes. I couldn't remember about the light, since it hadn't been dark when I left, but I was sure of one thing. I hadn't pulled the drapes shut . . . and they were pulled now!

"I think someone's in there," Fitz added. "Has that sliding door ever been fixed?"

"Not yet. It's hard to open, but it can be done. It can't be locked." And, I remembered with a sinking feeling, I'd opened the door earlier when a bird crashed into the glass, and I'd gone out to see if it was okay. And I didn't remember putting the rod brace back in place. . . .

I tried not to panic. Whoever it was, there was a logical solution. We didn't have to rush in like gangbusters.

"The detective is coming. We can wait for him."

"I don't think so." The faint light around the edge of the

drapes grew fainter still, then disappeared. "I think he's going to escape out the back. Wait here."

Fitz dashed around the side of the house. Wait here? No way! I dashed after him. A shadowy figure ran across the back-yard. Fitz raced after him. The figure reached the line of cedar trees and bushes at the property line. I heard an *oof* and a curse as Fitz dived in after him.

Thuds. Thumps. Crashes. The two figures stumbled out of the bushes, entwined to make a four-legged monster.

"Fitz, be careful!" I yelled.

A little late for that, with the other guy, bigger and heavier than Fitz, using his weight to force Fitz to the ground. Frantically I looked around for a weapon, some way to help. What? A floppy forsythia branch wouldn't do it. Neither would the daisies growing underneath. But then I stumbled over something . . . the burglar's flashlight!

Big flashlight. Heavy flashlight. No cheap stuff for this top-of-the-line burglar. I picked it up and circled the entwined fig-ures. One was trim-bodied. Fitz. I didn't want to make a mistake and clobber him. The figures wrestled across the lawn, both panting and grunting, Fitz's agility was all that was keeping him from going down. I held the flashlight with both hands, took aim at the one who wasn't Fitz, and whacked with all my strength.

The figure went down. No *oof* this time. It was a silent tumble. Something fell out of his hand.

The flash drive.

Fitz rolled the limp form over and felt the throat. "He's breathing, just knocked out."

I turned on the flashlight, the strong beam showing no ill effects from being drafted into battle. "It's Mr. Findley." Still wearing the gray suit, much the worse for wear now. "He came to steal the flash drive."

Which meant it definitely wasn't irrelevant after all.

I heard a car out front. DDS Molino had arrived. I started to head that direction, but Fitz grabbed me and wrapped his arms around me.

"You pack quite a wallop, lady. I like that."

"Isn't that what a sidekick is for?"

"I think we can dispense with the sidekick business." He tucked a strand of hair behind my ear and smiled. "From now on, it's sleuth-'n'-sleuth, partners and equals."

"No more sleuthing. We've got this killer. I'm retiring."

38

Joella set Tricia A. on the sofa and pushed a chair up beside her. At five weeks she shouldn't be able to roll off by herself, but she was one energetic, mind-of-her own baby. Fitz was in the kitchen, making a new chicken-and-rice dish, trying it out on us before using it for guests on the *Miss Nora*.

Mr. Findley was in jail, charged with murder. Seems hiring a killer is as frowned upon as pulling the trigger yourself. He wasn't admitting anything outright yet, but his two goons had been more talkative than Trudy Vandervort's parrot. They'd been picked up the morning after the shoot-out, their location revealed by a K-9 named Ruger. Bright guys. In the dark they'd gotten lost and couldn't find their stashed vehicle.

Their information, plus what was on the flash drive, had nailed Mr. Findley. Plus there was a clincher with the goons. Ballistics tests on one of their guns showed that it had fired the bullet that killed Jerry.

And now I knew what Mr. Findley had done, and why that article in the paper about Fitz and the identity theft had set him off. DDS Molino wasn't confiding in me, of course, but it was all over the news about a big identity-theft ring that had been cracked.

Seems Mr. Findley had been supplying a team of crooks down in California with information from the F&N files. He had everything they needed from insurance applications and records. Names, addresses, Social Security numbers, birth dates, credit-card numbers, even bank account numbers. He was paid for each name, plus a cut of the profits when the names were used. The going rate for a credit-card number was five hundred dollars.

He'd been careful to use out-of-state names only, nothing local, so it wouldn't be connected with F&N here in Vigland. Fitz's information had been stolen when he lived in California and had his house insurance through F&N. Apparently it had shaken Mr. Findley considerably when Fitz's name turned up in the local article. Then when I, the woman who owned the limo where Jerry had been killed, showed up working at F&N again, Mr. Findley was sure I'd been in cahoots with Jerry and knew way too much.

Although Jerry hadn't been in on the scheme, he'd found out about it and used the information to force Mr. Findley to cut him in on the profits and arrange for his new job in San Diego as well. Jerry's computer and CDs were never found, but the incriminating information was all there on the flash drive. Names of people provided to the identity thieves, how Mr. Findley had done it, everything. Jerry had spelled it all out.

"Dinner's on," Fitz called.

This was a little going-away party, because this was the last night Joella and the baby would be living in my duplex. God had provided. Friends of a couple from church had hired her as a live-in nanny for their two kids, the perfect job for her, because she could keep Tricia A. right with her. And the church was going to help with the medical bills she owed too.

I was glad for her, and she wouldn't be all that far away—

just on the other side of Vigland—but I was going to miss having her and Tricia A. right next door.

Though she assured me we'd still see each other at church. Providing . . . ?

Oh yes, I'd be there. I was digging deeper into my discoveries about God and Jesus, begun the night Tricia A. was born.

Elena had showed up for our meeting the night after our adventures with Mr. Findley in the backyard. I could see why she was worried. In her husband's things she'd found a photo of herself and Jerry taken with a telephoto lens. It confirmed to her that Donny had known about her and Jerry and meant he'd probably killed Jerry. I was happy to assure her that Donny was not the killer. The last I heard, they were working things out and moving to Texas for a new start together. I hoped it worked.

The limo sat out in the driveway now. New windshield, new passenger's side window, new wheel and tire, all paid for out of F&N's severance check. Not all the repair work the limo needed, but all I could afford right now. Because there'd been a number of other expenses.

I'd jumped through all the hoops. I'd had the limo's title transferred and proper insurance set up. I'd dealt with the Utilities and Transportation Commission and the Department of Licensing and various county and city departments. I'd worked my way through applications, fees, business licenses, tests, a physical, and an eye exam. I had an advertisement in *The Vigland Tides* and listings with the chamber of commerce, various resorts in the area, and every business connected with weddings.

And now—ta-da!—I had *this*. I laid the box of freshly printed business cards on the table, and Fitz and Joella gathered beside me to see.

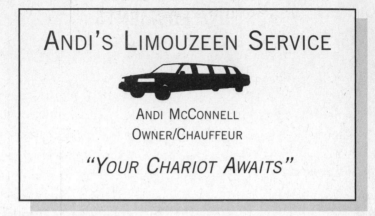

ANDI'S LIMOUZEEN SERVICE

ANDI MCCONNELL
OWNER/CHAUFFEUR

"YOUR CHARIOT AWAITS"

On the back of the card was a list of my services offered, along with my phone number and a post office box number, since Fitz had advised I not use my home address.

"Impressive!" Joella said.

Fitz draped his arms around me. "You're going to make a mint."

Yes!

There was still one small problem . . . but who's going to notice two little bullet holes in the trunk of a limousine, right?

ACKNOWLEDGMENTS

With thanks to Mark and Karen Norris of the Norris Limousine Service in Shelton, Washington, for all their helpful information about limousines.

With thanks, too, to Ivan Leith for showing us around his sailboat, to D. Niksich for letting us see inside his houseboat, and to both for answering my many questions.

Contact the author at P.O. Box 773, Merlin, OR 97532. Or visit her Web site at www.lorenamccourtney.com